THE
LAST DAYS
OF VIDEO

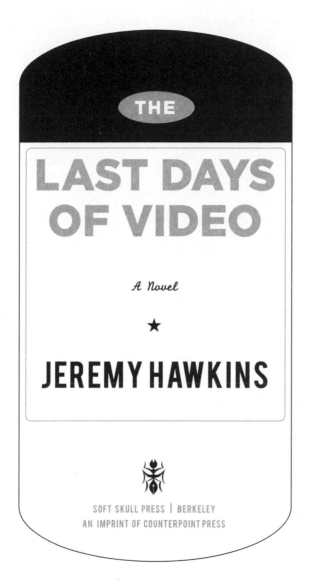

THE

LAST DAYS
OF VIDEO

A Novel

★

JEREMY HAWKINS

SOFT SKULL PRESS | BERKELEY
AN IMPRINT OF COUNTERPOINT PRESS

523/352

This book is a work of fiction. Names, characters, places,
and incidents either are products of the author's imagination or are used
fictitiously. Any resemblance to actual events or locales or persons,
living or dead, is entirely coincidental.

Library of Congress Cataloging-in-Publication Data

Hawkins, Jeremy, 1978-
The last days of video : a novel / Jeremy Hawkins.
pages cm
ISBN 978-1-61902-485-4
1. Video rental services—Fiction. 2. Motion picture audiences—Fiction.
I. Title.
PS3608.A89335L38 2015
813›.6—dc23
2014033912

Cover design by Jarrod Taylor
Interior Design by E. J. Strongin, Neuwirth and Associates, Inc.

Soft Skull Press
An Imprint of COUNTERPOINT
2560 Ninth Street, Suite 318
Berkeley, CA 94710
www.softskull.com

Printed in the United States of America
Distributed by Publishers Group West

10 9 8 7 6 5 4 3 2 1

For Mom and Dad.

And for Clyde.

"Oh, Fortuna, blind, heedless goddess, I am strapped to your wheel," Ignatius belched. "Do not crush me beneath your spokes. Raise me on high, divinity."

—JOHN KENNEDY TOOLE, A Confederacy of Dunces

STAR
VIDEO

HOW TO TRY IN BUSINESS
WITHOUT REALLY SUCCEEDING

The blue and yellow thing leaned over the road, a glossy robot poised to attack. It was tall, top-heavy, terribly real—a pristine anachronism on this otherwise dusty stretch of West Appleton—and it had materialized overnight, fifty yards from Waring Wax's shop.

The blue and yellow thing was a sign.

The sign read, "Blockbuster."

Waring's eyes burned. Tears. He pressed his brow into the crook of his elbow. He had not wept sober in over a decade.

A Blockbuster opening on College Street? It would kill him.

Waring turned away from the sign, and facing West Appleton's small business district—the snooty organic grocery store, two trendy thrift shops, three cafés, three deep-fried sandwich shops, seven taprooms, and no fewer than five yoga/naturopath healing studios—he spat out a minute-long fusillade of profanity. During this barrage, several pedestrians edged to the other side of College Street to avoid him. He couldn't blame them. He knew what they saw. They saw a short, sweating, babbling crazy person who was assembled of Hollywood's most disagreeable features: Humphrey Bogart's overbite, Fred Astaire's trapezoidal forehead, Leslie

Neilson's bowlegs supporting Jack Black's potbelly, and Chaplin's dark, frizzy hair, now gone Clooney half-gray. And, of course, Tom Cruise's lamentable height.

Arthur-era Dudley Moore, plus twenty extra pounds around the gut, might have been the ideal choice to portray Waring Wax in 2007.

Yes, Waring understood why the pedestrians circumvented him. But he didn't care, so he sneered at them anyway, and this sneering finally helped quell his ridiculous tears. He stopped cursing. He heaved for breath. He lit a cigarette and began sucking it down.

It was ten a.m. and already over eighty degrees. The August sun scalded Waring's sallow skin, a pain that he appreciated. Fresh sweat trickled down his already soaked back. Then a city bus swept by, kicking a gritty gust against his face and whipping his cigarette out of his mouth.

"Could have done without that," Waring muttered.

He listened as the offending behemoth receded behind him. If one were aboard this bus, carrying a cattle load of chirping undergrads, one would enjoy a six-minute air-conditioned trek between the disparate worlds of West Appleton and Appleton (combined pop.: 34,867; w/ students: 45,572). The bus route started here, in West Appleton's quaint-if-somewhat-low-rent business district, then coursed over the blue-green trickle of Nile Creek that demarcated the border between the two towns, then passed the picturesque and preposterous mansions of the Historic District, through Appleton's not-at-all-low-rent and more-than-somewhat-commercialized business district—where a new Blockbuster made a hell of lot more sense than *here*, Waring thought—and finally to Appleton University, that small, old, and consistently average institution that is the crown jewel of Ehle County, North Carolina.

Finally, after successfully consuming a full cigarette, and without looking again at the Blockbuster sign, Waring stomped across his empty parking lot and entered Star Video, his beloved grungy palace. He switched on the neon OPEN sign. Then he took up his station upon his director's chair behind the long black counter, at the register labeled "Cashier du Cinéma," and he started a John Ford Western. One of his part-time employees, Rose, had called in sick that morning, so he'd have to pull an all-day shift. But it didn't matter. It's not like his social calendar would be thrown into turmoil.

And anyway, business was slow. Over the next few hours, only the regular morning porn renters filtered in, wearing their abashed but resilient expressions, wordlessly swapping out their shame. Then at noon arrived the normal vanload of old biddies from Covenant Woods, the nearby retirement tank, for whom Waring reluctantly submitted to playing tour guide, as he was forced to almost every week whenever he couldn't pawn the job off on someone else. "No, don't worry, we won't sell our VHS tapes," he told them in annoyance as he showed them for the hundredth time to the British TV Mystery section. "Yes, I'm totally devastated that Bob Barker retired," he lied as he guided another old biddy to *March of the Penguins*, the same videocassette she rented every week.

But the old biddies were oblivious to Waring's harsher-than-average disdain. Or perhaps they weren't oblivious. Perhaps they just didn't care, because they'd grown accustomed to him, and because they needed his help navigating his imposing store, with its twenty-feet-high warehouse ceilings, its labyrinthine metal shelving, its thousands of titles, its sections and subsections and sub-subsections (Martial Arts, Bruce Lee, Bruceploitation), its plague of dust bunnies swarming like Tribbles, and its rickety loft/employee break room looming over the front counter, seemingly ready to collapse at any moment. And the Porn Room, into which these old biddies, on more than one occasion, had accidentally wandered.

Yes, the old biddies needed his help. But that didn't mean he had to be nice about it. Especially not today.

So Waring rolled his eyes at them. He sneered at the porn renters.

He scoffed in one way or another at every single customer, no matter how innocuous his or her offenses. But of course, as West Appleton's famously cantankerous drunk, Waring's mood went unnoticed.

Then, at four p.m., Alaura Eden—the longtime manager of Star Video—arrived for her evening shift, and Waring was relieved that she didn't immediately mention the Blockbuster sign. He hoped Alaura hadn't learned of the corporate villain's encampment. Would never learn of it at all.

"Hot day out there, huh?" Alaura said, tossing her jangly purse under the counter.

"I'm having a drink in my office," Waring replied, and he walked away.

Star Video closed at midnight, as usual. Shop lights down. *Run Lola Run* on the store TV, for the grinding music. Waring was back on the floor, mildly tipsy, sitting in his director's chair and totaling that day's paltry receipts at the counter. Alaura, who was shelving movies nearby in the New Releases section, chattered about how great an employee Jeff was going to be (apparently Waring's objections to Jeff, the tall Richie Cunninghamish undergrad suck-up Alaura had recently and unaccountably hired, were meaningless) and, as usual, about her sweet boyfriend du jour, Paul or Pierce or Peckerdick, though, lest we forget, Peckerdick had threatened to punch Waring in the very recent past for a drunken offense Waring thought best left forgotten. But at least Alaura hadn't mentioned . . .

"So is Blockbuster a big deal?"

Waring laughed bitterly. Then he muttered something about being tired/headachey/gassy, and leaving that night's paperwork unfinished, he retreated again toward the rear of the store, through the Porn Room, into his small windowless office.

In his MicroFridge he found a six-pack of Budweiser—lukewarm because the fridge hadn't worked in months—and he pounded two in a row. He collapsed into his creaky office chair. Then he looked up and saw Alaura standing over him. Today her dark brunette hair—long on top, clipped short on the sides and back—was slicked back into a rather amazing pompadour, a sexy punk rendering of Travolta in *Grease*. Her arms were crossed, displaying the immaculate sleeved tattoo on her right arm: a giant squid slithering its purple tentacles from shoulder to wrist. She wore a black Misfits tank top and tight black jeans, and Waring's eyes lasered in on the chubby Buddha tattoo on her neck, beaming his contented smile. Conversely, Alaura's face was irate and beautiful.

"Waring, are you having money problems?"

Because, you see, Waring and Alaura had a longstanding deal—*We take care of each other*. He had paid for her lawyer, for example, in the early 2000s for several absurd pot charges. Covered her rent when she'd roadtripped with that hairy guru pervert. Forgiven her for her other impromptu spiritual escapades (vanishing for a week or two to study Hinduism, Shamanism, Insane Clown Posse-ism). And once he'd even paid down her student loans when they'd gone to collections—she'd materialized on his doorstep, weeping, pleading for help, and cursing at herself in the most heartbreakingly sincere display of self-loathing he'd ever witnessed. He'd helped her. Gladly. Of course that was all years ago—she had repaid him for all of it. She'd pulled her life together, or seemed to, she hadn't wept on his doorstep for years, and thank Christ she'd given up those absurd religious quests, but still . . .

Still there was the silent bargain—*We take care of each other.*

Though Waring knew Alaura paid the greater price for their friendship. Appeased the customers he trampled upon. Hired new employees whenever old ones finally gave up. Fed him. Stuffed spearmint gum into his mouth to mask the smell of alcohol. Shoved him in a cab when he was too drunk. Instructed him when to buy new clothes. Everything.

In the end, he gave her nothing but money.

"No," he said. "I'm not having money problems. We're fine."

"But our bank account is getting really low."

"You know I have money, Alaura."

"And Blockbuster is obviously a big deal," she persisted. "Is that why Clarissa Wheat from Guiding Glow Distribution has been leaving messages?"

He looked again at Alaura—her pouty lips and pert Jean Seberg nose and angry eyes overlaid by concerned brow. Her heart-shaped face framed by the office door.

"Every single day, she calls."

But Waring didn't want to think about it. About Blockbuster, about money, about the downturn in business, about Clarissa Wheat from Guiding Glow Distribution. (And why *was* Clarissa Wheat calling? That was more bad news. Waring *needed* his feeble distribution deal and its measly wholesale discount, not to mention that Guiding Glow was currently allowing him to operate at a considerable debt. But Clarissa Wheat: a hideous Christian prude whom he had grudgingly screwed a year ago, though in truth he couldn't remember the particulars of her visit, such as conversations or copulation, because he'd been tanked. Perhaps nothing sexual had happened, which was possible, he supposed, given her Skeletor-like countenance and her obnoxious biblical proclamations, and especially given that his member hadn't functioned reliably since the early 1990s. But the point: Clarissa Wheat could cancel his distribution contract with a wave of her bony hand, effectively shattering the narrow margin upon which Star Video currently skated. And that, as they say, would be that.) No, he wanted to drink, so he chugged another beer, and he mumbled, "Don't worry, Alaura, everything is fine," and very, very soon, yes, he started to feel the booze, and he wasn't hearing Alaura. He was talking to her but not participating in the interface. Alaura, the only person he gave a crap about, the quirky country girl from Sprinks, North Carolina, turned hipster West Appleton power goddess . . . but now he didn't have the energy. This wasn't one of those times when *Waring Wax acts for a moment like a human being to gain sympathy*, this was instead when *Waring drinks*, which he did.

Alaura finally left the office.

He guzzled another beer.

Finally the warmth of the booze was pulsing again through his face, so when he thought about Blockbuster, he felt only a painful twinge that became easier and easier to ignore—because fuck it, he owned the ancient, rundown strip mall that housed both Star Video and Pizza My Heart, as well as the half acre on College Street where the building stood, and he owned his own house. Yes, they were shitty properties, but he *owned* them, so he'd never end up destitute. And when he thought of his family, all he saw of his father was a mound of wet clay, and of his brother a false, toothy smile, and of his mother a swath of gray and white—that cloudy headshot from her unsuccessful acting career that had adorned the mantle of his childhood home, a proud memento of her failure. And of his ex-wife, Waring saw nothing of her physical form—only the never-good-enough apartment in New York. And the bars he had frequented. And his office. And that last flight from the city, when he had decided, once and for all, that he actually didn't care about money, or working in an office, or owning things, or being married, or impressing people at dinner parties—especially dinner parties. He really didn't care, all he'd ever wanted to do was own and operate a video store, that had been all he'd ever dreamed about, and he had wept on that plane, and cursed, and told whoever would listen that his wife had left him for another man, that he'd been fired from his job by that same man, that he was leaving New York forever, and that life as he knew it, thankfully, was over.

An empty beer can slipped from his fingers and pinged loudly against the concrete floor—Waring jolted awake, surprised to find himself in his office at Star Video. It was two a.m.

He unearthed a half bottle of cheap bourbon in the bottom desk drawer, under the credit card bills (unpaid). He kept drinking, and later, on his couch at home, he passed out during the first long tracking shot of *Touch of Evil*.

The next morning, after a shower and a change of clothes (in his head he heard Alaura reprimanding him for his odor), Waring stumbled down College Street through the harsh whiteness of day. He needed a drink. But coffee first.

Waiting in line at the Open Eye Café—a large, trendy study spot for Appleton University students—Waring realized that he was surrounded, once again, by a hoard of people all transfixed by tiny glowing terminals. The laptops: rectangular screens blooming blue-white light, like a field of illuminated gravestones, brighter than the sun streaming through the windows. And all the damn cell phones. At one table he saw three emaciated college girls, each wearing a pink tee shirt and plaid pajama pants, each gaping like zombies at their one-inch screens, tapping away with their thumbs, lost in an ether of idiocy.

And . . . good God . . . was one guy actually watching an episode of that god-awful *Two and a Half Men* on his laptop? Wearing headphones, plugged in like an android?

Then, as if to intensify this horror show, Waring spotted Alaura's boyfriend, Peckerdick, in all his graduate-art-student glory. The kid wore paint-splattered pants and a black hemp shirt that fit a little too well, his gym-sculpted muscles somehow belying his commitment to the painter's craft. What was Alaura doing with this guy? After Peckerdick had threatened to punch Waring that drunken night not long ago, Alaura had defended her boyfriend, arguing that deep down, Peckerdick was kind and complex. Waring knew what that meant. It meant that Peckerdick performed oral sex and listened to Yo-Yo Ma while he painted. He listened to *This American Life*. He probably wept in joy during Peter Greenaway movies and worshiped the collective works of Terrence Malick without discussion. Peckerdick was, according to Alaura, "wise beyond his years." But Waring didn't buy it. The guy was clearly a rich kid pretending to be evolved. And he was only twenty-three years old. Way too young for her.

Then Waring saw—Peckerdick was sharing a fruit pastry with a blonde girl in a powder-blue tee shirt. Some high-breasted sorority chick. Peckerdick forked a hunk of pastry toward the girl's shimmering lips, and as the airship reached its dock, he made eye contact with Waring.

Peckerdick leaned back in his chair, frowned.

Waring pointed a finger gun at him. "I knew it," he mouthed.

Smiling at his discovery and resolving to lock it into memory so as to tell Alaura posthaste, Waring ordered a red eye. He paid the purple-tattooed twit who always sneered at him, and he thought, *Life sucks, but not as much as people*, and he wanted to say, "I know a girl with tattoos who knows a thing or two." But he didn't say it. He was tired, and anyway, being rude in the Open Eye might get him kicked out, again, and this was one of the few places where he tried to behave. He was spoiled on espresso. And wasn't that the best sort of business to be in? To sell a truly addictive product to your customers?

Two nights later, from the safety of Star Video's loft—referred to by those in the know as *The African Queen*—Waring listened to a staff meeting that Alaura had hastily arranged. He had spent the entire day in *The African Queen* drinking and smoking and reading a fascinating biography of D.W. Griffith (Waring supposed *someone* had to invent the establishing shot, but unfortunately it was a crazy racist) and just for fun watching *Thin Man* movie after *Thin Man* movie, and he had no intention of participating in the pointless meeting. *The African Queen* itself was tiny, only seven feet by seven feet, nothing more than a rectangular wooden crate supported by the shelves behind the front counter where all the DVDs and VHS tapes were stored, and further secured by several rusty cables. The vessel's name was etched upon its berth in black stenciled letters, and the walls of the loft rose high enough that, when seated on its dusty yellow couch, one was hidden from the large store below.

The loft's television—a fifty-inch flat-panel, high-definition screen—was Waring's lone concession to modern technology at Star Video. Because no matter how you sliced it, these new televisions were amazing, though he hadn't yet figured out how to attach the thing to a VHS player . . .

He peered over the edge of *The African Queen*. Five employees. Apparently someone had just quit; he did not remember who. But Alaura, sexy as always. And the new kid (Jack? Jed? Jessie?), that tall trim smiling Richie Cunningham suck-up. The names of the remaining three, which Waring was astounded he could remember, were Dorian, Farley, and Rose. Dorian was a small effeminate kid of indeterminate age—his complexion was so polished that he might be either twenty or thirty-five—and he was the store's expert on musicals and concert videos. Dorian spoke softly and had a habit that Waring admired of rolling his eyes when he was annoyed. Farley (documentaries and dramas) was huge, almost three hundred pounds, but unlike his nickname-sake, Chris Farley (or perhaps Farley was his real name?), he could never maintain energy levels high enough to parlay his obesity into merrymaking, let alone go a half hour without sitting down. Rose (cartoons, especially classic Looney Tunes), a tiny, oily girl who resembled a mouse, wore huge hooded sweaters even in the summer, and she snarled if anyone violated her ten-foot personal space.

"We all love movies," Alaura was saying to them. "Working at a video store isn't a glamorous gig. But if you're like me, you'd rather watch movies than do anything else in the world. Anything. And yes, I know what that implies . . ."

Waring watched as his employees chuckled at her corny insinuation and, he knew, in embarrassed agreement. That was Alaura's great talent: hiring certifiable cinephiles, those crackbrained personalities for whom the flickering screen was better than sex.

"This is a special place for *all* of us," Alaura continued. "This is a college town. Ape U's right down the road—" (more chuckles for her deployment of local slang for Appleton University). "But the point is," she said, smiling, "this is an artsy, progressive bubble in an otherwise stupidly Republican state. And Star Video is the only local store that stocks foreign and independent titles. We carry over thirty thousand movies. It's the best selection in North Carolina. We're an important part of the arts community in Appleton and West Appleton and Ape U. And we're an independent store. In-de-pen-dent. We do things *our* way. We stock the movies *we* want. When Waring bought this place over ten years ago, he turned it from a crappy little closet that only stocked mainstream releases, where you couldn't even find fucking *Seven Samurai*, into a goddamn cathedral of movie worship. *That's* why this store is special."

The employees all nodded.

Waring belched quietly.

"I've worked here for nine years," Alaura went on. "Since the nineteen freaking nineties. And if Star Video closes—I'm not saying we're going to close, because we're not, because Waring tells me that we're doing fine—but if we did close, then something special about this town would be lost. A piece of its heart. I really believe that, stupid as it sounds. So, we're making a few changes. We need to improve customer experience. Jeff and I have discussed some ideas. Would everyone like to hear them?"

Not really, Waring thought.

Then he remembered that there was something he needed to tell Alaura. Something from a few days ago? Something about a fruit pastry . . . there was another character involved . . . it was very, very important . . .

But damn it all, he couldn't remember! The thought was gone like so many other memories. Washed away in the current of booze.

"It's time to try customer incentives," Alaura was saying. "Like specials, prizes, giveaways."

Gimmicks? Waring thought.

He flopped back onto *The African Queen*'s couch. He cracked open another beer.

"Business is pain," he proclaimed in a whisper. "Anyone who says differently is selling something."

Then he realized, of course, that the real quote from *The Princess Bride* is, "*Life* is pain . . . Anyone who says differently—"

He drifted off to sleep.

Waring awoke in *The African Queen* the next evening, confused, having expected sunlight to needle the painful space around his head. Had he slept an entire day? Or awoken in the interim? He sat up, groaned, could not find a beer. Printers churned below. Coins clattered into the Cashier du Cinéma. Computers bleeped.

He stood and looked down at the floor. A quick scan—twenty customers. The New Releases section was nearly full. Friday was their busiest night.

Was it Friday already?

He looked at Alaura. Strangely, she was wearing a blue country dress. And what was wrong with her hair? Some sort of wig? Pigtails?

Next to her stood the new kid—straw protruded from the neck of his shirt, and a black hat flopped on his head.

Rose wore a huge lion's mane made of yellow yarn.

"Oh, Christ," Waring said. "Costumes?"

The Wizard of Oz played on the store's central TV.

The new kid—boring name?—he bounced around, scratching at his chest where the straw seemed to irritate him, always that damn frantic smile hanging on his face. Twitchy like a little bird. Muscular and youthfully handsome, except for those pimples. And he was clearly enamored with Alaura—always looking at her, always cowering whenever she addressed him, always attempting to impress her with his stupendous effort. But who could blame him? Look at her. She's amazing. Sexy pigtails. Tattoos. Lips and eyes painted severely dark. Steampunk Dorothy. Alaura was at her best here. She addressed all the regulars by name. Outside Star Video, on the street or in the bars, she always frowned, tough as nails. But here, in the store, she pranced around happily, fully equipped with fire and music, and enjoying every second of it, enjoying that people enjoyed being around her. That every customer hoped *she* would be the one to help him or her. Alaura was a West Appleton icon.

Waring overheard her recommend a Match Anderson movie to an Ape U student. Match Anderson, the young Hollywood director who had lived near Appleton as a teenager and had gone on to make one amazing indie thriller, *Losers*, and two Hollywood-financed flops, *A House on the Edge of Reason* and *Changeless*, the latter of which had taken eighteen months to film and that not even Hugh Jackman's loss of sixty pounds could save. Just because Match Anderson was a hometown boy made good didn't mean Alaura had to recommend his crappy movies to every damn customer . . . But look at Alaura, just fucking look at her, long tattooed neck, swaying hips, wonderfully filled-out ass, giving a little wink or a knowing grin, having fun, laughing, making a little joke, tapping her fingers in rhythm to "Yellow Brick Road" while a customer signed a receipt, doing a silly dance as she retrieved a DVD, saying something slightly risqué under her breath to a customer she thought could take it, always including the customer on something, always giving him or her some individual glimmer of her inner light.

She loved working here. This was her home. It wasn't only about money. He had to remember that.

He should go down and help; Alaura was now directing calculated glances at him, her lips pursed into a dark strawberry. He only
replied with annoyed shrugs. He didn't have the energy. He was
hungover. He lit a cigarette. The damned customers, he thought,
the damned fools. He knew that the night's biggest renter would
be *The Devil Wears Prada*, out that week. Already he had witnessed
the gaggles of Ape U girls prancing in and giggling and gaggling
and excitedly clutching their stupid Anne Hathaway vehicle. And
who the hell is Anne Hathaway anyway? Out there are wars in
Afghanistan and Iraq and daily terror plots and Dick Cheney running the damn country, not to mention the ever-present potential
of food poisoning or nuclear annihilation, and you want milky *meh*-
inspiring Anne Hathaway? Maybe they would rent a second movie,
but would it be something decent, something made with respect for
the craft of filmmaking, something classic, or, God forbid, something foreign, or independent, something about a character's inner
journey? There's a lifetime's worth of entertaining and well-made
movies out there, but would any of these customers make the right
choice? Of course not. And the male customers, men of all ages,
renting their action movies, occasionally venturing to Oscar winners but not usually, usually they would debate for three seconds
between a Vin Diesel vehicle and a Steve McQueen vehicle, and
they would choose Vin Diesel, every fucking time. And yes, *Little
Miss Sunshine* was an "indie" film that rented well, and *The Departed*
rented well, too, and that was another solid movie and it'd been
that year's Oscar winner for Best Picture, as if that meant anything.
But what about all the other classics? Why did most people rent the
absolute dreck? Waring could not believe that at this point in his
life, the customers he respected most were the little old biddies who
rented British movie after British movie after British movie (the
Colin Firth–Merchant Ivory whores), because at least they'd chosen
a niche they longed to exhaust, and the pimply teenage boys who

could not get enough of anime and sci-fi and horror, because at least they watched movies outside of the mainstream . . .

Waring watched his customers—the good and the bad, the worthy and the lame. Their faces blurred together, time-lapsed.

They were in *his* store. Renting *his* movies.

For better or for worse, this was his home, too.

Oh, Jesus. Was he crying again?

"I want to speak to your manager," one of the customers said.

Waring focused—Alaura smiled at the customer, a short man whose face was a little too tanned for his white hair and his white teeth and his white Nike track jacket. "I want to speak to your manager," he repeated, louder, as if Alaura had been too stupid to catch it the first time.

"I am the manager, sir," Alaura said calmly.

"Then I want to speak to the owner."

"Sir, I'm sorry, but I'm afraid you'll have to pay this late fee."

"But I've told you, it's a mistake."

"Sir, someone else on your account might have—"

"So your computer never makes a mistake?"

Alaura glanced up at Waring—her expression indicated that she was confident in the computer's assessment.

The customer shook his head, bubbled with anger. "I want to speak to your *man-a-ger*."

"Again, sir, I am the manager."

Thatta girl, Waring thought.

Alaura smiled pleasantly. The customers around them had quieted.

"So your computer never makes a mistake?"

"I don't think this is a mistake, sir."

"Your computer never makes a mistake?"

The new kid—Jeff was his name?—materialized next to Alaura. Waring watched her look up at the new kid, at his floppy hat, at his tawny neck gone red with hay scratches, at the frightened expression on his young, blemished face.

"Please calm down, sir," Jeff said in a deep, quivering, Southern-twanged voice.

The customer rolled his eyes. "I want to speak to whoever is in charge."

"No you don't, sir," Alaura said.

"I mean, you really don't," Jeff agreed sincerely.

"Yes," the customer said, "I do."

"Well, sir, that can be arranged," Alaura said. "Waring!"

Waring swiped away the last of his tears. Then he cleared his throat, climbed out of *The African Queen*, and descended the rusty spiral staircase—his footsteps a little heavy for dramatic effect.

This should be fun.

"Dorothy, Scarecrow, I'll take it from here," he said when he'd arrived at the counter.

"Are you the person in charge?" the customer asked.

Waring stepped in front of Alaura, stared the customer dead in the face.

"Owner," Waring corrected. "I'm the owner."

The customer extended a hand over the counter. Waring frowned, held out a limp set of fingers that the man immediately grabbed and shook, jostling Waring's entire body.

"I'm Adam," the man said, now speaking pleasantly. "Adam Pritt. I own Quick Dick's, the running shoe store in Browne Mill Mall. Surprised we've never met."

"Mm?"

"I only say that because, like you, I'm a local business owner. Started my place with nothing. I know the value of customer service."

"Customer what?"

"This employee," Pritt continued as if he hadn't heard Waring's quip, "who I understand is a manager, refuses to waive some late fees that I did not accrue."

Waring looked at the computer display of Adam Pritt's account information. The total of his outrageous late fee was six dollars. And a note in the comments section:

```
MAJOR asshole, always problem with
late fees. No breaks.
```

"Well," Waring said. "The thing is, you have a late fee."

"Excuse me?"

"Your hair is perfect," Waring observed, squinting at the white quaff atop Pritt's head. "Like the spoiler of a Lamborghini."

The man ran his fingers over his spoiler.

"You have a late fee," Waring repeated. "A whopping six dollars."

"But—"

"No buts."

The man laughed contemptuously. "I've never been treated like this."

"The treatment is free of charge."

"You know, it's almost cheaper to *buy* these movies on Amazon."

"Then go to Amazon, Tarzan."

"And I hear Blockbuster doesn't even charge late fees."

Waring leaned forward. "Then. Go. To. Blockbuster."

Adam Pritt (Adam *Prick*, Waring thought) was speechless.

"I hear Blockbuster also has a discount for dramatic hair. They give free Twizzlers for being repeatedly rude." Waring took a breath. "People like you amaze me. I recognize you. I've seen you skishing around on your bicycle, with all your bicycle buddies. Bragging at the Open Eye about your workouts, your four-by-four hundreds, your ten-by-ten millions, or whatever, in your tight sweaty shorts that seem designed to mechanically lift your balls in my direction." Waring cradled a large pair of invisible orbs from his waist toward Adam Prick's face. "And all the while you're sweating on the couches, so there's absolutely nowhere for me to sit in that place to enjoy my red eye that hasn't been tainted by your balls."

"I'm leaving—"

"That's an idea!" Waring cried. "Go in peace. And thank you for this opportunity, because it's been a while, but I think it's time for our 'firing a customer' dance."

Shifting his weight from foot to foot, Waring raised his hands in the air and waved them like a deranged Grateful Dead fan.

—Sometimes you *have* to fire a customer—

Alaura snorted in laughter, and she leaned forward, hands on knees, wiggled her glorious round bottom near the microwaveable popcorn display, nodded her head to a silent beat, and said, "Uh-huh, yeah, uh-huh, yeah," over and over. Her fake pigtails flopped in front of her face.

Waring glanced at the new kid. He was dancing, too—sort of hopping in place and pounding his fists . . . the mashed potato?

Maybe not such a bad kid after all, Waring thought.

Customers around them covered their mouths in astonishment.

"Oh, go to hell!" Adam Prick said to them all.

Finally he stormed out of the shop.

The other customers clapped as the door closed behind him.

Waring took a bow.

And Alaura collapsed on his shoulder in laughter—he could tell that she wasn't thinking about Blockbuster or money or how she was so much better than this place—and he held her up, hoping to memorize the sensation of her weight.

That night, Star Video grossed $1,100. One of their worst Fridays ever.

The following evening Waring entered Ehle County Social Club, one of the many dive bars he frequented and the location, he now remembered, of his recent debacle with Alaura and Peckerdick, the embarrassing particulars of which now came back to him in a sandy rush. Shit. Idiot. Sticking my tongue in her ear. Deserved to get punched. Didn't deserve Alaura defending me. Whatever. Just forget about it. Waring approached the bar, and when the bartender (to whom Waring was always polite because he resembled a young Joe Don Baker and didn't take shit from anyone) asked compulsorily how his night was going, Waring responded, "I'm scared I might be bankrupt, and I don't know how to save my shop."

But Young Joe Don Baker wasn't interested. Nor, Waring imagined, was anyone else.

Four hours later, after five pints and two whiskeys and an entire pack of cigarettes, and after abandoning a crossword puzzle upon seeing evidence, in that same crossword, of the progressive degradation of his own handwriting, Waring started walking home. Very drunk.

Time was slippery and amorphous, like the sidewalk under his feet.

Then he was lying on the street. Which was strange, he decided. Where was he lying? How had lying occurred? He had been walking home. Yes, he had made it to his own driveway.

He heard a familiar skishing sound.

Finally he managed to look up. Gliding in a circle of which Waring was the focal point were three muscular men on bicycles.

They all wore tight, ball-toting shorts.

They skidded to a halt.

Waring squinted at them, pulled them into focus. Below the unzipped collars of their body-hugging shirts was a large insignia that read: "Blockbuster."

One of the men was Adam Prick.

"What the fuck do you want, you dickless wonder?" Waring spat.

Another of the men, a tall rangy guy with dark skin and black hair, said, "Waring Wax, your day of reckoning is approaching."

A NIGHTMARE ON WARING'S STREET

Jeff sat in the Appleton Starbucks nursing a third cup of coffee, trying (failing) to focus on his *Introduction to Business Administration* textbook, and trying (failing) to ignore the pretty coed sitting by the front window. He chugged coffee because it was the college thing to do. But now his arms and face trembled, and his stomach gnawed at its own wooden insides. He understood now that three cups was way too much. And the girl made it worse somehow. She was stunning—a runner's body, tanned skin, glossy blue soccer jersey with three white stripes down each sleeve. She stared at her laptop, entranced, nibbling her lower lip.

Concentrate, Jeff told himself—in his textbook a lengthy sentence lay broken and jumbled, despite five attempts to comprehend it.

After failing to concentrate for the sixth and seventh time, Jeff glanced again at the runner/soccer player/genius and saw, much to his surprise, that she was now looking in his direction.

He turned, studied the wall behind him. Hanging there was a huge, creepy lithograph of a horse. Obviously she was looking at that.

He shut the textbook. Agitated sigh. Almost midnight. The café would close soon. He had watched the girl for two hours in the hopes that . . . what was he hoping? That she would approach *him*? That on one of his many trips to the bathroom a pen might slip from her table and he might valiantly retrieve it? That if any other such bizarre twist of fate were to draw them into conversation, he wouldn't make a total fool of himself?

He pushed the textbook into his backpack, stood, and, emboldened more by caffeine than by anything resembling confidence, he approached her table. She looked up from her computer. Her thoughtful frown vanished. She smiled.

Smiling back as casually as possible, Jeff said, "Hello?"

"Hi!" she responded brightly, and she produced a sweet little laugh.

But the laugh was so little and so sweet that it demolished whatever Jeff had planned to say next.

Long, painful silence.

Then the cell phone on her table rang—some recent Beyoncé tune—probably one of her nine million friends.

"I just wanted to say hello," he pronounced over the noise of the phone.

"Sorry, it's my mother," the girl said. "I should probably answer."

"Cool, I talk to my mother all the time." He chuckled at nothing, hoping to obscure the absurdity of this comment, then repeated: "I just wanted to say hello."

"Okay?" she said, her expression now straining at its edges.

And without thinking, Jeff's gaze rose to the door. He lifted his hand in a brief wave of farewell, and he exited the café still wearing, he now realized, the same deranged smile he'd been wearing all along.

Jeff walked quickly across College Street and onto Appleton University's campus. There he passed darkened class buildings—some gothic and corniced, others new and glass-fronted—and he trudged up to the one-hundred-year-old clock tower that crowned the university, where he'd made a habit of loitering moodily over the past few nights. The clock tower, along with the craggy live oaks surrounding it, was the postcard image that had helped sell him, and many other freshmen, on Appleton University. But tonight, the postcard had lost its romantic luster. It was just a redbrick monolith displaying the painfully slow passage of time. Standing there, looking up at the thing, Jeff didn't feel at all like loitering moodily, hoping someone would talk to him, and scribbling nonsense in his journal like the stupid undergrad he was.

So he considered walking the quarter mile to his dorm. But he was too jacked on coffee to sleep. And his roommate, who was a basketball player, had made no secret of his preference to be left alone with whatever new girl he'd probably be bringing back to their room.

Almost without thinking, Jeff moved west, off campus and back onto College Street. There the sidewalks swarmed with smilers and drinkers, all of them attractive, all of them friends with one another, all the young women showing off their flawless legs and end-of-summer tans, all the young men wearing expensive shirts and yapping on cell phones and screaming guttural insults at each other like steroidal jocks. Jeff tried to avoid their gazes, and he crossed the street to elude bars brimming with laughing women.

And all the while he muttered to himself, chastised himself for his infinite rottenness—his failure so far to make *any* college friends, his struggles to keep up in his freshmen classes, how for no good reason he'd skipped church last Sunday (tomorrow, he *had* to go to Tanglewood Baptist tomorrow), how he was just a country bumpkin in this big bustling town, a lamb amidst the wolves, a fool in the king's court.

And most of all he reprimanded himself for his humiliation with the café girl. Stupid virgin. Catching his reflection as he passed the darkened shop windows of College Street, seeing his pitiful, zitty face . . . and somehow *not* seeing that his trim frame and muscular shoulders might be attractive to many of the females who terrified him . . . Jeff knew, beyond a shadow of a doubt, that the person looking back at him was a total virgin loser.

He'd lived in his musty dorm at Appleton University for thirteen days, and his life now mirrored every corny college movie he'd ever watched—*Van Wilder*, *Real Genius*, *Old School*, and his favorite, *PCU*, which he believed was an underrated classic—but his life lacked any of the exciting, redeeming plot elements of that genre: parties, laughter, topless girls, loveable sidekicks, incremental triumph. Part of him had truly believed that because he was so well versed in College Freshman Plotlines, he'd also be immune to social awkwardness, homesickness, fear of maniacal professors. But he wasn't immune. Not at all. Occasionally his newfound freedom enthralled him (Momma never would have allowed him to walk aimlessly until one a.m.), but mostly it was weirdly repressive. The sheer number of choices. The glut of opportunities. Thousands of people who already seemed to know each other, and Jeff—exactly as in high school—too tongue-tied to make friends.

He had thought college would be different. And it was different. It was worse.

He clenched his fists and belted out a high-pitched, Bruce Lee squeal, and he kicked a pinecone with kung fu rage, sending it chattering across the pavement in the grubby West Appleton neighborhood where he now found himself.

So many clichés, he thought. Why couldn't he just relax? Be a normal person? Was he incapable of happiness? Only his job at Star Video was going well. Thank God he had found the place. Thank God Alaura had hired him. He needed the money, even if Star Video only paid minimum wage. But all those movies! He had already used his free rentals to watch ten films he never would have had access to back home in Murphy, North Carolina, the crappy mountain town where he'd spent his entire pointless life. His Star Video

THE LAST DAYS OF VIDEO

coworkers were cool, if a bit strange. Alaura was amazing, of course. And Waring . . . well, what could you say about Waring? Waring was bonkers. He was mean to Jeff. He complained constantly. He insulted customers. He was always drunk, or at least smelled like it. And he seemed completely disinterested in the welfare of his own company—Jeff had hoped to learn how to run a successful small business, but instead he had learned that some businesses survive *despite* their owners. Nothing about Waring made any sense.

But still, something about the short, strange, cranky drunk was . . . interesting. Waring seemed to know everything about movies. If a customer mentioned some random director, most of whom Jeff had never heard of, Waring could list all of that director's notable movies, *Rain Man*–style, all while still making rude quips to whomever he was condescending, and all while not removing his gaze from whatever movie he was watching, whatever book he was reading. Waring was brilliant and ridiculous in equal measure, and even though customers understandably disliked him, they always, without fail, left with the movie they wanted.

And Alaura liked Waring. That had to mean something.

Then Jeff saw Waring. Twenty yards ahead. Lying on the pavement. As if Jeff had conjured his boss just by thinking about him.

Waring rocked back and forth on his back like an upturned turtle. Yelling incoherent phrases.

Three handsome men on bicycles, laughing.

Seconds later: Jeff stood between Waring and the cyclists, who were parked side by side, ten feet away, like robber cowboys from some old Western. Jeff did not remember deciding to intervene. Or running toward them. Or even how he had arrived on this street in the first place. But here he was, breathing quickly, shoulders painfully tense—Bruce Lee somersaulting in to save the damsel in distress.

Jeff thought again of the café girl. Of her perfect skin.

"What's going on?" Jeff said to the men—his voice shaking, very un-Bruce-Lee-like.

"Who's there?" Waring hissed, staring blindly at the solitary streetlight directly overhead. "What do you mean, day of reckoning?"

"No. It's Jeff from Star Video."

"Jeff who?"

"You just hired me."

"I just what?"

A cyclist interjected: "Don't bother, kid. He's dead drunk."

It was Adam Pritt, the angry customer, Jeff could now see, from last night.

"What's going on?" Jeff said to him.

"Nothing, kid."

"Don't call me kid. I'm not your kid."

"Hey, relax."

"Don't tell me to relax," Jeff said, his voice unsteady. "What's going on?"

"What's your name?" said another of them. This man was impossibly handsome, with dark hair and a chiseled jaw. He leaned casually on his handlebars, sweat beaded his forehead, and he took a drink from a glistening water bottle.

"Not saying my name," Jeff managed.

"Fair enough. But why do you care what happens to this . . . guy?"

"He's . . . he's my boss."

"Wait, you really work at Star Video?"

"Yes."

The man emitted a long descending whistle, as if the concept of employment at Star Video was the tallest tale he'd ever heard.

"Listen, kid. We found him like this. Honestly, he was on the ground when we rolled up."

"I don't believe you."

"No? Do you really think this is the first time Mr. Wax has ended up drunk on the street?"

To this, Jeff could not summon an intelligent counter.

But he stood his ground, tried to stare down the cyclists. Wealthy men. College-educated men. Perfect complexions. The muscles on their arms and legs linked together like intricate machinery. They were preened and polished, light-years away from the good old boys Jeff had grown up with. Streetlight glinted off the gears of their expensive, space-aged bicycles. Precision equipment. And for some reason, this all called to mind Jeff's small, dingy, piece-of-crap television back home in Murphy. The eight-inch screen. How for years he had stayed up past his bedtime, set the TV on his bed, covered it and himself with a sheet like a kid reading a book, and secretly watched any movie he could find. Good movies or bad movies, *Star Wars* or *Starship Troopers 2*, he didn't care. The warmth from the cathode ray tube had comforted him, helped him forget about his rotten life, about his father, who was a drunk living in some holler and whom Jeff had only met five or six times, and about his mother, who was always right in the next room, and who never left the house and hadn't had a job in years, morbidly obese and fuelling her broad hatreds with Fox News and whatever pills for whatever condition she was suffering from that week.

Movies were his refuge, his escape, his closest friends, his only friends.

"Waring's my friend!" Jeff snapped suddenly.

"Calm down, kid," the handsome cyclist said.

"*You* calm down!"

"There's no reason to—"

"Shut up!"

The dark-haired man sighed, sat up, tested his pedals.

He pushed off and glided toward Jeff, who now, for some reason, found himself paralyzed.

The man punched Jeff in the mouth.

Jeff's vision rolled over white.

Seconds later, when he was able to open his eyes, Jeff saw the three cyclists slipping away into the darkness.

"Good luck with that job, kid!" his attacker called out, and the other men laughed as if this statement had made any sense.

Seconds later, they were gone.

Blood still pounding in his ears, Jeff attempted to help Waring stand. But the old man yelled, "No!" and Jeff released his arm.

Waring rolled to his stomach, groaned, pushed on the asphalt.

More than a minute later, Waring stood unsteadily and looked up and down the street. He seemed even shorter than normal to Jeff, who towered over him by almost a foot.

"They're gone," Jeff said.

"Mm," Waring croaked. "I'm going inside."

"Okay, but . . ."

"But what?"

"But I helped you."

Waring: no response.

"Is this where you live?" Jeff said, looking at a small, decrepit ranch house that eerily resembled his and Momma's duplex back in Murphy. "Can I help you inside?"

Waring hobbled on his own up the dusty driveway toward the house.

"They were messing with you," Jeff explained.

Waring climbed the house's front stoop, fumbled with his keys.

Jeff's voice cracked into a yell: "Aren't you even going to say *thank you?*"

Silence.

Finally Waring looked back, and he called across the weedy lawn: "You're the one with the crush on Alaura, right?"

Jeff's mouth swung open. He felt his face warm over immediately.

"She's out of your league, Sasquatch," Waring continued. "And don't even think about telling her about this."

Jeff shrugged. He looked up at the dark, hazy sky and mouthed a prayer for emotional support.

"Oh Christ," Waring said. "You don't believe in God, do you?"

Without thinking, Jeff responded, "My . . . my family's Baptist."

Waring looked up to the heavens himself, and after teetering backward and almost falling over again, he said, "I guess we need all the help we can get. Pray away."

Then Waring hocked a loogie into a nearby bush, turned, entered his house.

"Good night," he said, almost too quiet for Jeff to hear, and the door smacked closed behind him.

JEFF, LIES, AND VIDEOTAPE

The next morning, Jeff found himself sitting in a straight-backed chair behind the rear pew at Tanglewood Baptist Church. He was exhausted. Freaked out. Ashamed.

To his right sat three suited men—the other ushers—chewing on their gums, actively ignoring him.

Jeff didn't want to be here. But his minister from home, Pastor Fiennes, had e-mailed Tanglewood's minister, Pastor Herring, and Pastor Herring had somehow located Jeff on Appleton University's online directory and e-mailed him that week with a request to fill in as usher. And how could Jeff say no, electronically or otherwise, to a Google-savvy Baptist pastor?

Jeff's worst fear had already been realized: As he had escorted congregants to their seats, many of them had first smiled, then squinted, then glared at his swollen upper lip, where he'd been punched, quivering on his face like a purple mouse. *Who is this thug we've admitted into our church?* they surely thought. *This mountain trash?* The other ushers had avoided eye contact with Jeff (or eye-to-lip contact), and it seemed inevitable that Pastor Herring would soon be informed of Jeff's condition and proclaim from the pulpit,

"Son, I'm afraid this isn't working out. You need to leave. And of course I'll be calling your mother."

Pastor Herring trolled on and on, the same old sermon about taxation/homosexuality (bad) and Billy Graham/George W. Bush (good), and Jeff struggled in his agitation to settle his thoughts on God. To mingle with the Spirit. But like always, this process felt disjointed, perhaps even rudely presumptuous, and he thought, as he had been thinking often lately, that if God is this huge, unknowable, all-perfect entity—the glue that binds together the universe—then why would He bother with tiny pathetic humans on the tiny planet Earth?

The other ushers were standing. Jeff stood as well, two steps behind them, certain that he looked like a bloody, punch-drunk boxer.

An usher with a bulldog's frowning face handed Jeff a brass bowl—the collection bowl? At Berry Baptist in Murphy, they used small plastic baskets.

It must have been an hour later when he reached the last pew and discovered Alaura Eden.

Had Alaura been sitting there the entire service? Only yards away from him? It couldn't be her. But it was. She was dressed like a countess from some black-and-white movie: a rounded fascinator with a black lace veil draped to her nose line and a high-collared jacket rising almost to her ears. Her tattoos were hidden. Hands crossed in lap, back erect, chin pulled in, eyes closed—as if she were preparing for a posed photograph.

When her eyes opened, flashbulbs went off in his mind.

Her hand—gloved in gray satin—rose to her mouth in surprise.

Hi, Jeff mouthed silently.

Recognizing him, she laughed. A Julia Roberts outburst. A happily terrified cackle. So loud that Jeff knew he should be embarrassed for her, and for himself, but he wasn't.

He saw the heads of nearby congregants turn in their direction. One man with close-cropped white hair shook his head and scowled.

But Jeff didn't care.

He smiled back at Alaura, and he gave her a little wave.

"I go to church once a month or so," Alaura said. "Different churches. Methodist, Catholic, nondenominational. Sometimes I even drive over to Raleigh or Durham. Leave early, cruise the streets like a gangster"—at this she giggled irresistibly for a moment—"until I find a church that strikes my fancy."

Jeff nodded, blissfully confused. Alaura had removed the cap with the veil and her high-collared church coat, revealing a more Alaura-typical band tee shirt. But who are the Ramones? Jeff wondered. They were walking slowly down College Street, from Tanglewood Baptist in Appleton toward Star Video, where they were both scheduled to work at noon. It was the first week of September, and a break in the heat promised by the Weather Channel had never come to pass. It was over ninety degrees. They passed the huge antebellum houses of the Historic District, each adorned with silver Historical Society plaques, their perfect lawns bursting with dahlias and gladiolas and daylilies, clearly competing with one another in some heated bourgeoisie gardening competition. Then Jeff and Alaura crossed the concrete bridge over the pottering strip of Nile Creek, lined on both sides by smooth boulders and weeping willows, and they moved into West Appleton, which seemed a world away. They passed dingy student apartment buildings, a locally owned organic taqueria, a locally owned deep-fried sandwich shop, and several other restaurants with patios chattering with activity—students and locals who hadn't gone to church, which Jeff could tell by their grubby clothes and hungover expressions—everyone drinking frosty pints and laughing, not a care in the world.

Once again, Jeff was struck by how happy and relaxed everyone was . . . happier and more relaxed than he ever seemed to feel.

"I went to church as a kid," Alaura was saying. "Usually alone. Sprinks only had two churches, one Baptist, one Methodist. But I guess I always found church, I don't know, intriguing. The search for truth, et cetera."

Jeff nodded again. "We always go to church."

"You and your parents?"

"Me and my momma." Jeff quickly corrected himself, "My mother. She's real religious.

"Not my daddy. His is the Church of Coors Light Almighty. He's not a bad drunk or anything. Just an always drunk. He's a good man.

"My mother's a good woman. She's . . . pretty strict, I guess. Didn't want me moving down here. But I think she's doing okay about it."

Alaura nodded. "So your parents are divorced?"

"Um . . . um," Jeff stuttered.

"Sorry. I didn't mean to pry."

"That's okay," he said, struggling to recover his composure. "Uh . . . yes, my parents are divorced. My dad . . . I don't really know him."

"I never knew my mother," Alaura said.

A pause.

"So," Alaura said softly. "College must be a big change for you."

Jeff looked up and around the town, at all the activity and happiness. He smiled. "This place, Appleton, West Appleton, it's a different world—"

Then they saw Blockbuster, and another silence fell between them.

In the course of only a few days, the building had completely transformed. It had been retrofitted with royal blue paneling along the outside, the parking lot had been paved dark black, and the walls inside had been painted a glossy, antiseptic white. At this rate, Blockbuster must be opening soon, maybe within a few weeks, or even a few days.

Both Alaura and Jeff stared at the building as they walked past, but neither spoke a word. Star Video quickly appeared, moments later, on their left.

"So what the hell happened to your lip?" she finally asked.

"Um . . ." but Jeff's voice faltered again. For some reason he couldn't remember the lie he had prepared. Like last night when the café girl's sweet laughter had incapacitated him.

He didn't want to lie to Alaura. But he also didn't want to risk his job by incurring Waring's wrath.

"Sorry," she said. "You probably don't want to talk about it."

"Um?"

"A man of mystery, I can dig it. By the way, I saw that you checked out *Killing of a Chinese Bookie* a few days ago? By Cassavetes? That's awesome. What did you think?"

All at once, Jeff's nervousness redoubled—he didn't want her to know he had hated *Chinese Bookie*, hadn't even finished it. That it had been dull and sort of amateurish and kind of morally gross— all those strippers and drinking and gambling, not to mention the Chinese bookie, who apparently gets killed, though Jeff hadn't made it that far before passing out.

"It was okay," he muttered.

"Okay?"

"I mean . . ."

"No, Jeff. Never pretend to like a movie that you didn't like. But when we get to the shop, I have to show you something."

"Huh?"

"Part of your movie education."

In Star Video, Alaura and Jeff relieved Rose, who had opened that morning and who had been watching Looney Tunes on the store's central TV.

As she was leaving, Rose stopped at the door, turned back, and said, "Have a nice day, Jeff."

Surprised, Jeff looked at her; this was the first time she had ever spoken to him directly.

He smiled awkwardly to her in farewell.

"Here," Alaura said, breaking his attention from Rose. "You need to watch this. Cassavetes."

She inserted a VHS tape into the store's dusty player.

"Our DVD of this is scratched," Alaura explained. "It's awesome we still have it on VHS."

"Oh," Jeff said. "Is *that* why we still carry videotapes? And are we ever going to start carrying Blu-ray—"

"Waring's noncommittal on Blu-ray. It's fucking annoying. But let's talk about this movie, Jeff. It's Cassavetes."

"But I just don't think Cassavetes is for me," Jeff admitted. "I've watched some of his movies, but I—"

"Say that too loud, and Waring'll fire you."

"What? Is Waring here?"

"I don't know. He's probably passed out in *The African Queen.*"

"Oh."

"Cassavetes is maybe a little too indie for Waring," Alaura said, rolling her eyes. "A little too fast and loose for his tastes, but he still—"

"His tastes?"

"Classics," she explained. "Old movies. That's his jam. He's got wide-ranging tastes, of course. You've probably noticed he knows more about movies than God. But I'm not sure that he's actually *enjoyed* any movie made after 1979."

"But didn't Cassavetes make movies, like, back in the sixties?"

Alaura shrugged. "Jeff, you need to watch this. I know you love movies. That's why I hired you. And you've got a more-than-decent foundation of movie knowledge, enough to help most customers—"

Jeff: giddy with gratitude.

"—but you have a ton to learn. I'll give you the same lesson that Waring gave me, and the lesson that my boyfriend fell asleep during."

"Boyfriend?"

"Pierce thinks Cassavetes is overrated. Not visually stimulating."

"I just think his stories are, I don't know, boring."

Alaura shook her head. "They're not boring. They're different. First off, his dialogue."

"But I mean . . . I didn't like the dialogue."

"Watch."

On screen, two men walked on a beach, Peter Falk and some other guy, and a few young children ran around them. Jeff had watched this particular Cassavetes movie a few days ago, *A Woman Under the Influence*. But he could not remember this scene, must have dozed off or zoned out.

> OTHER GUY: What a day, Nick. I haven't been to the
> beach without my wife in years. We used to live in the
> water when I was a kid. "Fish," they called me. I was thin,
> see. Lips all blue. Shakin'. I was always lookin' for girls.
> My kids, they're all grown up now. My brother, Marco,
> he's a college graduate. Communist. Couldn't keep a job.
> Too many big ideas. Reads too much. I say let the girls
> read. They love to read. You know what I mean?
>
> FALK (angry): Okay! Let's enjoy ourselves, okay?
>
> OTHER GUY: Okay.

Alaura pressed pause, and the VCR whizzed to a stop. "Nick's in a bad mood," she explained.

"Which one's Nick?"

"Columbo."

"Oh, right."

"His wife is crazy, and he accidentally injured this guy at work. He's had a really, really shitty day. So, what do you think?"

"Of what?"

"Of the scene, silly."

Alaura smiled beautifully.

Jeff chuckled nervously. "It doesn't make sense what the other guy is saying."

"What doesn't make sense?"

Jeff looked at the TV screen, static trembling now over a frozen long shot of Falk, running on the beach after his daughter.

"Let me watch again," he said.

Alaura rewound the videocassette, paused it expertly at exactly the right moment, and played the scene again.

After, Jeff said, "I mean, his sentences don't fit together. Talking about fish. His brother the Communist? 'I say let the girls read.' What does that mean?"

"Have you ever read a transcript of a real conversation?" Alaura asked. "No one talks like they talk in movies or books or television. In real life, we constantly make mistakes. Speak in fragments. Self-edit. Go back to the middle of a sentence and start again. Follow a new train of thought."

"Okay?"

"That's what Cassavetes does. He writes more like people talk. All those pauses and random observations are intricately scripted. That other guy, Peter Falk's friend, he's yammering, trying to fill space, because Falk's in a terrible mood. Falk just injured a guy by accident, so his friend is nervous, saying whatever comes to mind. Cassavetes doesn't write Hollywood dialogue. No one actually sounds like Aaron Sorkin writes, you know?"

Who's Aaron Sorkin? Jeff thought. "What's wrong with Hollywood?" he said, suddenly a bit defensive, though he had no idea why.

Alaura's body quaked in silent laughter—one of her many disarming expressions. "Nothing's wrong with Hollywood, Jeff. But that's just one way to do things. It depends on the movie."

"Oh."

"Let's watch it one more time."

They watched the scene one more time.

"The other thing is the actors," she continued. "Cassavetes didn't direct his actors at all. Never gave them advice, even if they begged for it."

"So?"

"So if Peter Falk said, 'What's going on in this scene, John Cassavetes?' then Cassavetes would answer, 'You're standing here, and she's standing there,' and he would stare into Peter Falk's eyes, like this."

Alaura stared intensely into Jeff's eyes.

Jeff's diaphragm wrenched in terror, and he looked off at the floor.

"Nondirective directing," Alaura explained. "That's what it's called. That's how Cassavetes got those strange, realistic performances."

"Oh."

"Didn't you watch the commentary on *Chinese Bookie*? Or at least Google it?"

"No."

Alaura shook her head like a disappointed parent. "Watch it with the commentary. And find a book. There's tons at the Ape U library."

"Okay."

"But don't get *too* into film theory. Because, to put it politely, those guys sometimes miss the fucking point. Still, with good movies, you have to put in effort."

She ejected the videocassette, then inserted a DVD into the store's other player. It was the early-2000s indie thriller *Losers*. But instead of selecting a scene, she played one of the special features— Match Anderson, the young director of the film and, as Jeff had learned, a North Carolina native, was being interviewed on stage at some film festival. Anderson wore a wrinkled brown jacket, and he had dark Steve Buscemi circles under both eyes. The no-name, non-union actors from the film sat to Anderson's right, and a bodiless voice asked them questions.

"Listen to what he says about movies," Alaura whispered. "He really gets it."

"Who?"

"Match. Match Anderson."

Jeff looked at her strangely, then back at the screen. Match Anderson, in response to a question that Jeff had not heard, said:

"I've lived in movies since I was a kid. For me it was television. The movies on late-night television and the sitcoms and everything all the way down to the micro-narratives of commercials. I wrote out the plots. Seriously, when I was kid. I wrote out what happened scene by scene in *M*A*S*H* and *Married . . . with Children* and music videos and fucking bubblegum commercials. They all tell stories."

Reaction shots of the actors. Jeff glanced at Alaura—she was smiling at the television.

"We all lived *Losers*, okay?" Match Anderson continued. "This movie nearly killed a few of us, and I think everyone appreciated the toll it took on me. It's so much work, making a movie. Maybe that's a useless platitude, but it's so much fucking work, it's hell, and you don't know if in the end what you're doing is any good. Though this felt good, didn't it?" Sincere nods from the actors. "It felt right during shooting. And maybe that's all you ever have. That's all I had. I had a lot of work and a *feeling* that we were doing something good."

Reaction shots of the audience: snooty, cerebral approval.

"Watch," Alaura whispered.

"But that's not what I'm trying to say," Match Anderson muttered. He frowned and rubbed his temples with his thumbs, apparently distraught, it seemed to Jeff, to his emotional core. "That doesn't answer your question. Shit. What am I trying to say? Why are you listening to me? I can't talk about movies. No, I can't. Here's what I'm saying. What I'm saying . . . there isn't enough time in life, enough room in the artist's life, to get everything out. To film even 5 percent of what it is to be human. Because there's so much variance, so much drama and absurdity. So many shades of meaning, so many versions of emotion, and so many moments . . ." Match Anderson leaned forward, gripped the arms of his plastic chair. His eyes watered. "The amazing moments! Moments upon moments. There's no time, no words, no images to describe, to capture, even to summarize what it is to live, what reality *is*. No matter what, we fall short. All artists fall short. Filmmakers especially. No matter what, our attempts fail. Only briefly, very briefly, do movies succeed. I mean, sometimes you have to question this entire filmmaking enterprise, don't you? Your first principles as an artist? And at best, if you're really looking at it closely, if you're really being honest with yourself, an entire movie might intersect once or twice with what I'm talking about. With reality. Or with truth. And it's futile, isn't it? Our brains are too small. And if we don't have a clue how to live, how can we make movies about life?" His voice cracked into a whisper. "The answer is we do the best we fucking can. The best we fucking can."

The audience erupted in applause.

Match Anderson looked at them, wide-eyed in surprise.

Then he stood and left the stage.

The screen went black, and Jeff felt an indescribable ache in his chest—he did not understand the crazy speech, nor why Alaura had played it for him, nor her obvious fascination with this particular director. He turned to ask for an explanation.

But she was already ejecting the DVD and starting another movie.

This moment of silence, he realized, might be the perfect opportunity to tell her about the bicycle gang. How he had intervened and rescued Waring, even if he'd also chickened out and gotten punched in the face like a coward. But it would be simple—just tell her. There was no reason to lie. He could ask her to keep it a secret. He knew she would agree. Alaura was cool like that. Waring would never now.

But then he noticed that, for some reason, Alaura's expression had turned soft and distant, like she was about to cry.

He wanted to talk to her, but he had no idea how.

WHY FIDELITY

Pierce, Alaura's boyfriend of two months, began gathering and packing his possessions while she slept. He removed his toothbrush from the bathroom, his CDs from the stereo case, a quarter bag of barbeque chips from the kitchen cabinets, and he slipped it all into an orange duffel bag.

Awoken by the whistle of a zipper, Alaura climbed out of bed. She wiggled into a long E.T. and Michael Jackson tee shirt (an original) and walked into her living room.

"I need caffeine," she said. "How much did we drink?"

"Um?"

She looked at Pierce—he stood by the couch, fully dressed, and stared at the duffel bag at his feet.

"What are you doing?" she asked.

"Packing."

"Looks like you're already packed."

"I guess so."

"Why?"

"School started, like, three weeks ago," he said.

"So?"

"So I've got portrait studio this week."

"So?"

"So I have to go."

"You have to go?" she said.

"I *need* to go."

Alaura walked into the kitchen space of her small apartment and found a diet green tea in the refrigerator. Three quick sips. Then she flipped the "On" button on the Mr. Coffee, turned back to Pierce.

He stood there, not saying anything, in her tiny and shabbily furnished living room. At twenty-nine years old, she knew she should have a nicer place. One with a porch or at least bigger windows, one without undergrads living above, below, and on either side of her. She should have a larger television, and a better computer, and window blinds that weren't plastic and warped and cracked. Her movie posters should at least be framed rather that hung with that blue adhesive gunk on that cheap 1970s wood paneling. There was a reason she brought very few men back to her apartment—Pierce had been one of the only exceptions.

"What do you mean you need to go?" she finally managed.

"I mean, I think it's time—"

"Wait," she said, and she raised her palms as if signaling a car to stop.

"I'm sorry, Alaura."

Her eyes began to burn. She let her arms drop and said, "Are you trying to break up with me, Pierce?"

"I'm sorry."

"You're sorry?"

"Yes."

She saw that his face was calm—beautiful tan skin taut over square jaws. His hands were jutted in the pockets of his wrinkled, paint-covered pants, and a sandaled foot nudged against the duffel bag.

She walked toward him, placed her hands on his cheeks.

"No," she whispered.

"I'm sorry."

"Don't, Pierce."

"This isn't working," he said.

"What?"

"Because I'm not happy." He eased away from her. "We've only been together a few months, and we're arguing."

"But we're not arguing," she said.

"Yes, we are."

"No, we're not."

"Yes, we *are*."

She stepped toward him again, pressed her hands to his chest, guided him onto the couch. She sat on his lap, laid her arms over his shoulders.

"Wait, Pierce. This doesn't make sense . . . talk to me . . ."

But he hesitated. She felt the muscles of his shoulders stiffen, and they exchanged a glance that, if caught on camera, would have conveyed no information because their expressions were virtually flat. But a communication passed between them nonetheless. And she remembered how he had held her last night, spooning her after sex—she knew that in his mind, that moment, the way he had squeezed her tighter than normal before falling asleep, had been his farewell.

But one last fuck hadn't been out of the question.

She stood up.

"You basically slept here all summer," she said, her voice now frigid, channeling a generic indifferent bitch from the movies: Annette Bening in *American Beauty*, Goldie Hawn in *Overboard*, Bette Davis in, well, everything.

"And it was really fun," he said.

"Fun?"

He squinted a little, grimaced—he knew he had misspoken.

She set her hands on her hips, spoke with mock pleasantness:

"Yes, loads of fun."

"I had a great summer. A *really* great summer."

"I get it, Pierce."

"You do?"

"Absolutely. I'm your manic pixie dream girl, summer edition."

He frowned. "I don't know what that means."

"Of course you don't."

"What the hell, Alaura? I'm not trying to be a jerk."

"I'm sorry, is this upsetting you?"

At that, Pierce stood up. He shook his head vigorously. "You know what? Whatever. I tried to be nice. But I'm done. All you ever want to do is drink and watch movies. There are other interesting things to do, you know? Oh, and don't even get me started on Waring. That psycho. I don't trust that guy, and you shouldn't either. I mean it."

What the hell was he talking about?

"You need to get—a—life!" he whined with ridiculous, childish menace. "Oh, and let's watch another Match Anderson movie for the fifth time and talk about how wonderful he is, blah blah blah."

She almost sobbed, but she swallowed it. "Fine, Pierce."

"I never promised you anything," he said. "I'm only twenty-three years old, okay?"

"I'll definitely keep that in mind."

"And if you want the truth, Alaura, you're just too . . . just too . . ." and he waved an upturned palm at her crappy apartment, at the ten hanging plants, doorway beads, wallpapered indie-movie posters, three ornate crucifixes. In the same motion he included her, from head to toe, and she knew he meant to indicate how obvious it was that her tattoos and punk hair and age and probably the width of her hips did not fit with his grand plans for the future.

She crossed her arms. "By the way, your Star Video membership is cancelled, dickhead."

"I'm not a dickhead, okay? I'm sorry. Leave it at that."

"Get the fuck outta here."

Pierce picked up his duffel bag, walked toward the door.

And though she knew she would regret it, she ran at him—as pathetic as Scarlett running after Rhett. She cursed, spat, struck him with her fists, fists that, upon contact, opened and grabbed at the soft black fabric of his hemp shirt. She pushed and pulled at the same time. But it was almost like she wasn't there—his trajectory never wavered, he shook his head and laughed in cruel annoyance, frankly not giving a damn, and in a few seconds, he was out the door, his sandals clucking down the steps toward the parking lot.

She lay on the carpet and curled into a ball.

"Idiot," she said.

Mr. Coffee hissed. She poured a cup, returned to the carpet, leaned back against the wall.

A moment later, she noticed she was crying—but she forced it away.

She took her antidepressant. She took her antianxiety. Then she decided to meditate; it had been months—a year maybe—but perhaps meditation would help. At first she attempted vipassana, tried and true. But soon her mind wandered from her breath to images of Pierce, now her *ex*-boyfriend, to how he painted shirtless, to his spontaneous handstands, to his diatribes on obscure artists and theorists, and of course to how stupid it had been of her to say "I might love you" last week, after only a few months together, even though she might have meant it.

She tried the Osho meditations, focusing on the gap between breaths, imagining a blue crystal beneath her nose. Then a shamanic incantation, without success. Then the bits she could remember of the Mishnah. She even considered a few Sun Salutations . . .

But her hangover was too heavy for any of it.

So she gave up. She stared at her popcorn ceiling. A low-angle *Citizen Kane* shot. Charles Foster Kane, after being caught in an affair with what's-her-name (the crazy opera bitch) and losing the election, walking around his newspaper office. Waring had taught her, years ago, that Orson Welles had famously achieved the extreme low-angle shot by cutting a hole into the studio floor, and the wide lens had distorted everything further. The shot is all curved ceiling, like the roof might fall, or like the ceiling is the warped stage upon which Welles acts with what's-his-name (his friend who hates him). And all the campaign posters. "Kane" all around him. Ks everywhere. Surrounded by his own failed self-image.

She tried to think of another word that started with K, but for the life of her, she couldn't conjure a single one.

I'm going crazy, she thought. So she found a three-quarter-inch roach in the ashtray, turned on Turner Classic Movies.

She had met Pierce in a grocery store, not a bar, a novel accomplishment that added legitimacy to their admittedly short relationship, which, as she thought about it, was sadly one of the more successful in her life. He was young, but he was a grad student, and he seemed smarter than average, and polite, and built solid like a wrestler, and he was shopping at Whole Foods in Appleton. Lots of meat— organic steaks, flounder cuts, long clips of chicken legs. Pasta, rice, peanut butter, deli bread. Rather boring fare except for the three six-packs of exotic beer. He would not admit until a month later that he normally shopped at Food Lion in West Appleton "because of the prices," and not for another few weeks (in an offhand remark) that he had only gone to Whole Foods that day "to look at the ladies." He actually used that word, *ladies*. What kind of ladies? Alaura asked. Ladies like you, he said. But she knew what he meant. He meant edgy tattooed ladies. And yoga ladies. And hipster ladies. Or the older women. The sexy organic moms. The business-suited Raleigh lawyers. Basically, ladies who don't shop at Food Lion, where all the snooty artists in town bought their shitty fucking beer.

And there was Pierce's friend, Tony, who had visited West Appleton a few weeks ago. Tony was an economics undergrad, and he was a loud frat boy, which had all but confirmed Alaura's suspicion that Pierce himself had once been a frat boy, or a wannabe frat boy, and that his current persona as a starving artist was, quite likely, a gross affectation. This theory explained a lot—particularly his brand-new Subaru station wagon, his loft condo, the Amex card he bandied about, and the family photograph on his fancy new iPhone of him with four other attractive and well-adjusted citizens standing before a large log cabin. "It's where we spend Christmas," he had explained with unpersuasive embarrassment. Hearing that, she had wanted to jump out of her skin; she'd never had luck with rich boys.

But he was also very, very sweet. A tremendous smile. He listened to her like no one else ever had. And he was gorgeous. So it couldn't really be *that* bad that he had money, could it?

But another warning sign: though Pierce was a technically talented artist, his paintings were lewd and pretentious—lizards copulating with snakes, snakes copulating with birds, monkeys drinking tea and diddling one another under miniature tables.

Fuck!—she should have fucking known. God, her life was fucked. Was she going to turn depressed again? Would she have to battle again with her shrink to tweak her medications, lie again that she did not drink more than one drink a night?

Actually, a glass of white wine sounded like a great idea.

Her phone rang at two thirty.

Could be one of her friends. But she wouldn't answer. Maybe tomorrow, go out for drinks with the girls—but not today. Not even if it was Constance, who had warned Alaura from the beginning that Pierce was bad news. And definitely not if it was Michelle, who now had three kids and a huge house and a husband built like a Viking god.

Maybe she could hang out with Karla, her best friend. But it wouldn't be Karla calling. Karla never called first; Alaura had accepted that. And anyway Karla had been incognito for weeks, off at that life-training place in Raleigh that sounded weird even by Alaura's spiritual-seeker standards—the Reality Center it was called? But maybe Alaura would give Karla a ring anyway, soon, because Karla was not the kind of friend you let slip from your life—she was a successful metal sculptress, she was beautiful, she attended weird life-training things, she lived in a renovated farm house, she ate homegrown vegetables, she seemed to get everything exactly right—

Alaura checked her voicemail—just Waring bitching that she was late for work.

Waring, who was probably running out of money. Selfish asshole.

As she hung up the phone, Alaura's gaze came across the screener DVD of the movie *Chop Shop* sitting on her purple end table. She picked up the show box. Studied it. More often than not, advance-released DVDs like this were terrible movies . . . essentially junk mail from film companies hoping to convince you to buy their worthless crap. But *Chop Shop* had been a critical success, and it was directed by Ramin Bahrani, who'd been born in North Carolina, and the film had not shown in either of Appleton's dinky theaters. It might be a good renter if she decided to order multiple copies. But she had to watch it to know.

So she poured a second glass of wine and thought, *What a relief, to have a decent movie to watch.*

Two hours later, Alaura resolved to go into work looking good. So she pulled on her best bra and a tight and ratty tee shirt and fingerless gloves and a red plaid kilt, cemented her hair up and back in crazy anime spikes à la *Dragon Ball Z*, and she did her makeup heroin-chic, with sick dark eye shadow like Daryl Hannah in *Blade Runner*.

So she was feeling tough and sexy and a tad drunk as she drove down College Street in Waring's unregistered Dodge. The car was a rusty, hissing monster that Waring parked behind the store and that Alaura had begun "borrowing" two weeks ago in retaliation for the ear-tongue/fight-with-Pierce incident. She hated driving this clunker, but all in all, she wasn't feeling half bad about things when she saw—

Blockbuster had opened for business.

She pulled the car to a stop, flipped on the hazard lights. She examined the place. Glared at it. Shit. This wasn't possible. That huge Blockbuster sign had only appeared a week ago. Now the place was open! She had watched them laying the carpet, constructing the shelving, carting in box upon box of DVDs, all of it coming together precisely and without a hiccup, like a color-by-numbers painting. Still . . . it couldn't have happened this fast. It just couldn't!

But it had. At least twenty-five customers milled the aisles. Mostly college students. The store looked bright and inviting, with cool splashes of blue and yellow everywhere. Flat-screen televisions, visible from the street, displayed trailers for new and upcoming releases. A decently sized selection, from what Alaura could see. But no VHS tapes in yellowing plastic cases, of ancient titles not otherwise available on DVD. And likely no Independent Film or Documentary sections. Certainly no Anime section. No Criterion section. No pornography. No *African Queen*. And no eccentric employees with tattoos and refined movie tastes. Only ignorant vanilla undergrads wearing matching uniforms—those goddamn navy polos.

"Fucking wankers!" Alaura bellowed in her best *Trainspotting* brogue, and she gunned the Dodge toward Star Video.

When she entered the shop, the floor was empty. Jeff stood behind the long counter watching *Harold and Maude*, slack-jawed, a wild look of pleasure on his face. Handsome Jeff, tall Jeff, frightfully young Jeff—his lips moved as if he were conversing with the television. On screen, Bud Court screamed, and Ruth Gordon fell through a trapdoor. But Alaura ignored the movie because she hated to enter scenes, especially interesting scenes, midstream.

"Has it been this slow?" she said, flipping her purse under the counter.

Jeff snapped to attention. "Oh, hi. Yes, ma'am."

"How much have we done?"

"About two hundred dollars."

"Fuck a monkey."

"The new Blockbuster opened," he said in a low voice, and Alaura noticed that, today more than ever, Jeff averted his gaze from her. She hoped this was because of her unparalleled beauty.

"I know," she said. "I saw."

"Blockbuster was on campus today, handing out free rental coupons. They're giving away PlayStations and Blu-ray players."

"Christ."

"Alaura!" Waring yelled from *The African Queen*.

Alaura sighed—already she was exhausted by Waring. "Time to face the music," she said, and she dragged herself up the loft's spiral staircase.

Through the blue-gray fog produced by Waring's fuming cigarette, Alaura could see that he was drinking a beer and reading a fat hardback book, while *High Fidelity* played on *The African Queen*'s flat-screen. Waring looked up from the book, which Alaura knew would be some film-history text or celebrity biography, and his face slackened into shock and awe.

"Hello, nurse!" he said as his eyes scanned her up and down.

"Oh Jesus, shut up."

Then Waring's expression twisted quickly into an and-where-have-you-been-young-lady grimace.

"Sorry," she said as she plopped onto the couch beside him.

"Sorry for what? For being late? Yes, I'd say *late*." He coughed into his fist, then turned his book face down onto the loft's cluttered coffee table. "In the meantime," Waring went on, "I've been stuck with Blad, aka Captain Annoying. Have you seen his employee picks? He actually picked *Bring It On*."

Alaura shrugged but did not remove her gaze from the movie, enduring her midscene entry.

"Blad is Jeff's new nickname," Waring informed her. "You look amazing, by the way."

"I asked you to be nice to him, Waring. And *Bring It On* is a good movie."

"It's literally impossible that *Bring It On* is a good movie. And I am being nice to him. He still has a job, doesn't he? Which reminds me, I might have to fire Farley."

Alaura's face tightened, but she quickly released the expression, hoping to leave her makeup undisturbed. "What's the problem now?"

"Listen," Waring said with sudden theatrical Waxian urgency. "Farley was just up here filming with some little digital camera thingy. First of all, him being in *The African Queen* with his, well, girth and everything, is not exactly safe. Which he knows. Which I've told him. And when I asked him what he was doing, he said, in that wheezy voice of his, 'Uh, I'm getting footage for some stupid documentary about modern technology and the state of the video store industry and some other crap.' He's out there now. Filming, not working. So clearly I should fire him."

"Not like you care, Waring, but Farley's in school for documentary filmmaking."

Waring reached for the remote and paused *High Fidelity*.

"You're over three hours late," he said. "And you didn't call."

She took the remote from him, pressed "Menu."

"Is something wrong?" he said.

"No."

"Why are you so late?"

"No reason. I watched *Chop Shop*."

"And?"

"And it's fucking incredible. I think it'll be a good renter, so I'm ordering ten copies."

"But something's wrong."

"Why is Jeff's nickname Blad?" she asked with a curl of annoyance. "That's not even a word."

"Blad is fun to say, that's all." He squinted at her. "Are you going to tell me what's wrong with you?"

"No, I'm not."

Alaura felt him staring at her for a long time.

Then he smashed out his cigarette in the overfilled ashtray.

"Whatever," he said. "Sorry you overslept or your life hasn't turned out the way you wanted or yadda yadda yadda. Stay up here if you want. I was watching this *High Fidelity* thing again. Something about it is just . . . not . . . good. I mean, the book was good, I read it back when the movie came out, but I don't know. Maybe it's because John Cusack looks so stocky. He's sort of built like Edward G. Robinson—"

"I don't care."

"Fine, jerk face. And FYI, Blad is short for bladder infection. I don't remember why." He grabbed his book off the coffee table, climbed over the edge of *The African Queen*, and began to descend the staircase. "Stay up here if you want," he called back. "It's not like we have any customers anyway."

Alaura spotted a bottle of Sierra Nevada, picked it up, popped it open against a corner of the coffee table. She lit a cigarette. Finally good and ready, she restarted *High Fidelity*, which she had seen years before and which she would soon reevaluate as a flawed but endearing portrait of music store snobs, who were in many ways similar to video store snobs, and that Waring had probably been offended not only by Cusack's fading charm (he *was* too beefy to be that neurotic), but also by the basis of the movie's humor (that the characters' snobbishness was fundamentally ridiculous). None-theless, she found herself drifting easily into the mesh of the film, into the interdependent professional and romantic plot threads, because being engaged with a film was her favorite craving, the relief of images, the dependable escape, the conflicting empathies, the forming of plot hypotheses, the subverting of expectations, the satisfactions of suspense, all of it, all the tricks of narrative, all the lies they use to tell the truth. This was her truest religion, her most reliable form of meditation, and she knew it.

"Are you okay, ma'am?"

Alaura's attention jolted from the movie onto Jeff's face floating above the wall of *The African Queen*. She was crying again. Eye shadow probably ran down her cheeks. So she turned away from him. On screen, John Cusack and some no-name actress were reuniting after the sudden death of her father. They sat in a car, kissing, their hair wet from rain. The scene was nothing spe-cial, not visually original in the slightest, but the expression on Cusack's familiar face, his amazement that the girl of his dreams wanted him back . . . Alaura had not been able to restrain the tears. Normally she preferred indie and foreign films. But even Holly-wood movies (especially Hollywood movies, she had to admit) could make her cry.

She paused the DVD.

"Jeff?"

"Yes, ma'am?"

"If you call me ma'am again, I'll rip out your eyeballs."

No response.

"Oh, you know what I mean," she said weakly.

"Are you okay . . . Alaura?"

"Peachy keen."

She massaged her temples, tried to straighten the neckline of her tee shirt. Still facing away from him, she said, "Did you need something, Jeff?"

"It's, well . . . Waring's on the phone. I think it's Clarissa Wheat from that Guiding Glow Distribution place again. It sounds like bad news."

Alaura: sarcastic puff of laughter.

Clarissa Wheat is calling, and it sounds like bad news, she thought. Waring's on an epic bender. Pierce just broke up with me. Pierce fucked me before breaking up with me. Jeff just saw me crying. My makeup is running. Blockbuster just opened. I live in a dinky town thirty minutes from the dinky town where I grew up. I've never lived anywhere else. Waring is a ridiculous human being, and he might be running out of money. I might lose my job. No one will ever hire a girl with these tattoos. There's a marijuana charge on my criminal record. I'm half-drunk in the afternoon. I haven't talked to Daddy in a month. I haven't visited Sprinks in six. I'm old. I'm gaining weight. My only marketable skill is . . . my only marketable skill is . . .

"Thanks for the update, Jeff," she said.

"Can I do anything?"

"You can leave me the fuck alone."

Silence.

Then she listened to Jeff descend the steps.

And now I've been rude to Jeff, aka the Nicest Kid in the World.

She'd apologize later. But not now. Now all she could manage was—resetting *High Fidelity* to the beginning of the scene with Cusack and the girl in the car and taking a huge gulp of beer.

Your life hasn't turned out how you wanted, Waring had said.

No shit, Sherlock.

THE DISCREET CHARM OF CLARISSA WHEAT

A few moments earlier, the store phone had rung, prompting
Waring to stare at it in disgust. He didn't want to answer, but Jeff
was nowhere in sight. So after four rings, Waring slammed down
his book, snatched up the phone, and offered the caller an annoyed
"Mm?"

"Waring Wax, please?" asked a sober female voice.

"He's retired. Or asleep."

"Excuse me?"

"I don't know where he is."

"Pardon?"

"Message," he barked. "This is where you leave a message."

"I must say, sir, you're being a little—"

"So sorry, *ma'am*. I've got a line of ten customers."

"Oh?" said the woman, her voice rising in what sounded like
pleasant surprise. "That's nice to hear. Please tell Waring that Clarissa Wheat from Guiding Glow Distribution called—"

Waring stood from his director's chair. His entire body cringed.
With his free hand, he punched the air as if battling a shadow, or
perhaps Clarissa Wheat herself.

"Wait!" he cried into the phone. "I see Waring! Just a sec!"

Waring had put off talking to Clarissa Wheat long enough. After a brief pause, he spoke into the phone using a ridiculously deep voice and, for some reason, a pinch of a British accent:

"Clarissa! How are you?"

"Waring, my darling."

"Darling?" he said, instantly confused.

"Waring, dear, I've been trying to reach you. I don't think we've spoken personally in over a year, since my last visit. Did a Blockbuster recently open near your store?"

"Oh, is that all?" He tutted a fake laugh. "It's a long way down the street. Miles, really."

"Still," she continued, "the board of Guiding Glow is concerned. There's a not inconsiderable balance on your account, and it's been growing as of late. And, to be frank, we're surprised that you didn't inform us earlier about Blockbuster, as it's quite likely to impact your earnings."

"I see, I see. Oversight on my part." His voice trailed off, and he punched the air again.

"Of course, we should have kept you informed ourselves," Clarissa Wheat said. "For that, I apologize."

"Um, apology accepted."

"We're concerned, as I can tell you are. We had a group prayer for you this afternoon."

"Why, thank you. I recently did some . . . some praying myself."

"How is business, Waring?"

"Fine!" he belted out assuredly. "A slight drop, perhaps, but that's to be expected at the end of summer."

"Really? I assumed with students returning—"

"Business should be ticking upward," he interrupted. "It's fine. I'm fine. We're all fine and dandy. I'll catch up on my account shortly, and there should be no drop-off in our ordering, none whatsoever, not any time soon, not at all."

Waring scoured his pockets for cigarettes but found none.

"We've planned a visit to West Appleton," Clarissa Wheat said. "It's been too long. There are some things I'd like to discuss with you personally."

"Discuss?" Waring said, then he laughed as if her suggestion were pleasantly offensive. "Not needed. Like I say, business should be ticking upward in the very near future."

"My dear Waring, I'm sure you're aware that many of the stores we contract with are posting losses. All across the country. Significant losses. And obviously Blockbuster isn't the only issue . . . the Internet and Redbox have hit us all harder than we calculated. As one of Guiding Glow's most, well, *unique* clients, we'd like to come take a lay of the land, see if we can offer any help. Things are changing, Waring. We need to prepare for the future."

"But I just don't think—"

"We've already purchased our plane tickets."

Waring's head wilted forward.

"That's fantastic," he muttered.

"And Waring?" Clarissa said. "I've missed you. I think about my last visit all the time."

A twinge of recognition. A murky memory. Waring visualized Clarissa Wheat, the middle-aged heron of a woman in a starched gray business suit—she was bony and bloodless and offensively makeup-caked. Something strange had indeed happened between Waring and this specimen during her first and only visit to West Appleton, one year ago, soon after Guiding Glow—the Christian corporation she worshipped and served—had purchased Star Video's original distributor for fiscal and propagandic reasons completely inconceivable to Waring. Clarissa Wheat had arrived without warning one evening when Waring was whiskey-hammered and working alone, and among her many un-Christianly shrill complaints, she had particularly harped on his new contractual obligation to provide a more family- and faith-friendly movie selection.

He remembered cracking up in laughter—at her deadpan suggestion that he now operated at the pleasure of the Almighty—then
realizing she wasn't joking at all.

But somehow, on that occasion, everything had worked out fine.
Waring had awoken in *The African Queen* the next morning, deathly
hungover, memory obliterated, but with the vague sense that his
distribution deal was secure.

"Barney and I arrive in three days," she said. "Tuesday, two o'clock."

"Barney?"

"My husband, Barney Wheat. Vice president of distribution?
Your employee, Ms. Eden, places her monthly orders with him. I'd
rather come alone, of course. But you know how Barney is."

The call ended, and at once, Waring resolved to make peace
with Alaura, who today had been distant and crabby and later than
normal to her shift, and who for some reason was in a particularly
anti-Waring mood. But whatever the issue, whatever it took to
win her back, Waring would do it, because Clarissa Wheat was a
problem, and now he really needed Alaura's help.

Jeff stepped down from *The African Queen*. Waring turned and
considered the preposterously tall, preposterously well-proportioned
youngster.

Had Jeff been talking to Alaura? Smiling at her? Existing for
even a second within her field of vision? Unacceptable.

Then Waring remembered that night last week: those bicycle
deadbeats. How Jeff had swooped in like a zitty Errol Flynn. But
you're not getting a thank you, Waring thought. I didn't ask for
your help. And if I find out you've told Alaura, then you're fired,
Opie Taylor. That whole incident is better left forgotten.

Jeff scurried onto the floor without looking at Waring—probably
to organize DVDs or to dust or to do something else in a preposterously productive way—and Waring's gaze scrolled across his
expansive store and came across Farley, who was standing near the
Criterion section.

Farley held his video camera. The camera was trained on Waring. Had Farley captured his entire conversation with Clarissa Wheat?

Waring sneered at the camera and its rotund operator. "Farley?" he said. "Alaura might not let me fire you. But that doesn't mean maiming is out of the question."

Farley smiled and gave Waring an enthusiastic, directorial thumbs-up.

THE ONE WHERE THEY PERPETRATE
A COMPLETELY RIDICULOUS SCHEME THAT
COMES TO BE KNOWN SIMPLY AS
"THE CORPORATE VISIT"

On Tuesday, three days after the bad-news phone call, Clarissa and Barney Wheat arrived at precisely two p.m., driving a rented minivan, and as Jeff watched Alaura welcome them outside the shop, he decided that he had never witnessed a couple dressed so identically who also looked so different. The Wheats wore matching three-button navy suits, crisp white shirts, red ties, and shiny gray shoes, and around their necks hung thick silver chains upon which dangled thick silver crosses, resting over their ties. But Clarissa Wheat was a head taller than her husband. And twenty years younger. She was rail thin where he was pudgy and folded. Her coal black hair was pulled into a tight bun, while Barney Wheat's hair was sporadic and disheveled and gray. A dopey, perpetual smile swung on his sagging face, while her lips seemed to disappear into a haughty point an inch below her nose.

As if the Wheats' arrival had initiated a dimensional shift, Alaura looked like a different person. She wore no makeup besides a swipe of dull red lipstick. Her hair lay flat and parted like a brunette Mia Farrow. And though the temperature was well over eighty degrees, she wore a white turtleneck sweater and a pale blue, ankle-length skirt—an outfit designed to cover her tattoos, Jeff decided, just like that morning at Tanglewood Baptist.

Jeff watched Alaura banter and smile with the strange couple. He watched her ask questions and nod thoughtfully at their answers. But her skin was pale. Her face looked thin. Shadowy circles hung under her eyes. Jeff had caught her crying in the loft the other day, and she'd been mean to him, but he'd probably deserved it, though he didn't know why. Since then she'd been hours late to every shift, and she no longer emitted that same bright energy with customers or employees or him.

"Look alive, freshman."

Waring stood at the counter.

Jeff could not believe what he saw.

"What?" Waring said. "This is a thousand-dollar suit."

But Waring's charcoal suit was wrinkled and crooked, too tight over the stomach, too loose in the shoulders. One button dangled like a dislodged tooth, and around the suit's neckline looped a weird ring of dark wet spots. His hair was combed back and glistening. Jeff smelled the heavy tang of Vitalis.

Waring looked like a member of the Brat Pack after too many calzones and a rough night in a country jail.

"Stop staring," Waring said.

"Sorry."

"Listen, Blad, I know you're not thrilled about this corporate visit thing. But you have to play along."

Jeff sighed. Waring had employed the phrase "You have to play along" at least five times that day. Which apparently meant lying to Clarissa and Barney Wheat. But lie about what? Jeff had no idea.

"None of that," Waring said. "No discontented exhales. No shrugs. Understand?"

"Not really."

Waring placed both palms on the counter, as if to stabilize it. "Alaura thought you should work today," he said, mostly to himself, "which was clearly a mistake. At least Rose would have stayed quiet. Meaning less likely than you to say anything, well, wrong. Listen, Blad. I mean Jeff. It's very simple. I buy movies at a cheaper rate because I'm part of a distribution group. Even a rinky-dink distributor like Guiding Glow affords us a minimum of a 25 percent discount. The concept is called wholesale pricing—"

"I understand wholesale pricing."

"Good for you. Now, listen. My original distributor was purchased last year by a Christian cartel called Guiding Glow. Those twits outside . . . they're Guiding Glow minions. They manage my account. In order to get them off my back, we have to convince them, first of all, that we're making money hand over fist, which we're not, and second of all, that we stock a, quote, faith-friendly selection, unquote, which I'm delighted to say we don't."

Jeff glanced at what had once constituted the front panel of the Foreign Film section—Kurosawa and Fellini and Godard front and center for every customer to see, as well as Bergman and Antonioni, who had both apparently died, tragically, astonishingly, on the exact same day earlier that year. Now this section was labeled "Spiritual Spotlight," and its shelves were filled with Christian DVDs, many of which Jeff recognized from his old Baptist youth group and as the horrible movies Momma watched when Bill O'Reilly or her favorite televangelists called it quits for the night. Predictable storylines, laughable production value, shameful acting, Kirk Cameron. And the documentaries . . . the unforgivably biased documentaries. Jeff had given up on this entire subgenre years ago and never looked back.

The sole reason the Spiritual Spotlight movies were kept boxed in Waring's office, Jeff had surmised, was for these rare Guiding Glow visits.

"Familiarize yourself with those titles," Waring said. "There'll be a quiz."

"Fine."

"And remember, the Porn Room is locked. For today, it doesn't exist. Obviously we buy our porn from a different distributor. To your knowledge, we haven't rented a single title with visible genitalia since *The Piano* was boycotted by all those anti–Harvey Keitel Jesus freaks."

Jeff nodded weakly.

Waring nodded mockingly in response. "Honestly, Blad, I don't understand your problem."

Then he exited to greet the Wheats.

"I don't understand *your* problem," Jeff muttered to himself, walking the length of the counter. "Ungrateful jerk."

No, Jeff decided at once. He would not lie. The way Waring had been treating him—the yelling and the insults even though Jeff had kept his stupid secret about the bicycle gang, without so much as a "thanks"—Jeff had had enough. If asked a direct question by the Wheats, he would tell the truth. That he'd made compromises to work here, that he'd withheld from Momma that Star Video rented pornography, that he'd be missing church this weekend because he was scheduled for a Sunday-morning shift with Alaura . . . Jeff was sickened by the scope of his own failings.

So today—though he doubted it would have much effect on his immortal soul—today, at least, *he would not lie*.

It's so nice to see you again!" Clarissa Wheat fluted as Waring approached her.

Waring cringed. He forced his WASPiest smile.

Clarissa Wheat stepped forward, kissed Waring's cheek, and pressed her hip into his. His back stiffened. He noticed that her ropey neck was as veined as a heroin addict's forearm. She smelled like a freshly mown lawn—not a bad smell, necessarily, but not how a human being should smell at all.

She stood leaning against him for a few beats longer than made any rational sense.

"Hell-ooooh!" Waring said, Seinfeld-esque, and he gingerly tapped her back.

"We're excited to be here," she said.

"I'm excited that you're excited."

"*Very* excited," she whispered, and she finally backed away.

Waring glanced at Barney Wheat—an oblivious smile dangled on the old man's face.

Alaura laughed awkwardly. "Mr. Wheat was just telling me about his extensive research on Coney Island carousels," she said.

Waring attempted an expression that wasn't outright horror.

"Fascinating!" Barney Wheat suddenly exclaimed, and the crumpled old geezer began bouncing on his heels like an automaton nudged to life. "Hand-carved and painted, those old carousels. Amazing mechanical invention. And a truly intriguing history, dating back to the Byzantine Empire—"

"Come now, Barney," Clarissa Wheat said. "We're not here about carousels."

"Yes, dear," he said, and the automaton stopped bouncing.

"I think carousels are interesting," Alaura said politely. "And it's just nice to meet Mr. Wheat. I speak with him every month when I order movies."

"I am aware of my husband's job description."

Waring watched the two women smile tightly.

Oh goodie, he thought. Now Alaura and Clarissa Wheat hated each other, for no reason whatsoever.

"That gives me an idea," Clarissa Wheat said, still eyeballing the younger woman. "Miss Eden, why don't you show Barney your sales floor. That way you can continue to be entertained by his wonderful carousels. And Waring and I can catch up."

"Catch up?" Waring said.

"Yes, that will give you and me time to . . ." and Clarissa Wheat pulled at the crisp white collar of her shirt with a knobby finger, "to go over the books. Don't you think, Waring? Isn't now a good time to, you know, *pore* over the numbers?"

Waring whimpered but found himself nodding.

A few minutes later, Clarissa Wheat sat primly upon the director's chair at Star Video's long counter, in the same place where Waring usually posted up when forced to wait on customers. Now Waring stood behind the director's chair, behind Clarissa Wheat, gnawing on his thumbnail while she studied a series of reports on the dusty host computer. She had been working silently for ten minutes, navigating the ancient computer system Waring had never forked over the money to modernize. This outdated system enabled him, however, to reset the shop's operating date very easily, effectively presenting Clarissa Wheat with financials from two years ago, when business had still been declining but was at least more impressive than this year.

"Interesting," she said, still focused on the computer screen.

"Interesting?"

"Very interesting."

"By interesting, you mean?"

"But Waring, these computers are simply prehistoric! A decade old at least. You're being left behind. They're not even hooked up to the Internet, are they? And are these dot matrix printers? My heavens!"

She stood up from the director's chair and faced him.

"Waring," she said with a thin smile, "you know I love the kitsch value of your store. And you were sweet to wear your Sunday finest, just for little old me."

"Sorry about the hair tonic—"

"But you'll have to work *very* hard for me to ignore the obvious."

"I see," he said, nodding assuredly. "Meaning?"

"I think you know."

"I do?"

"Oh, Waring," she said, and she sighed as if overcome by exhaustion. "Barney is a nice, sweet man. Very nice and sweet. He's been a good father. And a leader in our church. And he knows more about carousels than you could possibly imagine."

Waring nodded thoughtfully. "And what's with the carousels?"

"Exactly," she said. "What's with the carousels?"

"Huh?"

"Oh, Waring, I should have known. When I married Barney five years ago, I thought he had a quirky sense of humor. The way his mind jumped around, it always made me laugh. But then I realized, rather quickly, that he isn't quirky. He isn't funny."

"He isn't?"

"No. He's going senile."

"I see." Waring nodded. "I guess that explains the carousels."

Clarissa Wheat leaned back against the counter. "I'm lonely, Waring. And I'm tired of sweet, kind, nice old Barney."

Waring looked around.

Jeff was nowhere in sight.

Alaura's voice echoed far off in the store.

And of course there were no customers—that would be *too* convenient.

Clarissa Wheat's eyes fluttered shut. She did not move. She sat there silently, head tilted back as if praying upward, or perhaps waiting for a bucket of water to splash down onto her.

If Waring was going to do it, this was (unfortunately) the moment to act.

So he slowly guided a hand toward Clarissa Wheat. His palm met her hip, which under the crisp navy fabric of her suit felt stiff and crooked, and for a moment he imagined touching, of all things, Katharine Hepburn's back. This bizarre flash confused him, and he tried to understand why Clarissa Wheat's hip should remind him of Katharine Hepburn's back, which he had no memory of ever thinking about before.

He felt a hot pain in his wrist.

Clarissa Wheat was clawing him with her fingernails.

"What the hell?" he whimpered, gripping his wrist when she released.

"Honestly, Waring! What kind of woman do you think I am?"

"I'm not really sure."

She shook her head, grimly disappointed. Then she turned back to the computer. "I'm not understanding these numbers, Mr. Wax. Not to mention that Blockbuster is two hundred feet down the street, not miles, as you reported to me on the phone."

"But . . . but . . ."

"And is that *The Last Temptation of Christ* I see in the Spiritual Spotlight section?"

Waring bit his lower lip. Words began building inside of him. Angry words, dirty words, but all of them, he knew, truthful words.

"Don't you have anything to say, Mr. Wax?"

Clarissa tapped at the keyboard, her back to Waring, and Waring found himself withdrawing an invisible dagger and raising it high, ready and willing to plunge the blade deep into his bony nemesis's back. Like Hamlet, he thought, like Olivier (*way* too old to play Hamlet when he did!) about to kill Claudius, played by that guy, oh, what was his name, from *Treasure Island*? And though the blade itself was incorporeal, the fantasy Waring had conjured was more than a little invigorating, and he realized that his murderous gesture and the attendant expression of glee on his face must have looked rather incriminating when he heard Jeff yell:

"Waring, stop!"

"Just stretching," Waring blurted, thrusting his arms to his sides.

"Well hello, young man," Clarissa Wheat said brightly.

Waring looked at her. Her chin was tucked coyly near her shoulder. Her tiny mouth curled into a tiny smile on the right side of her face.

"Hello, ma'am," Jeff replied.

"And how do you like working for Mr. Wax?"

Jeff approached them. He set the DVD cases he had been holding onto the counter and said:

"Well, to be honest, ma'am, he can be a real pain in the you know what."

Alaura was smiling for the first time since Pierce had broken up with her; hard to believe it had occurred only three days ago.

But things were looking up. It turned out that Barney Wheat was the least of their problems, because he lived in a happy little world, all his own. The old man stared off toward the ceiling, muttered disconnected phrases, all but confabulating. A content yogic smile shined on his face. And if she asked him a question, he mustered the focus to answer, but he only seemed able to do so in the affirmative:

"Did you have a good flight?" she asked.

"Yes. Planes are so exciting."

A bit later: "Did Waring tell you that we're having cleaners dust between the grates, replace lights, polish the floor?"

"Cleaners. Wonderful."

And later: "Star Video is a staple of this vibrant college community."

"Oh, yes? Community? Fascinating."

At first Alaura had tried to steer Barney Wheat away from racier sections like Anime and Concert Videos. But now it was clear: Barney Wheat had no interest in movies. Alaura had always suspected this. When placing her monthly order with him, the only comments he ever made concerned movie ratings; she was now positive that his primary capacity at Guiding Glow was to consult a spreadsheet listing movie titles in one column and their corresponding ratings in another. Too many R-rated movies, and he would casually suggest a compromise. Thankfully, however, he seemed unaware that "Not Rated" or "Unrated" usually meant that the movie was too racy for the MPAA—Barney seemed to think that "Not Rated" was akin to "G."

They approached the Russ Meyer section, all those breast-heavy and self-consciously schlocky show boxes with the greatest titles ever conceived—*Common Law Cabin*, *Beneath the Valley of the Ultra-Vixens*, and *Faster Pussycat! Kill! Kill!*—the absolute pinnacle of campy sexploitation, and the absolute worst movies, besides outright porn, for Waring to have left on the floor.

But Barney Wheat didn't react. Instead he gazed at the bodacious babes, thumbed the silver cross around his neck, and smiled pleasantly—a conduit of spiritual detachment, carousels spinning in his mind.

"I'm really enjoying this," Alaura said happily.

"So am I, Ms. Eden."

"To be honest, Mr. Wheat, we were nervous about your visit. But you're so nice."

"Why, thank you!"

"What were you saying about carousels? Byzantine Empire?"

"Carousels? Yes, a long and fascinating history. Originally used to train horseback soldiers—"

But then Alaura saw something terrifying. Someone. Pierce. Pierce was in the store. Standing ten feet away. Her jaw clenched; her eyes closed.

She heard Pierce's voice:

"Why the hell are you dressed like that, Alaura?"

She opened her eyes. She stared at her ex-boyfriend.

Pierce looked pissed off.

And for some reason, he was holding a brick.

• • •

"So tell me, Jeff," Clarissa Wheat said, "how long have you worked here?"

Such a disgusting woman, Waring thought. And was she really flirting with Jeff? She had loosened her ridiculous tie, undone the top button of her blouse. She asked stupid questions and laughed at Jeff's stupid answers. She played teasingly with a strand of black hair that had fallen from her bun, twirling it on her Cruella de Vil finger.

And for fuck's sake! everything Jeff had said—every stupid thing—had been totally fucking honest.

"I've only worked here for about three weeks," Jeff said, easing back from her slightly and, Waring could see, squirming a little.

"And why exactly is Waring a pain in your . . . well, your you know what?"

"Well . . ."

"Don't be shy, young man. Please be truthful."

"Truthful . . . okay. He, um . . . he gets mad sometimes. Says rude things to me . . . and to customers."

"He's rude?" Clarissa Wheat said. "Whatever do you mean?"

"Well . . ." and for the first time Jeff looked guiltily at Waring.

Waring flipped him the bird behind Clarissa Wheat's back.

"He calls me Blad," Jeff said with a sudden defiance for which Waring, at his first opportunity, would kick him in the face. "And Sasquatch. And a retard. And he calls me preppy, which makes no sense, because I'm from the most rural mountain town ever. And yesterday he told a customer who was wearing exercise tights that she looked like a doll made of sausage links."

Clarissa Wheat turned briefly to Waring, frowned as much as her small mouth would allow, then looked back at the young traitor.

"Very good, Jeff," she said. "Just a few more questions. How familiar are you with the titles of the Spiritual Spotlight section?"

"Actually, I'm quite familiar."

"Oh?" she said, her voice rising skeptically. "So if I wanted an animated family film without all the moral fuzziness of those Pixar and Disney monstrosities, what would you recommend?"

Jeff answered at once, and he sounded, Waring thought, a little pleased with himself:

"I always liked the *Adventures in Odyssey* series. They were fun."

"Excellent," Clarissa Wheat chirped, nodding in agreement. "And what would you recommend to a parent whose teenage daughter is thinking of, well, engaging in illicit behavior with her boyfriend?"

Again, Jeff seemed to have the answer on the tip of his tongue: "The movie *Only Once* comes to mind, ma'am. And if you're trying to, you know, scare it out of her, there's an old documentary I remember—*Teen Sex: Challenge and Decision.*"

"Very good!" Clarissa Wheat said. "Jeff is a wonderful employee, Waring. He has the perfect blend of knowledge and compassion."

But what was this sensation now trickling through Waring's brain? It amplified with every word Clarissa Wheat spoke. The feeling clearly wasn't jealousy. Jealousy would require some affection for Clarissa Wheat. Jealousy would imply a slight or a loss in her approval of Blad. No, this feeling was disgust. Pure disgust. Disgust of a certain green hue. His normal level of disgust at the nightmare that was humanity now twisted and rotted by the power Clarissa Wheat held over him, and by that little side glance she now gave him every few seconds, a glance that asked, Are you jealous? No, you skinny old snake! I'm not jealous! And for a moment he thought of *The Godfather.* The classic moment when Pacino lies to Diane Keaton: after instructing her repeatedly not to ask about his business, he tells her that he didn't kill Carlo, and *wham!* the audience hates Pacino, the audience thinks, *You son of a bitch, for lying to your wife,* and in the next breath, the audience realizes that Pacino just had about seventy-seven people murdered. And for a moment,

Waring thought that yes, lying, acting, pretending, like Clarissa Wheat was clearly pretending now, could be just as disgusting as any other crime—and he realized he wouldn't be able to contain himself.

So when Clarissa Wheat opened her mouth to ask Jeff another coy question, Waring blurted: "Enough!"

He stepped between Blad and Clarissa Wheat.

"Enough what?" Jeff asked.

"Just go away," Waring barked at him. "Help customers or something."

"But there aren't any customers."

"Go!"

Jeff took a few steps back.

"What do you want?" Waring said pointedly to Clarissa Wheat.

"You know what I want."

She reached up and removed a bobby pin from her hair, and her tight bun fell loose.

Dark curls spilled over her shoulders.

"Don't you think we'd have more privacy in your office?" she asked.

"Oh, God," he said in a pained voice.

"I've thought about you often, Waring."

He felt his body deflate. "So the last time you were here, you and I, we actually, you know . . ."

"Oh, yes," Clarissa Wheat said, and her tiny smile rose so high that he thought it might pop off her face.

"And I was capable?" Waring went on ashamedly. "I was physically able . . . I mean, I didn't have any trouble . . . we were able to . . ."

"Oh, yes," she repeated. "You were absolutely *wonderful*, Mr. Wax. Now, as I recall, your office was back this way."

• • •

"But why are you here?" Alaura asked Pierce in a pleading whisper, standing so close to him that she could smell the turpentiney paint on his clothes. His face was as striking as she remembered, brown and glowing, but now it was tinged with an anger she had never before seen.

Barney Wheat inched closer to them with dazed interest.

"It's simple," Pierce said, "I want to discuss this brick."

"What are you talking about?"

"I'm serious, Alaura."

"But this is a business associate, and today has to go well—"

She turned to Mr. Wheat. His eyes quivered with confusion. She offered him a strained smile. At this point, she could only hope that Barney Wheat would forget these events as soon as they transpired. "I'm very sorry for this interruption, Mr. Wheat," she said soothingly. Then, turning back to Pierce: "Thanks for simplifying my emotions about our breakup, jerk."

"So now you're tough?"

"I am tough!"

She thrust two palms into Pierce's chest, stepping into the motion and sending him back several feet. He steadied himself by gripping the Spike Lee section. *She Hate Me* fell facedown onto the floor.

"What's your problem?" Pierce said furiously.

"You're a fake, that's my problem."

"What?!"

"I really liked you, you fucking fake!"

"So you have no idea why I'm here?"

"No clue, dumbass."

"You didn't throw this brick through my bedroom window?"

Alaura stopped short. She looked at the floor. She had been drinking quite heavily in the three days since he'd broken up with her. But surely she would remember throwing a brick through his window.

"And this was rubber-banded to it," he said. He handed her a dirty, wrinkled piece of Star Video receipt paper. A note in blocked handwriting read:

MEMBERSHIP CANCELLED, PIERCE!

"That's creepy," Pierce said.

Alaura had to agree.

"If *you* didn't do it," Pierce went on, "then tell that little freak Waring to leave me alone. Whatever he told you about me, he's wrong."

"Get. Out. Of my—"

Something breezed past Alaura.

It was Barney Wheat.

For a moment, Alaura imagined that the older man was swatting a bug away from the younger man's face.

But then Barney Wheat grabbed the collar of Pierce's black hemp shirt and said sternly:

"Ms. Eden asked you to leave."

Oh shit, Alaura thought. Pierce will kill him.

Pierce raised a hand to dispatch little Barney Wheat.

But Wheat took a deliberate step backward, yanked Pierce's collar, and pulled the younger man's shirt over his face.

"What the—" Pierce yelped, his arms flailing.

And with the grace of a dancer, Barney Wheat slid a foot into Pierce's path.

Pierce tripped over the foot. He contorted for balance. He squealed a pathetic sound—"Lueeeeah!"—and he dropped in a flapping heap.

His body impacted the linoleum floor with a sick crunch. The mysterious brick catapulted from his grasp.

The brick soared in a high arc across the room, spinning like a stick grenade—and clanged into the Sports Documentary section, a length of shelving that had been tottering, in need of repair, for years.

The tall metal grating shuddered. Bolts pinged to the floor.

"Of course," Alaura said.

The Sports section fell, like a gigantic domino, and slammed onto the floor.

Surfing documentaries and Pilates DVDs and Star Video's entire WrestleMania catalogue clattered to the floor like machine-gun fire.

Alaura turned to Barney Wheat.

"What fun!" Barney chirped, beaming at Alaura like he'd just won a giant stuffed gorilla at the county fair.

When Jeff heard the crash in the back of the store, his first thought was that the ceiling had collapsed. Such a dramatic end—the literal obliteration of Star Video—seemed appropriate given the shoddy state of the building. Five minutes ago, Waring and Clarissa Wheat had retired to Waring's office, to do God knows what, and in Jeff's mind, disaster was imminent.

But when he crept toward the origin of the sound, he rounded a corner and discovered that it was the Sports section, not the ceiling, that had collapsed.

Out of nowhere, a shockingly handsome man in a black shirt appeared, knocking Jeff's shoulder as he rushed past.

"I'm done with you freaks," the guy snarled.

Jeff watched the handsome man flee.

Then he saw Waring emerge through the Porn Room doorway. There was a wild look of terror upon his ashen face. His shirt was unbuttoned, his round white belly was exposed for all the world to see, and his loosened belt buckle clinked with each step.

"Alaura!" Waring yelled. "Where are you, Alaura!? Are you all right!?"

Am I all right? Alaura thought. No, I'm not fucking all right.

She watched as Clarissa Wheat scurried out behind Waring, birthed by the same Porn Room doorway, both of them coming, Alaura knew, from Waring's office. Clarissa Wheat was in a state of undress similar to Waring—shirt loosened, missing one gray shoe, and her silver cross swinging between a surprisingly full and youthful-looking bosom—leaving little doubt as to what she and Waring had just been doing.

There they all stood, facing one another amid the shrapnel of the Sports Documentary section: Alaura next to Barney Wheat, Waring next to Clarissa Wheat.

"Clarissa, darling!" Barney Wheat said happily. "I've just met one of Ms. Eden's acquaintances. The poor guy took a nasty tumble, and now I don't know where he's gone."

"Oh hush, Barney," Clarissa Wheat said as she futzed distractedly with her hair, trying to push it back into a bun and apparently unconcerned about the display of her (again, Alaura noted) unexpectedly impressive body.

Barney Wheat smiled and teetered. Alaura placed a hand on his shoulder to steady him.

"Don't touch him!" Clarissa Wheat snapped.

Alaura removed her hand.

"She . . . she made me," Waring said, looking at Alaura.

"I have no idea what you're talking about," Clarissa Wheat assured him, and she approached her husband and took his hand, interlocking her fingers with his.

"You're lying!" Waring cried.

"Like you've been lying to us, Mr. Wax?" Clarissa Wheat said pointedly. "What is purchasing product on credit and not paying it back, except a lie?"

"I have no idea what you're talking about."

Clarissa Wheat shot him a startled glance. "Guiding Glow is a Christian organization, Mr. Wax, and your contract with us states explicitly that no pornography can be rented from any store under our distribution umbrella. And, of course, there's the issue of your back payments."

Alaura glared at Waring.

Waring looked down at the floor like a scolded child.

"I'm sure Waring just forgot," Alaura pleaded. "He can write you a check. Waring? Can't you just sell some investments or something and write them a check?"

"It doesn't matter, Ms. Eden. None of this is even the real purpose of our visit."

"What are you talking about?"

"We are here to inform you that, as of last Friday, Guiding Glow has sold its entire distribution network, including our two warehouse centers and our entire stock of DVDs, to Blockbuster Inc. It seems that they're expanding their DVD-by-mail business in hopes of competing with Netflix. They made us an offer we couldn't refuse."

Alaura gasped. She felt her own lips quivering.

"Oh, Waring," she managed.

Clarissa Wheat continued, "Star Video is in breach of contract. Your account has been terminated. We will continue to fill the orders you've already placed for the next two months, at which time you'll need to find a new distributor. Though incidentally, Mr. Wax, it doesn't appear that your credit is in any sort of shape to qualify you for a personal checking account, let alone a contract with Ingram or one of the others. No matter . . . at the end of those two months, your entire debt to us will come due. In summation, Mr. Wax—"

Alaura gripped Waring's arm to steady herself.

"—as of now, you are no longer associated with Guiding Glow Distribution. You are on your own."

THE
REALITY
CENTER

Articles

Appleton Herald
ONLINE

Editorial—Is Hollywood's sudden descent upon Ehle County worth celebrating?

Published: Sunday, September 16, 2007 at 3:30 a.m.

When [name of film studio omitted] announced last week that the cast and crew of a Hollywood production titled "Not Tonight, Joséphine!" would film scenes in Historic Downtown Appleton, we were all excited.

We were especially excited when the film's star was announced to be Tabitha Gray—one of the silver screen's highest grossing actresses. (Ladies, hide your husbands!) And of course we were excited about the likely boost to our local economy that the production would provide.

But has anyone stopped to ask, why haven't more details about this movie been released? Its other stars? Its director? Or anything about the movie's plot? Why all the secrecy? What if the movie portrays the South or, in a worst-case scenario, Ehle County, in a negative light? Will this be yet another film where Southerners are portrayed as ignorant, backwards, racist caricatures, who in the end will be grateful to be enlightened by benevolent interlopers?

The production refuses to answer any such questions. It seems content to arrive under a cloak of secrecy . . .

CLICK HERE FOR FULL TEXT

HOW ALAURA GOT HER GROOVE BACK

"Where's Karla?" Alaura asked Constance, an old drinking friend who was now (Alaura was just beginning to realize) a rather obnoxiously contented housewife.

Constance stared back with a frozen frown, as if to say: *Karla is your weird friend, not mine.*

Alaura and Constance were drinking mimosas in a hipster diner in West Appleton. The place boasted mismatched flatware, waitresses with Bettie Page hairdos, and paintings of dancing skeletons on the walls. Roy Orbison's "In Dreams" slithered from the jukebox, masking, but not completely blocking, the muted trombone of Constance's yattering voice, like Charlie Brown's teacher.

"*Whah-whah-whah, whah-whah-whah-whah film crew?*" Constance asked.

"No, I don't know anything about the film crew coming to Appleton," Alaura responded. "Just because I work in a video store doesn't mean I know anything about the actual film industry."

"*Whah-whah-whah, Tabitha Gray whah-whah?*"

"Aren't we here to talk about my life, not Tabitha Gray?"

"*Whah-whah, whah-whah Not Tonight, Joséphine!*"

Alaura sighed. "That's probably a fake title. I think *Not Tonight, Joséphine!* was the working title for *Some Like it Hot . . .*"

But her voice trailed off.

It wasn't that Alaura didn't care about the movie crew coming to Appleton. She did care. But she couldn't help thinking that *it just didn't matter*. Star Video had lost its distributor. Waring was broke (or "maybe broke"—the bastard still wouldn't admit the full extent of his life's train wreck). In two months, Star Video would have to start buying movies from somewhere new, probably Walmart or Target, since it was likely that no legitimate distributor would ever touch Waring with a ten-foot pole.

And she'd been drinking a lot. Too much. She'd smoked an entire pack of cigarettes yesterday. She'd been getting stoned, sleeping until noon, spending all day on her couch, avoiding work (because *screw* Waring), and, perhaps most worrisomely, she'd been watching DVD after DVD and weeping at every ridiculous plot turn. But nothing seemed to help. No meditations. No combination of chemicals. No movies. Not even catching up on fun shows like *Lost* or *Deadwood*, on silly but brilliant shows like *Boondocks* or *The Venture Bros.*, on pretentious but obligatory shows like *Six Feet Under* or *The Wire* (though *The Wire* was turning out to be amazing) . . . none of it offered any solace, a definite indicator of looming depression.

"*Whah-whah-whah,*" Constance was saying. "*Whah-whah watched that Tabitha Gray movie on Netflix last night, whah-whah where she's a grave robber—*"

"Wait, what did you say?" Alaura asked.

Alaura focused on Constance, who was tall and plain and always smiling, with limp blonde hair, broad shoulders, and a long, Sarah Jessica Parker face.

"The one where Tabitha Gray's, like, a gun-toting grave robber who knows karate," Constance said. "Her, you know, *breasts* are bigger than her head. And she's, like, stick-figure skinny. How could she even lift a rifle—"

"No," Alaura interrupted. "You said you watched the movie *on* Netflix?"

"Oh." Constance winked. "My husband, he's kind of a nerdy techie guy. He uses these hummadinger cords attached to our computer. I'm not sure what they're called. But you plug them in, and you can watch movies on Netflix."

"You mean, like, on your computer?"

"No! On our TV! It's really neat. Netflix just started doing it. You press a few buttons, and zoosh, there's a movie playing on your TV."

"Any movie?"

"No," Constance said. "They don't have a very good selection, but *whah-whah-whah, whah-whah* . . ."

Alaura tuned her out again. All at once, the implications crashed down on her. It didn't matter if Netflix only offered one crappy Tabitha Gray movie online. Soon it would be ten other movies. Then a thousand. Then ten thousand.

Every movie ever, zooshed directly to your television.

Of course she'd heard about this. She'd known it was coming in exactly the way Constance had just described. But now it was here, like a wrecking ball on its downward descent to demolish Star Video.

Alaura looked again at Constance. Her friend was now telling some senseless story, laughing about her husband/children/recent technological acquisitions, and she seemed completely unaware of Alaura's distress. Alaura sighed. She had always attended to Constance's complaints—about money, career, children, boyfriends, marriage, love affairs, everything—so she had not felt selfish initiating this bitch session. Not one bit. Now, for once, she needed Constance's help.

But brunch was not going according to plan. Thus far, Constance had seemed more interested in pointing out Alaura's life errors, past and present, than in providing the compassionate understanding Alaura had always given her. Constance demanded that Alaura quit Star Video at once. She suggested job-search websites and wardrobe intervention. She stated again and again that she had "never liked that Pierce," and she babbled that this confluence of events was "an excellent opportunity for cleansing," a vaguely nauseating notion that Alaura, despite her background of religious wandering and herbal experimentation, did not understand in the slightest.

Slowly Alaura was realizing that this "friend" hardly knew her anymore. How had that happened? True, Alaura hadn't seen Constance at all over the summer because of how much time she'd spent with Pierce. But still . . . somehow Constance had become a minor character in the drama of Alaura's life, unworthy even of backstory, multiple scenes, hard focus.

"Where *is* Karla?" Alaura repeated, this time to herself, and she gulped a mouthful of mimosa, then signaled their waiter for a refill.

Karla: her best friend. Karla had been out of the picture since beginning that weird life-training stuff over two months ago. But if anyone could straighten out this mess—straighten out Alaura's life—it was Karla.

Ten minutes later, Karla floated into the diner.

As always, Karla was devastatingly beautiful, luminescent, the top 1 percent of the top 1 percent, her arms and hips barely on the healthy side of anorexia, her face narrow and firm like a graphite-framed structure designed to support her significant lips. She was the only redhead Alaura had ever known who did not look like an anemic alien—Karla, Princess of Pallid.

The tablecloth rose and settled when Karla took her seat, as if by ghostly breeze.

Men at nearby tables looked beyond their wives at the new glowing creature.

"I have to tell you the most amazing thing," Karla said, staring deeply into Alaura's eyes.

Karla's voice broke the spell of her own entrance, and only at that moment did Alaura perceive that there was something very different about her friend. Karla sat more upright than normal. Almost rigid. She wore a broad smile rather than her usual sexy glower, for at heart she was a temperamental metal sculptor, given to rumination and self-criticism. And she gazed with otherworldly intensity into Alaura's eyes, which was not necessarily out of character, though the creepy duration of the eye contact certainly was.

"Are you okay?" Alaura said worriedly, finding it impossible to disconnect from Karla's glistening green orbs.

"Oh, my dear, *dear* friend. You're the first person I thought of."

Karla hugged Alaura.

Alaura felt the embrace shaking—her friend was weeping.

"What is it, sweetie?"

"Oh, Alaura," Karla said, leaning back and reestablishing eye contact. "I've had the most wonderful, wonderful experience. Something has happened to me that has changed my life forever."

"Are you crying?"

"These are tears of joy!"

A man rushed toward their table waving a handkerchief like a surrender flag—Alaura shooed him away.

"I've just finished the Advanced Experience at the Reality Center," Karla explained. "The most amazing month of my life!"

"You mean that life-training stuff?"

"No, Alaura. It's not training. It's experiential learning. They show you, Alaura, they really show you. How to achieve transformation. How to live with intention. *Real* intention. And once you have real intention, you know how to *be*. That's what I'm talking about, Alaura. Being."

Alaura realized she was nervously chewing her pinky nail. She forced her hand toward the table.

"You have to come, Alaura. If you never do anything else that I ask, please come with me to the Reality Center. It's exactly what you need, Alaura."

"What makes you think I need—"

"Because I heard the sadness and pain and loneliness in all those voicemails you've been leaving me. And I know what your problem is."

"My problem?"

"You hide in movies, Alaura. You escape into fantasy. You're a victim of the fracturing of our modern world. We're all cut off from one another. And movies are how you cut off yourself. You live through a television screen. Through other people's stories. Alaura, the Reality Center has taught me that you must run *toward* your intention, not away from it, because the future is today."

Alaura's face warmed in embarrassment—both for Karla, who sounded pretty much like a crazy person, but also for herself, because something about what Karla was saying was not entirely bonkers. Alaura *had* been watching too much television, almost twelve hours per day, too many movies, polishing off the last of Almodóvar's and Cronenberg's crazy films like she'd planned to do for years, and binging on shows, finishing one DVD then starting the next almost immediately.

And, as Alaura thought about it, all the wine and weed and cigarettes probably qualified as "escaping reality" as well.

"Please come with me to the Reality Center," Karla pleaded, smiling her intensely beautiful smile. "I know that you're *meant* to do this, Alaura. There's a glorious being of light within you, just begging to emerge."

"A being of light?"

"A majestic being of light," Karla said. "Our society is at a turning point, Alaura. Those who are willing to embrace the truth, and embrace one another, will lead us toward the future!"

Alaura looked across the table at Constance. For once, Constance wasn't smiling. Her lips were sewn shut. Her neck was tight as a rope. It was sweet, Alaura thought, how Constance was so obviously put off by Karla's weird earnestness. And Alaura realized that, despite today's awkwardness, Constance *had* been a good friend to her. Always a lot of fun, always honest (in her own way). One botched summer hadn't erased all of that.

Still, Alaura could see clearly how Constance rarely allowed her to talk about herself. Constance never asked questions. It was always Alaura's job to listen—somehow Alaura had fallen into the role of caregiver with Constance as well.

Karla was different. She radiated compassion. She was complicated but caring. She looked at life through a spiritual-artistic lens. She spent her days creating art and meditating and reading bizarre texts—the letters of Gauguin, the journals of Anaïs Nin, the Bible. And years ago, Karla had been the only one to listen—really listen—when Alaura had gone through her period of religious wandering, from Christianity to Wicca to Buddhism to Confucianism to all the others, and the corresponding history of tattoos—Santeria crucifix on her back, the Buddha and Chinese characters on her neck, Mother Goddess in the form of cephalopod on her right arm (which in truth had been inspired by an insane acid trip and a viewing of *20,000 Leagues Under the Sea*). Karla, trim and delicate as she seemed, was in fact tough and perceptive and wise. A spiritual seeker, just like Alaura.

She's an honest-to-God metal sculptor! Alaura thought.

A waitress with Zooey Deschanel bangs and black fingernails arrived with breakfast. Alaura had ordered a deep-fried sausage sandwich—she was shocked now that she had allowed herself such a greasy indulgence. She looked at the sagging thing on the plate in front of her. Everything about it disgusted her. The glistening exoskeleton. The twists of blue steam. Even the fanned slices of orange—fruit suggesting what? That this meal was somehow defensible?

The sandwich was like her life—disgusting and indefensible.

She turned to Karla.

"When?" Alaura said.

"Today," Karla responded excitedly. "There's a guest event at five p.m."

"Okay, I'll think about it."

A sibilant gasp across the table; Constance touched her mouth in horror.

Karla looked toward the ceiling. She beamed. Bright white energy spilled from her pores, filling the restaurant like a Klieg light.

"Oh, Alaura," she said glowingly. "Make sure to dress up. Something businessy. And come sober. And keep a positive attitude. Reality might seem freaky at first, but if you keep positive, it will change your life forever."

After breakfast, walking toward Star Video, her head spinning from Karla's bizarre proclamations and also still from the ramifications of being able to watch movies *on* Netflix, Alaura came across a crowd of twenty people gathered on the front lawn of Weaver Street Market, West Appleton's organic co-op grocery store. Standing on a small stage at the center of the group, under the shade of a sprawling oak, a young woman was reading a truly god-awful poem.

Such a display was not uncommon in West Appleton, especially now that the midday heat had finally dropped below eighty-five degrees. Alaura had noticed street musicians popping up everywhere, more people out walking and running and biking in the evenings, and there were more hula-hoopers and interpretive dancers/schizophrenics frolicking around. But what caught Alaura's attention this morning was not the crowd of people, nor the terrible poem (which was one of the most excruciating things she'd heard in a long, long time—all "raven of the night" and "blood splashed upon the moon"), nor that the poor girl reading it was visibly shaking in intense self-awareness of her own poem's awfulness. What caught Alaura's attention were all the tiny video cameras.

Four of them, to be exact. Little handheld things, no bigger than a cell phone. More than Alaura had ever seen in one place. They were called Flip Video cameras, and Alaura knew that they could be plugged directly into a computer. You could download your video and zoosh, post it online. Or you could cut together your own little movies, using free editing software. The cameras had been on sale since last year.

And now here they were, on the Weaver Street Market lawn, their small, rectangular screens shining like badges of light, all of them held aloft by skinny undergrads.

Not to mention that half the damn people on the lawn were chatting on their six-hundred-dollar iPhones.

Alaura realized that the tiny cameras were focused on the petrified bard, and that they were all capturing her crime on digital video. Digital video that would soon be uploaded, most likely, to YouTube.

The future is today, Alaura thought, and at that moment, she decided she had no choice but to go to the visitor's event at the Reality Center.

"Don't do it," Waring said, perched on his director's chair behind Star Video's counter. "Sounds like a scam."

Dorian—Alaura's favorite part-timer and Star Video's musical and concert film expert—was working, too. Upon his ageless face hung a calm, though concerned, frown.

"It does sound a little strange," Dorian said.

"Jesus, I shouldn't have told you guys."

Alaura had only stopped by Star Video to pick up schedule requests and to count change for the weekend. Though she'd skipped work all week, having gladly scheduled Waring for seven consecutive shifts, she could not completely suppress her near-maternal devotion to the store.

"Does it cost money?" Waring asked.

"Of course it costs money," Alaura replied flatly.

She looked at Dorian, who wore a neon pink blazer, and whom Alaura knew to be unfailingly polite and understanding. He gazed back at her with calm inquisitiveness, so she explained to him, more than to Waring: "It's not religious or anything. It's not a cult. They help you organize your life. Think positive. Experiential learning and all that."

Dorian smiled what Alaura always thought of as his gay-Buddha smile.

"Do what you gotta do, Alaura," he said. "As long as you're safe."

Then Dorian picked up a stack of Tabitha Gray DVDs, which he was using to set up a special feature display near the front of the store, and he strolled onto the floor to arrange them.

"Dorian's clearly an idiot," Waring said, standing up and approaching where Alaura was counting change at the Cashier du Cinéma. "And anyway, I think you're just trying to punish me."

"That might be true."

"What are you so angry about?"

She wheeled toward him. She stabbed a finger in his direction. "Are you *really* asking that?"

"I told you, I didn't throw a brick through Peckerdick's window."

"That's not what I'm talking about."

"What we've got here . . . is failure . . . to communicate."

Alaura glared at him. She took a moment to collect herself. "You think I'm in the mood for jokes, Waring? After everything that's happened. You lied about your financial situation. You lied about your credit. And now we're on our own. We're screwed. We have no way to buy movies. So what's the point of all this now?"

Waring forced a snorting laugh that Alaura knew to be an affectation of disinterest.

"Alaura," he said, "there's nothing to worry about."

"Of course there is!"

Waring smiled falsely.

She pointed a thumb at her own chest. "*I'm* trying to do something positive with my life," she said.

"Positive?" he said, wincing. "You know, this wouldn't be the first time you've fallen into some stupid religion in hopes of fixing your problems."

"This isn't a religion."

"When will you realize that you're just as miserable now as you were before all those religions?"

"I'm not miserable."

"The Reality Center? What kind of name is that?"

"Whatever!" Alaura turned back to her change count, but she had lost her place. She raked her fingers through her hair, which lay flat and oily on her head because she hadn't washed it in days. "I can take it for what it's worth, Waring," she muttered in exhaustion. "Maybe learn a few things that'll help me."

"I don't like it."

She sighed, shook her head, and looked back at him. Then she stepped forward to straighten the collar of his dirty checkered button-up.

She noticed his body stiffen. But he submitted silently to her attention.

A calm descended between them.

"I'll be fine," she said gently when she had finished. "But it would be nice if you could just . . . not give me a hard time."

Waring grimaced. He hesitated for a moment, then said:

"But it sounds so embarrassing."

"Come on," she pleaded. "Stop joking. Please . . . I really need you, just for a moment . . . to *stop being you*."

Waring backed away from her. His eyes were trained on the floor. He sat back down on his director's chair. He turned to face the host computer.

"I'm really mad at you, okay?" Alaura went on. "You've been good to me. I was fucked up a few years back, and you helped me through it. I'll always be grateful to you for that. But I know that you're aware of how completely psychotic you are. You're not like normal people. You're crazy, Waring. You *have* to know that."

Waring: no response.

"Having an affair with Clarissa Wheat?" she went on desperately. "Not telling me about your money situation. I mean, shit. You have to know that's all really, really . . . crazy and self-destructive."

"Fine," he said in a low voice. "I understand. You have legitimate reasons. You're mad at me."

He reached out and tapped the keyboard, one stiff jab at the "Return" key.

"I understand," he said again, his voice even softer.

"You do?"

"If you want to go, then go."

Alaura nodded.

She turned and walked toward the exit—she hadn't finished counting the change or picked up the schedule requests, and she wasn't going to.

"Good-bye," she said, and she left the store.

Later that afternoon, when Alaura entered the Reality Center conference room (windowless, clockless, gray), she found a group of thirty well-dressed Caucasians holding hands in a semicircle. Fifty or so other people—parents and siblings and friends—mingled inside the circle, all looking a bit dazed.

"Wind Beneath My Wings" played over loud speakers.

Weird, Alaura thought.

"This is wacko," hissed Constance, gripping Alaura's arm— Constance had told Alaura point-blank after brunch that she wouldn't allow her friend to go alone into "some insane asylum," thus inaugurating herself into an extended speaking role.

But the Reality Center was different than Alaura had expected. She had expected classrooms and PowerPoint presentations and Tony Robbins. Maybe guided meditation and macrobiotics. Or perhaps some Scientology-ish iconography. This didn't feel like that at all. The vibe in this room was very spiritual, but somehow not religious. A lot of hokey love in the air.

It reminded her of her favorite aspect of church as a kid—the church lock-in.

A small Asian woman with obviously enhanced cleavage led Alaura and Constance into the semicircle, and she instructed them to wait directly in front of Karla, a link in the chain of hand holders. Karla stood holding hands with two handsome men in their twenties, and her head was thrown back, like the rest of them, in cataleptic bliss. She wore a searing white business suit that called the transfiguration to Alaura's mind, and she mouthed the ridiculous lyrics along with Bette Midler.

On the walls around them hung a series of blue-on-white posters with simple slogans in bold letters:

THE FUTURE IS NOW

YOUR POTENTIAL IS YOUR REALITY

PROGRESS IS EVOLUTION

"Seriously," Constance whispered, "this is fucking crazy."

"Yeah," Alaura said. "Those posters are pretty *1984*."

"Whatever," Constance said. "This is just fucking crazy."

Alaura nodded. It was fucking crazy. But the cumulative effect of the hand holders ("graduates" they were called) was nonetheless impressive. These were real people, after all—not all of them could be loonies. Many of them seemed to wear Dorian's gay-Buddha smile, totally at ease and confident, if not contentedly homosexual. Were they all as convinced as Karla that they had figured out their lives? Unshackled their egos? Figured out their future? Had they finally put everything in order?

Karla, of course, came from a rich family. She'd never had to worry about money. She only worked part-time jobs. The bohemian-sculptress lifestyle made financial sense for Karla, so it was also perfectly reasonable for her to venture on mental and spiritual escapades like this potentially crazy Reality Center. But in the diner, Karla had seemed so centered. So happy. In the past, despite her intense positivity whenever listening to Alaura bitch about her shitty life, Karla had also harbored, it seemed to Alaura, a certain latent displeasure with the world. At times she was prone to bursts of witty cynicism born of sublimated rage (a pose that other bohemian artists in town seemed to respect intensely, and her looks didn't hurt), and this complex disposition made its way into her sculptures, large twisting things that defied gravity.

But now, standing here, Karla seemed like a different person—a mightier person. Even swaying silently with eyes closed amongst a bunch of weirdoes, Karla was someone to be idolized.

Mercifully, Bette Midler stopped singing.

"Thank God," Constance whispered.

"Hush," Alaura said harshly.

"I can't take this. I feel sick. I think I have to get out of here."

"Then leave."

Constance took another look around the semicircle. "Maybe I will."

"Go then."

"You should come with me, Alaura. Please don't get involved in this."

"Maybe I want to get involved," Alaura said. "I can just take it for what it's worth."

"But I've got a bad feeling."

"And I've got a bad feeling about *you*."

Constance's mouth dropped open—she turned and left the conference room.

Moments later, a woman's voice exploded over a loudspeaker: "Welcome, guests! The Reality Center would like to thank you for being here on perhaps the most important day of our graduates' lives. They have experienced one of the most exhilarating, frightening, and illuminating events they will ever experience, and now they are ready to reenter the world and help pave a new future for us all. You should consider it a singular honor that you have been chosen to share this momentous moment with them." (*Momentous moment?* Alaura thought.) "Graduates, open your eyes!"

Karla opened her teary green eyes, and Alaura, feeling a bit like a misguided apostle, smiled. They embraced. Alaura felt her friend's body shudder against her, cold tears glazing her neck.

JEFF AND WARING'S EXCELLENT ADVENTURE

It had only been seven days since The Corporate Visit and Alaura's subsequent "leave of absence"—a term Jeff had thought applied only to doctors and professors—but during that short time, without her guiding hand, Star Video had begun falling apart. It was shocking to Jeff how quickly things unraveled. He would arrive for a shift to find that none of that morning's returns had been shelved, and though business was slow, this still amounted to fifty or more show boxes, not including pornography. Then, when Jeff had gone back to Waring's office to retrieve a roll of quarters, he'd found no change in the money box and had to pay back customers with dimes. New membership forms hadn't been filed for a week (though there had only been two). No one had swept the floor or battled the dust bunnies or taken out the trash. They'd run out of Jiffy Pop. And that Monday, the day before that week's new titles were to be released, Jeff realized that no one had printed up the New Releases handouts, nor had anyone updated the New Releases whiteboard positioned by the front door, which was the very first thing most customers looked at when entering the shop.

So Jeff did what he could. He shelved DVDs and VHSs. He took cash next door to Pizza My Heart and pleaded for change. He swept the floors, changed the whiteboard, took out the trash. He scoured the file cabinets and found the phone number of their concessions distributor, and he ordered more Jiffy Pop, because how could a video store function without popcorn? And, on Tuesday, he used the dingy laptop he'd inherited from one of his redneck cousins to create a poor approximation of Alaura's New Releases handout, which he then printed and photocopied on Ape U's campus, at his own expense, using his student account.

Later that day, Jeff worked with Waring, and he found himself, as usual, the only one standing to help the few customers who entered. Waring never budged from his director's chair, and he hadn't bothered to thank Jeff for any of his extra work. Instead, Waring kept his gaze dispassionately on the television screen, today playing *High Sierra*, and he only occasionally emerged from his trance to belt out the title of a movie that a customer might be asking about.

"Night of the Living Dead," Waring grunted to one unsuspecting customer who'd approached Jeff with a question. "That's Romero's first zombie movie. *Dawn of the Dead* is better. They're both great. I was just reading that Romero says that the racial commentary in *Night* wasn't on purpose . . ."

Waring's voice trailed off, and Jeff led the confused customer to the Horror section.

Over the next few hours, as Jeff continued shelving and cleaning and assisting customers, he occasionally stole glances at the ragged little man, who seemed even more weird and distant, and possibly more drunk, than normal.

And slowly Jeff realized what must be going on in Waring's mind—he was worried about Alaura. He missed her. He might even be in love with her. It had been easy for Jeff to think of Waring and Alaura as an old married couple. As bickering, griping, sexless entities. But the truth, Jeff decided, was much more complicated.

"It's been years!" Waring said suddenly, some time later, when they were alone. "I thought she was over all that religious crap."

"Where is she?" Jeff asked in confusion. "What is the Reality Center?"

"I think it's some Werner Erhard knock-off."

"The director?"

Waring sighed, shook his head. "No, Jeff. That's Werner *Herzog*. Werner *Erhard* ran these life-training seminars in the seventies. I had no idea they were still around. The kind of thing where they berate you for hours, then empower you with mumbo-jumbo, then convince you to sign up all your friends. A pyramid scheme."

Jeff wanted to respond, but at that moment, a beeper went off on his hip. He scrambled to silence the device.

"What's that?" Waring said.

Jeff wrote something in a small notebook.

"Hey. You. Hick."

"I'm not a hick," Jeff said, but not as forcefully as he would have liked.

"What was that beeping?" Waring asked. "That's twice today I've heard it."

Jeff replaced the notebook and beeper in his jeans pocket. "It's for school," he said.

"School?"

"Psychology class. I'm participating in a study. It's a class requirement."

"They're studying the psychology of beepers?"

"No."

"Beepers are annoying," Waring proclaimed. "Also very out of date, from what I understand."

"They're not studying beepers," Jeff said. "They're studying happiness. Relative happiness or something. Every time the beeper beeps, I have to write down how happy I am on a scale of one to ten."

Waring stood up from his director's chair. "No shit?" he said with a strange smile.

Jeff nodded halfheartedly.

"What number did you write down?"

Jeff hesitated. He looked up to the television screen—Humphrey Bogart scrambled over the face of a blue-gray mountain—and said, "Seven."

"Seven? What about the last time they beeped you?"

"Eight."

"Why the drop-off?"

Jeff couldn't assemble a convincing lie, so he reluctantly answered with the truth: "Because Alaura won't be working this weekend."

Waring rolled his eyes theatrically. "Tough luck, Blad. And how happy would you be to work extra hours this weekend because Alaura will be out?"

Jeff considered the question. "Honestly, I might bump back up to eight. I need the money. And I like working here."

"Even if you have to work with *me* all weekend?"

"You don't really bother me anymore."

Waring held two fists in front of his face. "Tough guy, eh?" he said, then he dropped his hands.

Jeff shrugged.

They both turned their attention back to *High Sierra*.

A bit later, apropos only because Jeff had been trying to deduce it for a long time, he asked Waring:

"I was wondering . . . why do you own a video store?"

Waring scowled at Jeff, nostrils flared, as if he'd just been asked why he wore pants.

"Sorry," Jeff said.

Waring shook his head and looked back at the television screen. "Because it's Tuesday afternoon, and I'm watching a Humphrey Bogart movie," he muttered. "Obviously, because I love movies."

"Me too!" Jeff said happily. "Back home in Murphy, I had this small television, and I'd put it on my bed and cover myself—"

"I grew up in Manhattan," Waring said, cutting Jeff off. "It was a damn movie mecca then. In the seventies. Lots of amazing stuff happening. A new groundbreaking movie every week. My mother, she always took me to movies. That's what we did, we'd go around the city to see the latest Kurosawa and *Taxi Driver* and *The Towering Inferno* and whatever Vietnam movie was out that week. And man, if there was ever anything showing from the sixties or before, we'd always see that. Silent films, anything. This was way before video stores. You had to *go* to the theater. Or read your *TV Guide* to find out when movies were showing."

Jeff nodded.

"Video stores popped up in the early eighties, after my mother passed away."

"Oh," Jeff said. "I'm sorry."

"'Snothing," Waring said, and he shrugged disinterestedly. "But she would have loved video stores. All those movies, and a lot of them back then were the classics, because they were public domain. Betamax. Now that was a good technology. Way better visual quality than VHS." Waring clenched a fist and shook it at the sprawling store in front of him, as if in rebuke to all VHS tapes that might be paying attention. "Anyway, back then, I'd go all around the city, from video store to video store, looking for movies. Video Shack on Broadway, New Video in the Village, I'd hit all of them. I even worked at New Video for a few months, when I was about your age . . ."

Waring's voice trailed off. His wistful expression quickly flattened.

"What was New Video like?" Jeff asked.

Waring sighed. "It was great, okay? And that's why I bought Star Video. It was my lifelong dream."

Silence.

"But why *this* store?" Jeff asked tentatively. "Why all the way down to North Carolina?"

"Jesus," Waring said. "What's with the interrogation?"

"Uh—"

"Because I saw an ad in the back of a trade magazine, okay? The original owner of this place was selling out because he was old as dirt. And there was no competition in Appleton, and business was booming, so, you know, I did it."

"Oh."

"I saw an ad," Waring repeated. "And then some other things happened, and it just made sense, you know? You dream about doing something for a long time, and once you finally have the money to do it, which I was lucky enough to have, then why not fucking do it, you know?"

"Wow," Jeff said. "That's cool."

High Sierra's final credits rolled. Waring stood up and stuffed his hands in his pockets. Jeff noticed dark armpit stains on Waring's grungy gray button-up shirt. The shirt was rumpled, like he'd slept in it for the past few nights.

"Jeff?" Waring said.

"Yes, sir?"

"I was wondering if I could get your help with something."

"Sure. What?"

"What if I asked you to come to Blockbuster with me and plant pornography in their DVD cases?"

Jeff laughed.

Then he realized that Waring was completely serious.

At three p.m. that afternoon, Waring and Jeff approached the Death Star, aka Blockbuster. Five cars were parked on the Death Star's brand-new, coal-black lot, five more cars than were currently parked in front of Star Video. Through Blockbuster's crystal-clear windows, Jeff could see that ten or more customers perused the aisles and that no fewer than four employees wearing navy polo shirts were manning the front counter or shelving DVDs.

Jeff glanced at Waring, who was now scowling up at the huge blue and yellow sign that dominated College Street. Inside the angry man's wrinkled pants pocket, Jeff knew, was a stack of particularly vulgar pornography—*Real Raunchy Redheads*, *Lex the Impaler 2*, *Anal Blasters 6*, and others. Waring had printed DVD labels for mainstream movies like *The Prestige*, *The Passion of the Christ*, and *Bambi*, as well as for some of that week's new releases—*We Are Marshall* and *Death Proof*—and he had applied the labels to the porn. "Blockbuster stores their DVDs on the floor," Waring had explained to Jeff, "not catalogued behind the counter like us, so I'd say they're basically asking for it." Waring's brilliant plan, as far as Jeff could tell, was to infiltrate the Death Star and surreptitiously switch out the DVDs, so when customers popped in *Bambi*, they would instead encounter, well, Lex the Impaler's impressive physiology. All blame would then fall to Blockbuster—perhaps shutting them down, or in the very least, causing them to spend days searching every DVD case in their store.

Now that Jeff was here, about to navigate into the Death Star, he had no earthly idea why he had conceded to act as lookout for such an obviously absurd scheme. But it was too late. Farley was watching Star Video, filming again around the shop with his video camera, and Jeff was Waring's accomplice.

Yes, Waring's plan was ludicrous. Repulsive. Almost certainly illegal. But sometimes you meet a person like Waring . . . *who does whatever he wants*. No matter what. Damn the consequences. Ef the police. Screw embarrassment—embarrassment doesn't even fit into the equation. And these people—who really couldn't care less about you or anyone else—are so rare that we are drawn to them, Jeff thought, like scientists drawn to a near-extinct, if nauseatingly grotesque, species of bat. They have a unique power that we envy. We can't remove our gazes as they demonstrate their buffoonery. We are jealous. We ridicule their rejection of "normality" while simultaneously our chests ache with the possibility of letting go—letting go, for example, of the D grade Jeff had just received on his Intro to Business exam, his first college exam ever. Letting go of Alaura's likely hatred of him after The Corporate Visit, how he hadn't lied for Waring. And letting go, especially, of Momma's expectations, or rather her presumptions, and the presumptions of everyone else back in Murphy, that he would ultimately fail at Appleton University, that soon he'd be back up on the mountain and pumping gas or working at Kmart or cooking meth or whatever. All of which hung over him like a gray ghost.

How amazing would it be, not to care about any of these things?

As he wandered Blockbuster—keeping Waring's lookout, but a lookout for what?—Jeff studied the sparkling, intentional layout of the place. Every detail seemed designed to inspire a sort of heightened relaxation: cool fluorescents, waves of color and candy, clusters of giant flat-screen TVs playing *Toy Story*. The shelves were less cluttered (and thus less intimidating) than Star Video's. Not as large of a selection, of course, but much better organized . . .

The beeper beeped.

Jeff wrote down "8" in the notebook.

Waring legitimately wanted to puke. It wasn't just the colors of the place, which were cloying, corporate, sickly electric. And it wasn't just the light fixtures, which were so bright that they aggravated the fug of his hangover to the extent that his head might go all *Scanners* and explode. No, what really got Waring's goat was that *this* Blockbuster was exactly like every other Blockbuster he'd ever had the misfortune to enter, down to the alphabetized candy displays and twenty flavors of microwaveable popcorn and the stupid graphic art on the walls and the theft-detection scanners at the front of the store . . . as if this were some jewelry shop or high-end electronics store. Like anyone gave a damn about Blockbuster's crappy mainstream movies.

Then Waring saw a sign near the front counter, surrounded by yellow light bulbs and designed to mimic an old theater marquee. The sign read:

TIRED OF DRIVING? REGISTER ONLINE FOR TOTAL ACCESS (WWW.BLOCKBUSTER.COM) OUR DVD-BY-MAIL SERVICE!

So it was true. Et tu, Blockbuster? Going the way of Netflix!

Waring's stomach churned, and he considered the merits of relieving his nausea upon Blockbuster's floor. He took a deep breath. Then he crouched, removed a flask from his hip pocket, took a slug of bourbon.

When he stood up, he noticed a security camera clawing at the ceiling—it's insect eye zeroed in on him. He took a few steps. The camera swiveled to follow.

First he searched for *The Prestige*, but he found no copies in either Drama, Action, or New Releases (and there didn't seem to be a Why is Christian Bale Famous? section). Nor could he find *The Passion of the Christ*. Probably checked out, he thought, by one of those conservative nutsoes who used to picket Star Video's Porn Room years ago.

Bambi. They must have multiple copies of *Bambi*. He saw a sign labeled "Kids," walked there, found two *Bambi* show boxes.

He knelt to the floor as if to tie a shoelace, shielding his furtive enterprise from the camera. But when he tried to open the show box, it produced a tiny plastic groan and resisted his pull. He studied the box. It was secured by a yellow, magnetic tab. Waring yanked at the tab, twisted it, but the damned thing would not come loose.

"Sir, may I help you?"

Waring's entire body shook. *Bambi* fell to the carpeted floor. Waring scrambled, hastily replaced *Bambi* on the shelf, and stood up.

"I was just looking for—" Waring began, but his voice seized when he saw the fiend who had addressed him.

It was the tall, dark-haired guy from that night a few weeks ago. One of the three bicycle-gang men. Their leader. He was tanned and muscular, his skin smooth and clear like he had never come within ten yards of a deep-fried sandwich. He was at least six inches taller than Waring, and he wore pressed khaki pants and a navy "Blockbuster" polo.

"I could have guessed," Waring said, standing up. "So you're the owner?"

"Paulsen Crick, franchise operator," the man corrected with a cool smile.

"Could have guessed that, too. I actually *own* an independent video store. Own."

"Are we going to have a problem, Mr. Wax?"

"That's for you to say, cupcake."

The man continued smiling—as far as Waring was concerned—like a villainous bastard.

"What were you doing to *Bambi*?"

"We're fresh out of *Bambi*, and I'm craving cartoon tragedy."

"To give context to your own life?"

"Ouch," Waring said, forcing sarcasm.

Crick was formidable. Not as easy to intimidate as most dolts.

"Have you been drinking?" Crick asked.

"Not to your knowledge."

"You have quite a reputation in that regard."

"If I drink, it's only in response to some people's aggressive tactics to drive out a longstanding local business."

Crick laughed, mirthful pity spilling from his chiseled face.

"You really have no idea what's going on, do you?"

Waring shrugged like he couldn't care less.

"You will," Crick added. "As I said before, your day of reckoning is fast approaching."

"Good God, I honestly thought I'd hallucinated you saying that," Waring said with a laugh. "Adios, dipshit. Oh, and these are for you." He removed the camouflaged porn DVDs and tossed them on the floor in front of Crick, where they fanned out or rolled in every direction. "Someone dropped them off at Star Video. Make sure you put them back out on the floor."

And Waring strode triumphantly out of the Death Star.

Outside, he found Jeff standing on the sidewalk.

"Killer job on lookout, Blad," Waring snapped.

"I though you were right behind me," Jeff said. "I saw that guy from the other night. Does he work here?"

"Thanks for the support, Jeff."

They began the short trek to Star Video. Waring jammed his fists into his pockets, grumbled to himself. It was getting dark, and the air was unseasonably cool for late September. Or was he in need of a drink? Anyway, feeling that first chill of the year meant it was almost time for his biyearly clothing run, when he would purchase several identical sweaters and pants to wear for the entire season. Tomorrow maybe. He would go to the outdoor store in Browne Mill Mall that Alaura had mentioned. But no . . .

That shop, Quick Dick's, was also located in Browne Mill Mall. The fired customer, what's-his-name, Mr. Prick, he owned Quick Dick's.

And all at once, a few pieces fell together. Not the entire puzzle, only a vague outline. Mr. Prick and Paulsen Crick were friends. Biking buddies. And twice, Crick, franchise operator of Block-buster, had insinuated that Star Video would be going out of business, or some other looming catastrophe.

Was a conspiracy afoot?

But how could they know the extent of Waring's financial problems? Waring didn't even know himself. The stock market was booming these days, or at least he thought he'd heard that. Maybe his stocks had ballooned despite his neglect. Maybe he had become a millionaire and didn't even know it.

No, Waring thought. That was just stupid.

Almost as stupid as planting pornography in Blockbuster.

Back in his office, Waring cracked open a beer, drained it quickly. Then, on his desk, he discovered a stack of white tee shirts screen-printed "Cutters." An unsigned note in Alaura's handwriting, which she must have written before The Corporate Visit, read: "Bought these. Wear one tonight. Part-timers, too. Found them last week on eBay for ten dollars apiece. Free shipping."

Waring balled up the note, tossed it across the room.

"Ten dollars apiece!" he yelled at the ceiling.

How had it come to this? That spending fifty dollars on stupid movie tee shirts felt like it might break the bank?

And Alaura? What the hell was she doing? That was the worst part of all of this. She meant it, Waring knew. She was really angry this time. This time she was finally going to quit.

If Star Video didn't go out of business first.

He pounded another beer.

Yes, she would quit. Of course she would. It was only logical. She wasn't an idiot, like most people. She would flee this sinking ship, find a new job, find a new town, find a new boyfriend—some turd with a million dollars and a mountain climber's body—and she would marry him, and they would have sex, and she would never ever ever come to Waring again and say, "I need your help."

He closed his eyes.

Immediately he is on the airplane again, on that last flight from New York over ten years ago. He sees the chubby guy sitting next to him, that orthodontist or veterinarian, and Waring begs the guy to drink with him, buys them little plastic bottles of liquor, tells the guy about his wife leaving. "Can you imagine that?" Waring says. "You come home, and all her things are gone? Can you believe that actually happens? That she could actually leave a note? On the day you lose your job, a job that you hated more than life itself, but still, it sucks to lose it, and you come home *that same day* to find a little folded note taped to the wall? Hey buddy, hey friend, can you believe that actually happens to people?"

Then he is in a hotel room. A week later. Lying in bed. Surrounded by bottles and darkness. In North Carolina, in Charlotte. Earlier that day, he bombed an interview for a job that would have paid him a third of what he made in New York, a job he probably would have hated even more than his last, so he has no idea why he even applied. He's been in the hotel for days now—in fact the interview was days ago. He's drunk, he's hungry, he hasn't eaten since yesterday, and he's trying to muster the energy to walk down to the lobby restaurant . . .

When the phone rings.

He looks at the phone, hears its piercing squeal, and he answers—

"Bullshit," he hissed at himself, waking up, back in Star Video.

He opened one of his desk drawers. There he found a stack of account ledgers. All of them were blank. Looking at them, he remembered—in his first few years of owning Star Video, he had maintained rigid, daily accounts. The computer could do all of that for him, of course, but he had wanted a physical record. To feel his fingers running over the numbers. To have proof of the new life he'd built.

But at some point—five years ago? more?—he had stopped maintaining the ledgers. That would have been around 2002, which was the first year that DVD rentals had outpaced VHS rentals, and was, in many ways, the peak year of the video store industry. Even from Waring's naturally pessimistic point of view, business could not have been better. Everyone in the world had purchased a DVD player. And everyone in West Appleton rented from his store. He was bringing in twenty or thirty copies of the biggest mainstream titles: *The Fast and the Furious*, *Harry Potter and the Sorcerer's Stone*, *A Beautiful Mind*. Sure, there were hints of what was to come. Netflix was open for business, those bastards. And the damn studios were offering DVDs for ridiculously low sell-through prices—twenty dollars, sometimes less—instead of the traditionally high prices of VHS tapes—fifty dollars, eighty dollars, more—which had of course helped cut down Waring's bottom line, but which was also drawing customers away to Walmart and Target to buy DVDs. Oh, and lest we forget about the Internet, where he'd heard there was more free porn available than a night at the Playboy Mansion . . .

But still, business in 2002 had been churning along nicely. Waring, with Alaura's help, had built an incredible library of movies, and he'd grown the store from sixteen hundred square feet to over five thousand square feet, and he'd even made enough money to buy the entire building.

Maybe that's why he'd checked out. Because it had all been too good to be true.

Waring removed the ledgers one by one from the deep drawer. There were ten of them. All completely blank. He stacked them on his desk.

Then he saw his mother looking up at him. In the drawer, under where the ledgers had been, was a framed photograph of her. That headshot from her youth as an actress. He'd misplaced the photograph years ago. He lifted the picture, its heavy silver frame, and set it on his desk. The woman looking back at him was young, beautiful. Twenty-two years old. A dead ringer for Gene Tierney. But unlike Tierney, it was somehow obvious that the woman in this headshot was hoping, begging, desperate for stardom, and that this desperation would lead to her downfall. She was moments away from being cast in a role that would never come, and years away from going to her final reward, those last years during which she would complain endlessly about all the movies she should have starred in, and she would pull Waring out of school, several times a week, and take him to the movies. Always the movies.

"There's your reason, Jeff," Waring whispered.

He laid the picture face down.

From his MicroFridge he grabbed another lukewarm beer, snapped it open.

But he didn't drink.

Not right away.

Instead, he opened one of the blank red ledgers, sought out a pen, then picked up the phone to call his bank.

It was time to figure out where Star Video stood.

THE WRATH OF THOM

Alaura stood before her forty Reality Center classmates, who were all holding hands and sitting together in a tight bunch, like kindergarteners listening to their teacher read *Curious George*. It was Alaura's first full day of the Basic Experience, and ten days since beginning her retaliatory "leave of absence" from Star Video. On stage to her left, and seated behind a shiny music stand, was the cofounder of the Reality Center, Thom Trachtenberg.

The man looked a bit like Ricardo Montalban as Khan in *Star Trek II*—all chest and feathery hair.

Alaura felt weak. The air was too warm. She had skipped breakfast, and they had not taken a lunch break. And she had no idea what time it was; watches were not allowed. She had been standing for at least an hour, answering Thom's pointed, personal, often rude questions and revealing more about herself to these strangers than she had to anyone in years—though she supposed that was the point of Reality.

"Why won't you be honest?" Thom asked for the fifth time.

"I am," she replied again, rolling her tired shoulders, shaking out her hands.

"No. You are sabotaging your life."

"I told you, I'm trying to live a *good* life."

He raked her with an eye, and his voice rose: "Trying? See, you're wrong about fucking everything!"

She had adapted to his cursing, and to his bursts of saliva, but not to his constant incredulity. Was it possible for anyone to be wrong about *everything*? She had spoken of her past drug problems, of watching too many movies, of her various religious wanderings, of her job, of Waring, and of her stupidity at recently falling for Pierce.

But did those things sum up her life completely?

"You are the architect of your own future," Thom proclaimed. "So why do you work in a video store?"

"I told you, I . . . I . . ."

"I . . . I . . ." he said in mock imitation, then he paused for a centering breath. "Answer without thinking, Alaura. Why do you work in a video store?"

"I . . . I like movies."

"And?"

"I like helping people. West Appleton is a nice town. People know me."

"You believe people know you?"

"I . . . I guess so."

"Shit," he snarled, scowling at her. "We're trying to help you, Alaura, yet you resist. Are you saying that you crave popularity, that you crave approval, that you crave people telling you how sweet and interesting and unique you are? The hip, tough girl with tattoos . . . all of which makes me think that this video store is just a safe ego zone."

Alaura fired Thom a look of warning. But he was now consulting his notes with disgust. He was going too far, and none of the hand holders seemed interested in defending her. Instead, her class-mates murmured like bewildered yet hopeful congregants, and she considered, for the fifth or sixth time, simply walking out. They had told her they would refund her money at any point, but she wondered if that was true, if there was some loophole in the lengthy contract she had signed.

Thom said, "Basil, the young man who conducted your entrance probe last week, told me that you hate your life."

"He did?"

"Yes."

"I don't remember saying 'hate.'"

"That's what Basil reported."

"Thanks a ton, Basil."

"So," Thom said, "why do you stand for the video store?"

"Stand for?" she asked. "I'm sorry, you're moving kind of fast, and I don't really understand all the terminology—"

"It means," Thom said, gritting his teeth and looking over the class. "It means that you *stand* for it. That you believe in the video store so deeply that it defines who you are. I, for example, stand for the Reality Center because of the good work we do helping people realize their full potential. I also stand for the universal right of all people to exist. Do you understand?"

She did not. "Yes," she said.

"We have all agreed that our full potential is simply an innate characteristic of our being. And we have all agreed that the modern, interconnected world offers us two distinct paths: one toward solitude and loneliness, and the other toward communion and evolution. You say you hate your life, Alaura, and you work in a video store. Why do you stand for the video store?"

"I don't know. I've thought about quitting, but . . . Star Video is a part of me."

"Mmm," Thom said, sounding not unlike Waring. "And if you had an infected appendix, which is certainly a part of you, would you hesitate to have it removed?"

"I . . . I don't know."

"She doesn't know!" he said, smiling with satisfaction. "You're one big mass of 'I don't know.'"

I will not lose my cool, Alaura thought, and as quickly as she thought it, she began speaking—calm, even, like reading a grocery list: "Fine. I enjoy working there. I love it, actually. It might not be the best job, but it's mine. I'm good at it. Star Video is a cool place. It's a gathering place for film nuts. I mean, not like it used to be. There aren't as many regulars. But still. The store is culturally important, I really believe that. I believe in movies. I don't believe they're just about escape. Though I kind of see what you're getting at there." She pulled her left arm across her chest with her right hand, trying to stretch out her back. "There's a chance Star Video might have to close soon," she continued, "and I don't know what I'll do if that happens. It would be a disaster, for me, for West Appleton. I'm good at managing employees, and I'm good at dealing with my boss, who's totally insane. I know a lot about movies. Not as much as my boss, but I know a lot. I might not be a millionaire, but I'm secure." She knew she might be lying, or at least half-lying, and that her country accent was emerging like blood at the edge of a Band-Aid. "I got a place I can call home while I sort out the rest of my life. I'm a very spiritual person, you see. I studied religion in school. You could say I'm on a spiritual quest, have been since I was a child."

"Continue," Thom said.

His voice was now smooth, laced with wind.

"My mother left when I was young. I never knew her. We weren't churchgoing. My dad and I. He was a good man. Is a good man. Always working. I started watching movies when I was seven or eight." *Keep talking.* "We lived in a trailer by a river. Didn't always have a television. Every step, the whole trailer rattled. I would go to town and sneak into movies. There was only one theater. In retrospect, the movies were terrible. Six-month-old releases, never anything R-rated except a few action flicks. But I loved it, loved the dream, the lights going down, the movie coming up." *I haven't been to an actual movie theater in how long?* "My dad's good to me. I should call him more often. I should visit. I shouldn't be disconnected, like you say. I grew up close to here, like, thirty minutes from Appleton, in a podunk town, Sprinks, you've never heard of it. I loved the movies, even back then. My first boyfriend, he was a movie nut, too. I loved watching movies with him, at his house, on his big TV. His family was rich. But then he left, and my daddy encouraged me to leave, too, to get out of Sprinks, to go to college. I got into Appleton University. I'm done paying off my student loans. Anyway, as I kid, we didn't go to church, but on Sundays, I'd walk around town and peek in church windows. Listen to what they had to say. Since then, I've tried everything. But religions can let you down. Movies never do."

Silence.

She looked at her classmates — several of them had tears running down their faces.

Why were they crying? In sympathy? In pity? And what was the difference between sympathy and pity? Alaura couldn't decide.

Then, strangely, the foreign sensation that the tattoos on her right arm were horrible scars.

"You're a very smart woman," Thom said, away from the microphone, in a whisper meant only for her. "We can all see how intelligent you are."

Alaura frowned, but she stared at this new, polite incarnation of Thom.

His chest hair beckoned her. His crisp white shirt glowed.

"But your brain is merely a mechanism," he said, louder, for everyone. "It is not who we are. It is not our animus."

"Okay?" Alaura said, again confused.

"Your brain is telling you that if you just think hard enough, work long enough, probe deep enough, then you will at some point discover some *thing* that will give you permanent bliss. But this is a lie our brains tell us, the Lie of Completion."

That made sense.

"For example," Thom continued, "you've mentioned your problems with men."

Her brief comfort deflated. She had complained about Pierce and about her many other ill-fated relationships, though now she wished she hadn't.

"It is clear that you want a man in your life," Thom said. "But it seems to me, and I don't think I'm wrong, that you expect once you meet this mythical man that all matters will be settled. But that is not progress, Alaura. That is not true communion. Instead, you're like the struggling writer who thinks, if I get my novel published, then everything will be okay. You're like the executive who thinks, if I make vice president, then I can finally relax. You're like—"

"I get the point," she said flatly.

Thom reared back, suddenly enraged, his righteous homily exhausted. "You *get* the point? You get nothing! You hide behind your tough fucking image and your tattoos, as if they make you special, when in fact you are a deep dark hole into which you shovel alcohol and men and movies, hoping to fill yourself, hoping to avoid who you really are."

"I thought I was a being of light," Alaura said, lapsing now into full bitch mode.

"Why are you being defensive?"

"Because you're being aggressive."

"What are you scared of?"

"I'm not scared, I'm annoyed."

Thom's mouth dropped open like he had never heard anything so appalling.

"I have to pee," she said.

"Not until we're done."

"We've been doing this for an hour."

"And you still can't be honest."

"I am being honest," she said.

"What are you scared of?"

"Honest. Scared. Words and words."

"What are you scared of?"

"I have to pee."

"What are you scared—"

She walked from the stage, stomped through a field of gasps, broke several links in the bunched, hand-holding circle.

At the exit of the conference room, a young man stepped in front of her. He was young, maybe twenty-one, and pudgy.

"You can't leave," he said, his voice blurry and dumb. "The rules."

She hissed nonsense syllables at him. He backed away.

In the bathroom, on the toilet, Alaura watched an aimless bug wander the tile floor: a pen point upon white tundra. Her heart rate slowed. She unclenched her teeth. She focused on her breath—a blue crystal beneath her nose—but still she felt on the verge of screaming.

She had been the first to stand before the class. She knew she was being made an example of. The others would have it easier. But this was only the beginning. If she returned to the conference room, she'd have to resume the stage. She'd have to face Thom again.

Yes, Thom was an arrogant prick. His holier-than-thou shtick was insulting. His hair, basically a mullet, was ridiculous. But the Lie of Completion? That was golden stuff. The appendix thing, too. He had some good things to say. She should not have lashed out.

But of course, that was probably his angle: to push her, soldier-like, to a breaking point.

If so, if Thom really wanted total honesty from her, then why not tell him her deeper, darker secrets? Why not tell him, for example, about Jeff, young Jeff, whom she had briefly, briefly considered seducing despite (and maybe, weirdly, *because of*) his age and his innocence and his fervent, puppy-like devotion to her? His attention felt nice—she couldn't lie to herself about that; it felt good to be idolized. Jeff had a religious bent like her, and like her, he had been raised by a single parent in a nothing town. Jeff clearly needed help breaking out of his shell. He needed a real-world, freshman-year, mind-blowing experience. The kind of experience Alaura wouldn't necessarily, in a moment of weakness or generosity, be averse to providing.

Sometimes sex makes me feel better, and Jeff would probably appreciate me breaking off a piece, she might say to Thom. And she bet Thom would get a real kick out of her sick attraction to an eighteen-year-old kid.

That was honesty, right? Her base impulses? Her incredible narcissism?

What do you think of that, Thom?

But why was she reacting this way? Why was she so angry? Thom was just asking her questions. Was it merely her own answers that were pissing her off? True, Thom's methods were annoying. She'd been around the philosophical guru block—his tactics were as tired as his wardrobe and his feathered mane.

But the core of his message, though she hated to admit it, was undeniable:

You are the architect of your own future.

Which, if true, meant she was a shitty architect. Fuck. It *was* true. There was no other way to look at it. She'd settled for a life of drinking and men and movies in a tiny college town. She blocked herself off from the world. She'd wasted her twenties. She'd waited passively for something better to come along, some*one* better to come along, to fix everything, to complete her. The Lie of Completion. She'd known that Star Video was a dead end for years. But she'd been too asleep to translate that knowledge into action.

And now, she had morphed into an awful cliché: the aging sassy tattooed sexpot. If she was her life's architect, then the structure she'd designed was a slumping, decaying deathtrap, unsuitable for human habitation.

Like the building that housed Star Video.

And like Star Video, she had no idea how to fix things.

When she returned to the conference room, her classmates cheered. They whistled and hurrahed. They hugged her all in turn. She did not understand their reaction, but still she made her way to the front of the room, receiving their genuine affection, bolstered by their compassion. Going to the bathroom, breaking the rules in this way, was seen as a great triumph. They were proud of her. Which was stupid, Alaura thought.

But it was better than nothing.

She resumed her position on the stage. Her classmates gathered in a tight cluster at her feet.

Thom, upon high, smiled.

"Now will you tell us the truth?" he asked.

IT'S A MISERABLE LIFE

Having watched twelve or so science fiction and anime movies in the last week (not including what he watched in the store) and two trippy movies that morning alone (*Dead Leaves* had been a particularly twisted choice: gratuitous violence, thought-scrambling techno score, seizure-inducing artwork), Jeff felt profoundly off-kilter, shrouded in a purple fog. Nothing seemed quite right—even sunlight appeared chemical and fake. In this state of mind, he found himself on Ape U's leafy, bustling campus. He was sitting in Warlock Hall, a creaky early-twentieth-century building retrofitted with silver air-conditioning ducts snaking along every hallway, giving the place a space-station vibe. The office where he sat had one small round window, like a porthole, and it looked over a grassy quad, where girls were eating lunch and boys were trying, most of them unsuccessfully, to talk to the girls. On the desk in front of Jeff lay the beeper and notebook he had kept with him for the past two weeks (he had *al*most made it without Waring finding out about the beeper), and across from him sat the graduate student—a dark, barrel-chested Russian named Dorofey—who had run the experiment. Vaguely threatening,

Dorofey seemed both focused on and annoyed by the interview he was conducting, Jeff thought, like Agent Smith in *The Matrix*.

But at least Jeff could feel good about this sweet new tee shirt he was wearing. Soft and thin, scoured green cotton, in places brushed almost to transparency, and on the front of it a simple graphic of Richard Pryor's face, the comedian's hair like a black globe about his head, his mouth wide open in laughter. Jeff had recently watched some Pryor stand-up for the first time, and it had blown his mind, so when he had come across the tee shirt at a boutique near the Open Eye Café, he had purchased it immediately, and without guilt, using twenty-five dollars from his second Star Video paycheck. Jeff looked down at the shirt now, at the inverted image of Pryor on his chest, and for a moment, he felt a bit more grounded in space-time.

"What this?" Dorofey said in a gruff, thickly accented voice.

Jeff leaned forward over the desk and looked at the page in the notebook where Dorofey now pointed.

"Oh," Jeff said. "I made a note. I realized, uh, that I was making my happiness too high."

"Too high?"

"I made a note that you should take away two from every rating before that day."

"Take away?"

"I mean, you know, subtract?" Jeff explained, gesturing toward the notebook. "Too high. In there. Subtract two."

Dorofey set down the notebook. "Mr. Meeker, I speak English very well. No need for speaking slowly so I understand."

Jeff's face warmed over. "Sorry," he said.

Dorofey squinted at the younger man. "Did something happen, Mr. Meeker, on September the tenth to prompt you to retroactively reduce your level of happiness?"

"Nothing happened," he said.

"Then what's the problem?"

"Well, I'm not sure I should say," Jeff said.

"Why not?"

"I don't want to hurt your feelings. Or mess up your experiment."

"My feelings? Mr. Meeker, if there is problem, you should tell me."

Jeff settled back in the square wooden chair, a chair reproduced identically, he had noticed, all over campus. "Well," he began, "I guess I didn't understand the assignment, sir. I mean, what do you mean by happiness exactly? You never told us. You just gave us this slip of paper that said, 'Write down how happy you are on a scale of one to ten whenever the beeper beeps.' I mean, I don't walk around all day feeling happy happy. I don't think anyone does. So maybe you meant, I don't know . . ."

"Contentment?" Dorofey suggested.

"Sure, contentment. That's what I was thinking. But I wasn't sure. Then, on Monday, I pinched my finger real bad at work while we were repairing some shelving that had fallen down. I work at Star Video, you know, in West Appleton? And right when I pinched my finger, the beeper beeped. I didn't know what to write. I mean, I was in pain, so I wasn't feeling too happy. Maybe contentment, but I don't know. You didn't say to write down the reasons we were feeling whatever, but I did anyway, on the next page. I wrote down, 'Pinched my finger at work.'"

"I see that."

"I thought maybe—"

"Mr. Meeker, please get to point."

"Sorry. I just wanted to know what the goal of the experiment was, sir."

Dorofey removed his gold-rimmed glasses, folded them shut, and with a discontented huff slid them into his shirt pocket. He muttered something in Russian, then said, "The purpose of the experiment is to study relative happiness. How happiness fluctuates throughout the day. You, for example. Your happiness seems quite high in evenings, but not so much during day. Overall range of five points."

"Is that a lot?" Jeff asked, a little frightened by what the Russian's answer might be.

"Mr. Meeker, this is not a diagnostic tool. I am not telling you if you are happy or not."

"Oh."

"But your fluctuations do seem higher than other subjects I have interviewed."

Jeff heard himself gasp. "What does *that* mean?"

"Mean?" Dorofey said. "I don't know what it means. It means you seem fairly unhappy in the mornings, and fairly happy at night. This is not uncommon. Most people work in morning, go home in evening, and their happiness fluctuates accordingly."

Jeff felt a chill of fear. Was it possible that he was miserable and didn't even know it? "But, sir," he said, "I work in the evenings."

Dorofey nodded, squinted with momentary thoughtfulness. "So you like your job?"

"Yes, very much."

"At the video store?"

"Yes," Jeff said, taken aback by Dorofey's apparent disbelief. "I like working at the video store."

"Is not boring?"

"Boring? No, sir! We watch movies and talk—"

Dorofey held up a hand, as if asking for a high-five. His voice lowering, he said, "Mr. Meeker, I don't care about video store."

"Oh."

"What do you do during day that make you so unhappy?"

"I don't know."

Dorofey waited, stone-faced.

"I go to school," Jeff said finally.

"So you don't enjoy school?"

Jeff shook his head, thought of the string of awful exam and essay grades he had received lately, despite all his studying. Then he said unsurely: "No, I enjoy school."

Dorofey squinted. "Is a girlfriend?"

"A girlfriend?"

"If not school, usually young men are unhappy about girlfriend."

Thinking at once of Alaura, Jeff quickly raised and lowered his shoulders to indicate that his problem was most definitely *not* a girlfriend.

Dorofey leaned back in his chair, crossed meaty fingers over a considerable belly. "Listen, Mr. Meeker. This baseline phase of the experiment in which you participated was designed simply to measure how much self-reported happiness fluctuates throughout a day. That is all."

"Okay?"

"I'm sure you are familiar with famous lottery-wheelchair study?"

Jeff heard Waring's voice in his head say, *What do you think, buddy?*

"Very simple," Dorofey said. "Happiness research is relatively new, but my colleagues and I agree that human beings are not terribly smart at determining what makes us happy. In lottery-wheelchair study—a classic study referenced many places, including several Hollywood movies, I might add—in this study, researchers compared the happiness of people before and after they had won lottery or received major injury that put them in wheelchair. The result was that lottery winners were not any happier one year after winning lottery, nor were wheelchair folks more unhappy once they got used to their new condition. Happy people remained happy. Unhappy people, unhappy."

Jeff's vision blurred as he struggled to follow the Russian's words.

"It complicated," Dorofey continued. "Apparently, chronic back pain and long commuting time are better indicators for unhappiness than is blindness. And having one extra hour of sleep every night makes businessmen happier than doubling of their income. Do you see what I'm getting at?"

Jeff shook his head no.

"And if you want to, the phrase 'hedge your bets' against unhap-piness,"—Dorofey's eyes fell shut, and a chortling sound began to emerge from his throat that Jeff soon recognized as laughter—"then, then you should seriously . . . consider taking many naps . . . and against children. Naps make people happy. Children, on average, miserable."

Dorofey's weird mirth subsided, and he sighed in what seemed to Jeff like an unconvincing display of embarrassment. Finally Dorofey said, "Mr. Meeker, I shouldn't say this, but you strike me as a nervous and potentially unhappy young man. If you want to be miserable, go ahead, I do not care. But if you want to be happy, maybe make some changes in your life. This is modern world, after all. There are options."

"Options?" Jeff asked quickly.

"Many. Go out in world and do modern things. Post profile on online dating site. Get cute girlfriend. Use the Facebook or Meet-Together sites to find people with interests similar to yours. You're interested in film? Join film club. There are several I believe here at Appleton University. Or buy your own little camera and make your own little movies. I hear it very affordable these days. Then put your little movies on Internet. A documentary. Or a fun romance. Cast a girl and a boy and have them talk about things, have silly things happen. This formula always works. Who knows, you might get one million hits on YouTube, become famous."

Bewildered, Jeff opened his mouth to ask the Russian another question, but Dorofey again held up a hand and said:

"Time to leave, Mr. Meeker. Bye-bye. I have fifty undergraduates to see, and they all want to know why they're so damned unhappy."

Meanwhile, Alaura—though it was a bit embarrassing to admit, even to herself—felt like a new woman. She had been a student at Reality for four days, and while she still believed that many aspects of "the

Experience" were absurd, corny, over-the-top, useless (in particular, the constant hand-holding), nonetheless "the Experience" had
cracked open something inside her—what she could only refer to,
in Reality jargon, as "access to her innate potential." Karla was
right—they just showed you. They pushed you and asked you end-
less swirling questions until all of your defenses had chipped away,
leaving only your soft, frightened inside. Leaving only your future,
ready to emerge. They showed you how your decision-making had
formed your life—that you, and no one else, had formed your life—
for Alaura, it was most definitely how she'd isolated herself with
movies and drinking and unhealthy eating and smoking, her lack
of ambition, her worry about appearing both tough and sweet to
others, and her choosing to fall in love with shitty men . . .

   That night, she strolled through West Appleton (when was the
last time she'd actually *strolled*?) focusing on the contractions of her
muscles, conscious of an energy stirring in her belly, and observing
the goings-on of a Thursday in late September. It was eleven p.m.
The LED streetlamps, powered by solar energy collected during the
day, cast a bluish light over the nearly empty business district. The
first day of autumn had passed only a few days before, and already
some of the small retail shops had decorated their windows with
fake pumpkins and fake brown, yellow, and orange leaves, though
the trees wouldn't begin changing color for a month or more. A
handsome street musician played a slow, sad electric guitar, sitting on his own amp at the corner of College and Weaver Streets,
in front of Walk In The Clouds—one of West Appleton's many
yoga studios. Alaura sidestepped a crocodile of cackling young
women, a bachelorette party stumbling arm in arm from one bar to
another. Of course the bars on College Street were full—the upscale
places filled with blazers and sorority hair, preppy interlopers from
Appleton, and the not-so-upscale places, Alaura's places, with their
pretentious jukeboxes and craft beer on tap and a greater likelihood,
on any given night, for physical violence.

All of it beautiful in its own human, sweetly pathetic way.

Alaura had asked Karla to drop her off downtown, not at her apartment—she and her gorgeous friend, like little girls, had chattered, giggled, actually held hands in Karla's Lincoln Navigator on the forty-five-minute drive back from the Reality Center. Alaura had never felt so close to Karla, never allowed herself to be so relaxed in Karla's presence. And this was only because, Alaura now knew, she had been so weak and frightened before Reality, so unaware of how she sabotaged her potential, like a skittish animal conditioned to fear all external stimuli. But now, with four full days of Reality under her belt, Alaura was "standing outside the ordinary" (Reality's term), a "powerful goddess" (Alaura's term—such melding of belief systems was not openly discouraged), fearful no more. So she walked the streets of West Appleton, wasting the hour before she absolutely *had* to be at Star Video, to train Jeff how to close the registers—one of the last tasks keeping her connected to the place—and she couldn't stop smiling.

Her face ached from so much smiling. But even the ache was transportive to broader thoughts: the ache represented her new life, and looking at herself in the autumnal shop windows, allowing herself to smile her full Reality Smile, she saw that she was beautiful, while, at the same time, she knew that others, seeing this (manic?) expression, might think she was insane.

A giggle erupted from her stomach like an electric shock— *Other people!* she thought. Though her Reality Center instructors wouldn't admit it, other people, non-Reality people, were to be pitied. Loved, of course, but also pitied.

Love. She loved herself—she could honestly say that she loved herself. Despite everything, she loved herself! And though this thought, *I love myself!* was real and frequent and always accompanied, almost literally, by melodic trumpets and riotous applause from the invisible audience of her psyche, still she was the tiniest bit ashamed of loving herself so much. It was a hackneyed sentiment, she knew. So banal. But was this shame the last barrier Reality would help break down? When its philosophies finally came together, and the future finally revealed itself to her, would she finally love herself without embarrassment? Would the power that now rendered her unable to stop smiling soon narrow its focus, phaser-like, onto her life's true purpose? And she could see with HiDef clarity that she loved West Appleton. That was obvious. West Appleton was her home. She never wanted to leave. She had occasionally entertained the notion of moving away, of finding a new life somewhere else, anywhere else, anywhere far away from Sprinks and West Appleton, anywhere outside of North Carolina. But not now. Now she strolled and strolled, hands linked behind her back like a dictator surveying *her* town. Her people, West Appletonians, "Applets" (Waring's term), streamed around her—the pleasant drinkers (she hadn't sipped a drop of alcohol in four days—but they are having fun, aren't they?). Why would she ever leave? True, the shops that lined West Appleton's business district, a quarter-mile from Star Video, sold mostly expensive nonsense. Trinkets of no real value. Vintage clothing stores—but the skirts and shirts and scarves were all so pretty, she thought. Is it wrong to want to be pretty, to value beauty?—her thoughts, a mile a minute. But always returning to the Reality mantra—*I love myself, and I can create whatever I dream. I will never abandon this belief. I love myself, and I can create whatever I dream. I will never abandon this belief.*

She looked at the ornate analog clock high on the redbrick Community Center building—a clock she knew to chime a digital bell tune every hour—and she saw that it was 11:45. Star Video would be closing in fifteen minutes. She didn't want to be late.

Jeff kept surveillance on Star Video's parking lot—Alaura would be arriving any second. Business was slow. Nonexistent. He and

Rose had nothing to do, and, like always, Rose had remained silent during their entire shift. But that was fine. Since meeting with the Russian grad student, Jeff hadn't felt like talking to anyone.

Alaura arrived at 11:55 p.m., five minutes before closing. On time, for once. He hadn't seen her since The Corporate Visit. And . . . she looked amazing. Jeff was speechless—she wore a black dress, blood-red lipstick, gold sandals snaking up her legs. He was transfixed by the dress's spaghetti straps and the almost-fully-exposed tattoos on her back and right arm. And her hair—it was up in that amazing pompadour, rising three inches above her head, slicked back and shining dark.

"Hi," he said shakily.

"Hi there, Jeff." She presented an open-mouthed smile, teeth gleaming, as she glided around the counter.

"I . . . you . . . we . . ." but Jeff's stammering was silenced by Rose, who yanked her backpack from under the counter, slung it over her shoulder, and stomped (as much as such a tiny person can stomp) toward the door.

"Is something wrong?" he called out to her.

"Bye, Rose," Alaura said sweetly.

The door clanged shut behind the little girl.

"That was strange," Jeff said. "What's wrong with her?"

But Alaura hadn't seemed to notice. "Waring's not here, is he?" she asked with a cheerfulness that did not match her question. "I'm avoiding him."

"Um, that shouldn't be hard," Jeff said, confused. "He hasn't been around much."

"No?"

"Me and the other part-timers are basically running the store."

"What?"

"Well, honestly, me more than anyone else. Nothing seems to be getting done. I think there's a whole shipment of DVDs in the back that haven't even been processed."

He watched Alaura's face tighten, but a moment later she rolled her eyes and said brightly, incongruously, "Oh well, it's Waring's store!"

After this baffling response to what he assumed was troubling news, Jeff decided not to report the full extent of Waring's strange behavior: that for days he had been scribbling in a large red book, talking angrily on the phone, and storming in and out of the store without explanation.

"How's your leave of absence going?" he asked instead, bypassing the subject of Waring.

"Wonderful, Jeff. Absolutely wonderful."

Only then did he notice the dark circles under her eyes. "You look tired," he said.

"I didn't get much sleep these past few days."

"You look great, I mean," Jeff corrected himself. *You're such an idiot*, he thought.

"That's very sweet of you, Jeff."

"Uh . . . so you were at . . . uh . . ."

"The Reality Center," she said—and in the next breath, she launched into an impassioned monologue about her miraculous experience. Her voice brightened steadily as she spoke—she smiled, laughed, oozed gratitude at her great fortune in discovering "Reality."

But her fervor, well, it was just plain weird. Jeff had only witnessed such drowsy-eyed enthusiasm in church, or at tent revivals on his high school's football field in Murphy, and for the first few minutes of Alaura's speech, he suspected that she was acting. That this was all a big joke. Until it became clear that it wasn't a joke. She pronounced his name with worrisome frequency. She drifted on tangents. And the odd, new age phrases. She was now "aligned with who I really am, Jeff," an idea he could in no way comprehend. She was "ready to change my life, Jeff, to change our world." She was finally "embracing interconnectedness and running away from solitude, Jeff." She believed in "the magic of positive thinking, Jeff."

Reaching out and squeezing his arm, she said: "Look at how we're interacting now, Jeff. Right now, Jeff, this is the most powerful conversation you and I have ever had."

Jeff looked down at her hand, which felt warm and damp on his skin.

She removed it.

He focused again on her pompadour, which seemed to defy the laws of physics, and he was unable to look at her beautiful face.

Had she noticed his new Richard Pryor tee shirt? Did she like it? "Jeff?"

"Yes, ma'am?"

"Does it make you uncomfortable, me talking about Reality?"

Jeff froze in fear—like that night when he had been unable to defend himself against the cyclists. Other versions of Christianity were one thing—but experiential learning? The Reality Center? All he could think to say was, "So you're going back there?"

She pondered, breathed deeply. "There are two more levels of the Experience: Intermediate and Advanced. I've signed up for both."

Jeff managed a nod. "Do you mind me asking how much they cost?"

She told him the cost of each session.

"Oh my . . ." he said, but he captured "God!" in his throat.

"It's an investment in *me*," she assured him.

"I guess so."

"Don't worry, Jeff. If you're not interested, I won't talk your ear off about it anymore."

Jeff nodded, glad for this offer.

A moment later, Alaura hopped up and sat on the counter, facing the store's central television. Jeff had been watching *Forbidden Planet*. She pointed at the television and asked, "So you're a sci-fi fan, Jeff?"

"I guess so."

She smiled again, and with gentle fingertips, she adjusted the delicate fabric of her dress to drape more evenly over the curve of her hips. *"Forbidden Planet* is a classic," she said softly. "Great sets. Great costumes, too." Her eyebrows raised. "Jeff?"

"Yes, ma'am."

"Did you throw a brick through my ex-boyfriend's window?"

Jeff looked away—

"If you did, I'm not mad at you," she said.

Jeff said nothing. He looked at the television, where a giant, howling cartoon monster was being shot with purple lasers.

"And if you did," she said, "it's the sweetest thing anyone has *ever* done for me."

His stomach, pole-vaulting into his throat. Then he remembered, strangely, his quiz in Business Administration tomorrow; he needed to study.

"I've decided not to borrow Waring's Dodge anymore," Alaura said. "Could you walk me home? Maybe we could watch a movie at my place. Do you have class tomorrow?"

"Yes, ma'am."

"The Reality Center has this silly thing about movies," she went on. "They say movies cut us off from human contact. I'm pretty sure I don't agree. But still, if you and I watched a movie together, and we talked about it, that wouldn't be cutting ourselves off, would it?"

"I really don't know, ma'am."

She smiled, and Jeff realized that she had been ignoring his repeated "ma'am" slip-ups.

"Jeff," she said, "I *want* you to walk me home."

Once she had taken him through the steps of closing Star Video and bequeathed him his own key to the store, they locked up the shop and set off into West Appleton. They walked slowly—it had rained at some point, and volcanic steam rolled off the streets. And to Jeff's surprise, they did not speak as they walked. At first this worried him because he felt it was his responsibility to fill in the silence. But Alaura seemed content, smiled gently to herself, and he decided it was best not to bother her.

Eventually she motioned for them to turn right onto Cape Fear Drive. Small, close-set houses lined both sides of the narrow street. No curb—weedy lawns ran directly onto pavement. Like Waring's shabby neighborhood. She turned onto a driveway, and he thought they had arrived, but then they walked past the house, past a fenced-in yard where two yellow dogs trotted with them happily for a few yards. He realized that he was looking at her constantly, at her profile, at her lips that seemed so soft he would be frightened to kiss them too hard. Should he reach for her now, here in the dark forest, draw her toward him? Is that what she wanted? But she was so much older than him. Ten years, more. He didn't want to ruin this opportunity by acting too soon.

Two weeks ago—after overhearing Alaura leave a strained voice-mail message for a friend about her boyfriend breaking up with her—Jeff had looked up Pierce's address in the Star Video computer, Googled directions, and at three a.m., he had thrown a brick through the a-hole's window. It was maybe the craziest thing Jeff had ever done—and he had virtually wiped it from his memory, until Alaura had brought it up.

A small baseball field opened in front of them. The field was surrounded on three sides by kudzu-masked trees. Alaura led him onto the field. Strangely, she climbed the pitcher's mound, set down her large purse on the dirt, kicked off her golden sandals. Her eyes were closed. Her body cavity expanded and deflated several times. He stood beside her, several painful feet away, and listened to the crickets, to the breeze in the branches, to the drizzle from earlier draining onto the forest floor. Looking at her again, he felt his manhood straining against the elastic band of his boxers, where he had been repeatedly tucking it whenever she wasn't looking.

But what was she doing, standing on this weedy field? Praying some Reality Center prayer?

Then he noticed—her gaze had turned downward, and she was staring with a frown at his feet. He was wearing leather sandals with white socks underneath.

What was wrong with his sandals?

She left the pitcher's mound—he was confused—but five minutes later, they entered her apartment, which was just around the corner from the baseball field. She directed him to sit on the couch. She walked into her small kitchen, and he marveled at the movie posters (*L'Avventura*, *Amores Perros*, *Happiness*—all movies he would now have to watch), hundreds of books, the organized clutter, the odd smell that he knew to be incense because his dormitory often reeked of it. This was exactly the sort of bohemian Fortress of Solitude he had imagined.

From the kitchen, she asked if he wanted something to drink.

"A beer?" he said.

She brought him some fancy bottle with a purple label, which was like no beer Jeff had ever tasted. He loved it.

"What do you want to watch?" she asked.

"I mean, I *have* been watching a lot of sci-fi."

She grinned the mischievous grin he'd come to love, said: "We could get stoned and watch *2001*?"

But he only realized she was being sarcastic after he'd responded, "I've never seen it."

She found the movie on an orderly bookshelf holding at least three hundred DVDs. "I'm actually not smoking or drinking these days," she said matter-of-factly as she started the DVD, "because of the Reality Center. But we can still watch it."

Jeff nodded.

2001: A Space Odyssey's overture began, and Alaura disappeared into her bedroom. She was gone for a long time, but when she returned, the orchestra was still playing, and no images had yet begun.

Seeing her, Jeff felt a chill of aroused terror—she now wore tiny cotton shorts and a long tee shirt that, yes, he was sure, had on the front of it a graphic of a young Michael Jackson posing with E.T. He forced a chuckle, and she did a little curtsy for him. And for a moment he thought she might walk over and straddle him, right here, right now—so he prepared a hesitant objection, *I'm not sure, are you sure, do you really want to do this*, and he even considered confessing his virginity. Would that be the right thing to do? Would it keep her from expecting too much? Or would it scare her off?

She sat next to him on the couch. She brought her feet up onto the cushion and nestled her head onto his shoulder. He realized how rigidly he was sitting, tried to relax—but found himself unable to free his arm to drape it over her body.

He wanted to kiss her so badly.

This is only a little break, laying my head on Jeff's shoulder. A little break to think about what I really want. She was exhausted, after all, and in this state, could she really trust herself to know what she wanted? In the bedroom, after stepping out of her dress and before slipping on the tee shirt, she had caught a glimpse of herself naked in her huge oval mirror, and she had instinctively sucked in her belly, pushed out her tits, contorted her body into the mirage of her idealized self. But what the hell was she doing? This was wrong, to be ashamed. To fear what Jeff would think of her imperfect body. That was living through her perception of what others might/maybe/probably would think of her cellulitey legs. That wasn't being true to herself. That wasn't the new Alaura.

No, there was no freaking way she could hook up with Jeff. Out on the baseball field, she had felt a slap of doubt—for a moment she had been lost in blissful meditation, a moist warm breeze dashing her face, images of Jeff holding her, his tall frame over her, how they would laugh afterward and become true friends, though definitely not long-term lovers . . . then she had looked down and seen his leather sandals, with the ridiculous white socks beneath, and she had remembered Pierce, who was handsomer than Jeff and sexier and smarter and who had worn the exact same fucking sandals the day he'd broken up with her, and a thought had slipped in: What if Jeff falls in love with me? If I sleep with him, will it end up hurting him later? But I want this. This is what I want. Isn't it?

They watched *2001* together. She'd never really understood the movie, though she wouldn't admit that to anyone, because Kubrick was sacrosanct. As they watched, she muttered a few things to Jeff, a few trivia tidbits she'd picked up from Waring over the years, that the planets and moon aligned above the black monolith are apparently nowhere close to realistic proportions, and that *Planet of the Apes*, not *2001*, had won a special Academy Award for makeup design that year, which was totally absurd, and that Arthur C. Clarke himself had theorized that the Academy must have thought Kubrick had employed actual simians instead of actors. Jeff listened and asked her questions, and she answered as best she could. He was a sponge for movie trivia, just like she had been long ago.

She made it through the "Dawn of Man" sequence, when the story jumps ahead to the distant future of the year 2001 and Tchaikovsky plays lightly while spaceships spin around like Barney Wheat's carousels, and she felt her eyelids getting heavy.

She slipped easily into sleep, her head still pressed to Jeff's shoulder.

He decided to watch every second of *2001* and to get drunk on Alaura's delicious beer—he dislodged himself from beneath her, covered her in a red-orange chenille blanket, and, having totally forgotten his important quiz the next day, he resumed watching the movie from the floor. As the film progressed, he found himself increasingly angry and horrified—angry because *2001* did not seem to play by any rules, horrified because he realized he would never again experience this amazing movie for the first time. By the end, after Hal

9000 had been deactivated and Dave-the-unemotional-astronaut had jettisoned into the trippy wormhole, and after some space-baby thing had floated toward Earth, Jeff realized that he had no idea if he should stay the night with Alaura. Had she invited him to stay? If so, why had she fallen asleep? If not, was it because of the sandals he had worn, which she had stared at with such puzzlement on the baseball field? So many questions. And this Reality Center stuff was crazy. Really crazy. Finally he remembered his quiz. It was three thirty a.m., and he still needed to study. But he was drunk. Looking at Alaura, at her angelic face knitted with sleep, he didn't want to leave—he didn't want to leave. Those soft lips bunched together. The heavy smell of her. Her warm body under the blanket—

But if she found him next to her in the morning, she might think he was a creep.

So he turned off the television, adjusted the blanket over her shoulders, and with terrified softness kissed her on the forehead.

Ten minutes later, walking toward his dorm, he realized that he'd probably just missed out on one of the greatest opportunities of his life.

IT'S NOT EASY BEING GREEN

It was a Monday morning in early October when Waring finally comprehended the titanic forces working against him. He was drinking his red eye, reading a copy of the *Appleton Herald* that he'd found lying in the middle of his street, and ignoring an elderly customer who had been waiting outside for twenty minutes for Star Video to open. This in itself was not peculiar. What was peculiar was the article on C2, in the Local section, and the large advertisement on the adjacent page.

The article—"Vote on Green Plaza Tonight"—was typical, in Waring's view, of the trendy environmental mumbo-jumbo gushing from Ehle County in recent years. As one of the few liberal havens in an otherwise conservative state, Appleton/West Appleton had made a habit of trumpeting every miniscule improvement to environmental standards, and the article detailed a new environmentally friendly business plaza and arts complex that had been proposed in West Appleton. Green Plaza/ArtsCenter would be comprised of three buildings, the tallest of which would be six stories—four stories taller than the largest building currently located downtown. The bottom floors of the complex would be reserved for retail business, the top floors for apartments and offices and convention space.

"Ridiculous," Waring muttered to himself. The article boasted that Green Plaza/ArtsCenter would be built to some protocol from Japan and meet a triple bottom-line (sic) of environmental sensitivity, social equity, and economic viability.

The elderly man knocked again on the front door, made a muffled cry.

Waring studied the graphic. Green Plaza/ArtsCenter looked like a Frank Gehry abortion. Stacks, tiers, irregular angles, rumples, like a piece of paper that had been wadded up and flattened out and then folded into an origami pineapple. And there was a theme of V shapes that Waring could not understand—

Then Waring saw it. On the left side of the graphic was a small building that resembled Mexica Orienta, the Mexican-Chinese restaurant just across the street from Star Video. On the right side was Satane Motors and the train tracks. Which placed Green Plaza/ArtsCenter directly . . .

"What the fuck!" he yelled.

Carrying his newspaper, Waring stormed to the front door. The elderly man who had been knocking wore a pained expression, as if standing for so long had caused him significant physical distress.

"You were supposed to open a half hour ago," the man grumbled when Waring opened the door.

"Sorry," Waring said. "Soundproof glass. Listen, do you know this place?"

Waring held up the newspaper and pointed to a short paragraph at the end of the article, which read: "Board of Aldermen. West Appleton Town Council Room, Community Center. September 27, 7 p.m."

"The Community Center?" the old man said. "It's right up the road. Do you know where the West Appleton polling station is?"

"No," Waring said impatiently.

"I think you can see it from here."

"Where is it, gramps?"

"Across from Weaver Street Market? The building labeled 'Community Center'?"

"That big red building?" Waring said.

"That's the one."

"Right."

And Waring locked the door in the old man's face.

Waring had needed a week to organize his finances and a few days after that to digest the bad news. He had forgotten the names of various investments, had lost documents with account numbers. And over the years—without committing it to memory—he had apparently fired several of the people who had managed his investments. So, with nothing more than his name, his Social Security number, and a sense of annoyed determination, Waring had reconstructed the frame of his financial life.

The result, organized as neatly as possible in one of his old red ledgers, was not pretty:

1. Star Video's earnings were down 10 percent in the last year.
2. The shop was losing money every week and had been for some time.
3. His business checking account was nearly empty, hovering at a ridiculously low three thousand dollars, which would barely cover next period's payroll.
4. One of his business credit lines was maxed out, and another was close. If something wasn't done soon, the second credit line would not cover his upcoming payment to Guiding Glow, let alone all of the back payments to those Christian psychos.
5. Total debt, both to Guiding Glow and to the credit card companies, was close to twenty thousand dollars, which was

more or less the total of Waring's remaining soft investments: an old retirement fund, a mutual fund, four thousand
dollars in gold he'd inherited from his mother, a forgotten
money market account, and a few ancient stocks that had
remained level since the mid-1990s, despite the market's
recent performance.

All of which left him with little choice.

That afternoon, he placed a call he had been avoiding—to sell off
his remaining investments and to pay down his debt.

Leaving as his only assets (1) a Dodge clunker, (2) his house, and
(3) the building that housed Star Video and Pizza My Heart—the
rent for which, Waring now saw, he was hugely undercharging for.

And now, on top of all this, the county government was scheming
against him. Something was going on. And no matter what, it
would cost money.

He had broken even, but not for long.

That night, Waring stood in front of West Appleton's Board of
Aldermen—seven wealthy citizens sitting behind a tall curved
table that was positioned on a short stage. It was a small room,
with scalding, Blockbuster-esque lighting. Large ficus plants were
clustered in each corner of the room, as if to distract from the antiseptic vibe of the place, and a ridiculous flag hung from the ceiling
that read "West Appleton—Home of Understanding." Five rows of
metal foldout chairs, half-filled with citizens, were lined up behind
Waring, who was the only citizen now standing. No one else had
even raised a hand when they'd asked for opinions from "the public"
on the Green Plaza/ArtsCenter, because no one else, it seemed, was
currently concerned that his or her life was on trial.

Standing there, Waring felt like General Zod in *Superman II*,
about to be cast into the Phantom Zone.

"Isn't there some sort of process?" Waring said. "Some sort of procedure?"

This is our first public meeting on the subject, the head alderman answered into her unnecessary microphone. *You will have two weeks to file a grievance if you feel it is necessary.*

"But how was I supposed to know?"

The head alderman—a white-haired woman wearing a sunflower-yellow blazer—proclaimed in her amplified, God-like voice that letters had been repeatedly sent, and Waring suspected these letters lay either on the floor of his office or decomposing on his lawn at home. Still, he couldn't believe that Alaura would not be aware of these proceedings, or that none of his customers would have informed him. But of course Alaura had been distracted—first by that Peckerdick person and now by her stupid "leave of absence"— and most of his customers disliked him.

"Well," Waring said, clenching a podium for support, "I don't care. You can't have it. It's my property."

There is also the issue of back taxes.

"Eh?" He stuck a finger in his ear, wiggled it as if to dislodge an obstruction.

Property and business taxes, the head alderman said. *We've recently finished sorting it out, or we would have informed you earlier. It seems that you owe the county, not to mention the state and federal governments, a fair amount of money.*

"Says who?" Waring protested.

Says we, she said.

Someone handed Waring a small stack of papers. Waring leafed through them. They were tax forms—each page reporting more money owed than the last.

Your property has been chosen for many reasons, Mr. Wax, and the proposal has near unanimous support from this board and from various advisory boards.

Waring continued rifling through the tax forms.

The Arts Committee, for example, believes that a performance space for theater and music will act as a symbolic bridge between the communities of Appleton and West Appleton.

"But Star Video is al*ready* an important part of West Appleton's arts community," Waring said, using Alaura's words.

There is also a report from the Environmental Advisory Board, which states in no uncertain terms that the proposed Green Plaza/ArtsCenter will have a lower carbon footprint than the decaying building you currently own.

"Decaying?"

In fact, every single advisory committee we tasked with reviewing the proposed Green Plaza/ArtsCenter has returned in the affirmative. That is, against you. County approval is expected within the week. So unless you are willing to submit to negotiations for the purchase of your property by the county . . .

"Absolutely not!"

We will be forced to invoke our right of eminent domain and to seize your property without your consent, with due monetary compensation.

The head alderman announced the amount of said due monetary compensation.

Waring guffawed. Then he turned to look at the audience behind him, whom he had completely ignored until this point. He discovered a small crowd of blank disinterested faces.

To the head alderman, Waring said, "Eminent domain, meaning?"

Meaning we take your land.

"Well," Waring said, "I'll see you in court."

Menacing chuckles rained down from the Board of Aldermen.

Mr. Wax, it is very rare for anyone to successfully challenge eminent domain in North Carolina. In fact, it has never been done. If the vote passes tonight, the building of Green Plaza/ArtsCenter will most certainly come to pass.

"Not if I have anything to say about it."

In that case, I must ask the audience and my fellow board members to pardon me for my candor. Mr. Wax, your business is seen by many as a blight on West Appleton. Each and every member of this board has had at least one terrible experience in your store. We discuss it often—Star Video is something of a joke around here. You are an embarrassment to this town.

Waring: poleaxed.

That you provide pornography is also a serious issue. Everyone in surrounding counties knows that if you want pornography, you come to West Appleton.

"But the law allows it!"

Of course. We would never stand for censorship, Mr. Wax, and we are offended that you would even imply that. But now with the arrival of a Blockbuster in our town, the existence of Star Video feels a bit . . . redundant.

Waring, for once, was totally speechless.

After many months, we have come to a final vote. Do you have anything else to add, Mr. Wax? May we proceed?

Waring stared at the aldermen. Indeed he recognized several of their faces as people he had yelled at, cursed at, degraded over the years. They were all middle-aged, all wealthy-looking, all staring down at him with flaming, righteous eyes. He could smell their mingling perfumes and colognes, could imagine them watching *Pokémon* and *Snow White* with their children. They were entirely different from him—they were businesspeople, successful, motivated, having sought local office in order to better their community or run local scams. They thought of twenty things at once. There were hundred-dollar bills in their purses or wallets. They were him, Waring realized, before he'd left New York.

Waring looked again around the conference room—this had all happened so quickly that he had not taken in the space, and to his right, he was surprised to see Adam Pritt, the owner of Quick Dick's, and Paulsen Crick from Blockbuster. Pritt was smiling wickedly, Waring thought, like a diminutive Jack Palance, while Crick looked intensely bored as he tapped on a shining, futuristic-looking cell phone. Around them sat a band of similarly tanned and healthy men, and all at once, Waring knew with crystal clarity that they were *all* in it together—they were investors—they had probably conspired to keep news of Green Plaza/ArtsCenter out of the newspaper—they had been planning for months to take down Star Video. Today was, as Crick had warned, Waring's day of reckoning.

Then Waring saw Farley. His portly employee aimed a video camera at him from the back of the room; he was filming this entire debacle.

"You're fired," Waring said, pointing at the camera. "I mean it." Farley didn't respond, fiddled with device, zoomed in.

Those in favor, say "aye."

All seven aldermen trumpeted, "Aye."

Those opposed, say "nay."

Silence.

Waring yelled, "Nay!"

Final approval for Green Plaza/ArtsCenter is passed. Eminent domain for purposes of urban blight shall be exercised. Mr. Wax's objections have been noted, and if he decides to challenge the vote, then he will need to contact the county judiciary. Next on the agenda . . . we will discuss the recent application from [name of film studio omitted] *to film exteriors in West Appleton, starting September 30 and ending no later that October 17. This production has already obtained a permit to film in Appleton, in the Historic District and on Appleton University's campus. But I'm not sure we in West Appleton should be so hasty. I know we're all excited about Tabitha Gray and Alex Walden coming to town. And my daughter in particular is wound up about Celia Watson.* [Chuckles from all.] *But we've recently learned that the film's real title is* The Buried Mirror, *which to me sounds a little, well, suspicious . . .*

"Of course, because movies are evil!" Waring yelled, unable to think of anything more clever, and he stalked out of the room.

REALITY BITES

On Alaura's mind when she awoke that morning was (1) that today she would begin the Advanced Experience at the Reality Center, and (2) that after almost three weeks of mental debate following The Corporate Visit, she was ready to quit Star Video.

So at seven a.m., before walking down from her apartment to meet Karla, her ride to Reality, she called the shop to leave a voice-mail, certain that Waring wouldn't be there this early to answer.

"I have to quit," she blurted into the phone. She cleared her throat, realized she was more nervous than expected—she'd known it wouldn't be easy to quit, but she hadn't anticipated this pang of stomach acid, this dry mouth, this odd sense of weightlessness. But she'd resolved to do it, to finally do it, and to cover several mapped-out points in the message, so finally she continued, speaking quickly, "From Star Video. I need to do this, Waring. I'm sorry. I hope you understand. I'll work for the next few weeks to help you get on your feet. You *need* to hire someone. If the store's going to stay open. And find a new distributor. This is the best thing. For me. I'm almost thirty.

Years old. Thank you for understanding." She coughed. "And sorry to do this on voicemail."

When she hung up the phone, her legs felt painfully numb.

Later that morning at the Reality Center, after two hours of energy exercises and group cheering (she had to admit that she was tiring of energy exercises and group cheering), the Advanced class—smaller by 50 percent than the Basic class—was ushered into a room of cubicles with cream-colored partitions. The cubicles were numbered, and inside each of them, Alaura could see, was a shiny Mac computer and multiline office phone.

What the hell? Alaura thought.

Thom Trachtenberg, their mighty-haired leader, appeared as if by magic amongst the cubicles. He looked over the class with a benevolent smile, then began one of his typical motivational monologues. His voice rose and fell hypnotically. Alaura listened closely, hoping for some kernel of information, some sliver of philosophy that would bring everything together. But no such kernel, nor sliver, nor rational line of thinking emerged. Nor any of the vibrant, self-confident energy she'd enjoyed for the past few weeks.

Thom's speech lasted ten minutes, and the concluding gist of it was: "So we all know now how important it is to live with real intention, and the power of investing ourselves in the future, and in the well-being and interconnectedness of others. This is the power of love that we all feel around us, that connects all of humanity. I feel it. Do you feel it?" Alaura's classmates cheered, but Alaura, looking at the cubicles, could only manage a blunted "yeah-huh." Thom continued, "I think we all agree how powerful and important this message is and how simple it will be to change the world, one person at a time, if we get this message out there. Don't you want to change the world?"

Cheers!

"Well, we're going to help you do that. We're going to provide you with the platform. Here, today. We have made printouts for all of you, all the things you'll need to say to change the world, to get the message of Reality out to your friends, and that's what you're going to do, that's what *we're* going to do. We're going to call our friends and show them how to change their lives, to change their world."

More cheers!

"Does everyone have the iPhones we asked you to purchase in advance of the Advanced Experience?"

Hands shot up holding iPhones, like lighters at a concert. Alaura, meanwhile, fingered her own new iPhone, which was resting in her pocket.

"We want you to text, e-mail, Facebook, instant message, everything! The entire world is there for the taking!"

Even more cheers!

"And you get thirty dollars cash for each prospective classmate who completes Basic. Now go get 'em!"

The group dispersed gleefully.

As Alaura rounded a corner in search of her cubicle, #18, she felt a tingling all over her body, as if she were wrapped in a blanket of pine needles.

Recruiting? The Advanced Experience, the most expensive stage at the Reality Center, was about recruiting?

She found cubicle 18, sat down. On her desk lay a twenty-page printout.

"We're so happy you've decided to continue with us," a deep voice intoned behind her.

It was Thom Trachtenberg, standing with Karla. They both beamed majestically.

Alaura smiled back, said thanks, and they floated away, carrying their glossy teeth and amazing hair with them.

She began studying her script—in fact, it was a complicated

rubric, with pages of alternate responses to different objections a "prospective" might present. After fifteen minutes of studying, she felt prepared to make the first call. But a creeping fear had surfaced—she did not have many family members (only her father, really) or friends (a few old drinking buddies, the girls, Waring, maybe Jeff?). She knew lots of people, but . . .

They would *all* think she was totally fucking crazy.

But she had to try. Didn't she? And though she wasn't quite sure why she did it, the first call she placed was to Star Video.

Waring answered. "Well, well, well," he said upon hearing her voice. "If it isn't the deserter."

"Did you get my message from earlier?" she asked.

"You know I don't check the messages, Alaura."

"Waring?"

"What?"

"I have a question."

"I have a hangover."

Ignoring him, she read from the script: "I've recently experienced the most incredible thing in the past three weeks. And the first person I thought of was you. I've finally seen how I can change my life, Waring." She had almost said, *Insert name here.* "And I want to share with you the power, the *real* power—" she made sure to *add emphasis,* "of this experience. Have you ever felt lost in life, Waring?"

Waring was silent.

She repeated the question.

"Alaura?" he said finally.

"Yes?"

"Go fuck yourself."

She flipped the pages of her rubric, searching desperately for advice on how to manage hostile responses. "Waring," she muttered, "this is very important to me."

"Are you trying to recruit me, Alaura Eden? To this Reality Center shit?"

"I think it could really help you—"

"Shut up, Alaura. Shut up and listen to yourself."

"Waring, please don't."

"Why would you call *me* unless this is one of those cry-for-help things?"

"It's not a cry for help. It's not a cry for help."

"Well, that's convincing," Waring said. "I'm coming to get you. Now."

He hung up.

Twenty minutes later, Waring was driving with Jeff in the ancient Dodge, his eyes fixed on the streaming road ahead, a phantom ride down an undulating country highway lined with infinite pine trees and the occasional dusty gas station. They were driving to Raleigh. Waring had found the address of the Reality Center in, of all places, a phonebook, which now sat on Jeff's lap, opened to a small map of the state capital. Both Farley and Rose had agreed to work, at a moment's notice, and they were currently manning Star Video—that Waring had "fired" Farley a few days ago at the Board of Aldermen meeting was not mentioned. Nor was it mentioned that Farley and Rose had arrived together: Star Video's biggest and smallest employees had apparently been hanging out together at a café down the street, talking about Farley's video store documentary, which they were now both working on. But Waring couldn't concern himself with these lesser entities.

I might lose Alaura, he thought, but not to some cult.

"So this is your car?" Jeff asked over the rattling scream of the engine.

"I park it behind the store," Waring said, now regretting his decision to enlist this third lesser entity for backup.

"Why don't you drive it more often?"

"It's not registered. And I don't have a license."

"I have a license."

"So?"

"So maybe I should drive."

Waring considered the suggestion—he *was* driving too fast. And he was still soused from the night before. So he pulled the car over, and they switched seats.

"So what are we doing exactly?" Jeff asked as he eased onto the highway.

"Search and rescue," Waring said.

"But what's the actual plan?"

"We storm in, take her out."

Jeff pointed a finger at his head, imitating a handgun. "Take her out?"

"No, idiot. Remove her from the building."

Then Waring remembered the scene from *Pulp Fiction*, how Sam Jackson had said, "Take her out?" in the exact same way. The young joker was attempting to be funny, and Waring, annoyed that he had missed the obvious reference, barked at Jeff to speed up. When Jeff did not comply, Waring barked at him to pull the hell over. They reswitched seats, and a minute later, Waring once again careened down the highway, over an on-ramp surrounded by orange and yellow flowers, and onto I-40.

Sounding a little terrified (which wasn't an entirely unsatisfying sound in Waring's ear), Jeff said, "You really care about Alaura, huh?"

Waring sneered at the blurry road. He should have picked up a deep-fried ham sandwich for the drive—*that* would have helped with his hangover.

"I care about her too," Jeff continued. "But if the Reality Center is something she wants to do—"

"She doesn't," Waring said. "I heard it in her voice."

"You what?"

"She just realized it's bullshit."

"It is?"

"I told you, it's a pyramid scheme. She's actually paying them, probably her life savings, for the privilege of recruiting for them."

Jeff reported how much money Alaura had said she was paying.

"I mean, fuck!" Waring bellowed. "It's a business scam wrapped in new age self-help mumbo-jumbo bullshit. I knew it, and now she knows it, too."

"You got all of that from talking to her for, like, a minute?"

"She's my best friend."

Waring—realizing he had divulged more than he intended—lit a cigarette, focused on the road.

"But what *exactly* are we doing when we get there?" Jeff said.

"We go in, be loud and obnoxious, bring Alaura to her senses, and bring her home with us."

"You could really do that?"

"Do what?"

"How do you barge into a place? Where do you get the . . . the confidence?"

Waring glanced at Jeff, and he realized that the kid's question was entirely serious. Then Waring thought, for some reason, of his ex-wife. Her dark hair, her smart-ass sense of humor, her small body next to his in bed. Years ago, after their separation, he had planned to storm into her office in Manhattan and make a scene in the hopes of winning her back. But he had never done it. Because she hated him. All of his bluster would have been for nothing. That he'd loved her didn't matter.

But he could help Alaura now.

"I've got no advice for you, Jeff," Waring said. "You just fucking do it."

But Karla, did you follow a script?" Alaura asked again—she was straining to keep her voice calm. "In the diner, at brunch with Constance, when you first told me about Reality. Were you following a script?"

Karla frowned. "Where is this hostility coming from, Alaura?"

"I'm not hostile. I'm feeling strange. About recruiting."

"It's not recruiting, Alaura."

"It feels like recruiting."

"You're sharing your experience, Alaura, with those you love."

Alaura tried to roll her eyes, tried to act tough.

Then Thom Trachtenberg emerged from a door labeled "Private"; he walked toward them and laid a casual arm over Karla's shoulders.

"Hello, beautiful people!" he said. "Everything positive?"

Alaura watched Karla poke forward her perfect honeydew breasts, activate her internal radiance. "Alaura is experiencing apprehension with her goals for the future."

"Is she?"

"No, I'm . . . well . . . not excited about recruiting," Alaura said.

Thom shuddered with intense disappointment. "Recruiting?" he said.

"No," Alaura said, realizing her mistake. "Not recruiting. What I meant was—"

"Alaura, I think we're seeing some of your self-doubt springing forth."

"No, we're not. It's only that Karla used a lot of the same wording when she asked me to come here. The same wording from the script."

Thom's voice lowered: "It's a guide, Alaura, not a script."

"But the thing is—I don't have many people to call."

"Nonsense. I'm sure you have friends and family."

"I don't," Alaura protested, almost whining. "Really."

She looked down at herself, at the midnight blue Calvin Klein business suit she had purchased for today—she had never owned a business suit before.

Thom removed his arm from Karla's shoulders, stepped forward, and snaked his other arm around Alaura—a smooth transition from one acolyte to another. "Alaura," he said soothingly, now guiding her back to her cubicle. "It is *very* important that we take this step. It is only through helping others that we learn to love ourselves."

"Maybe that's true," Alaura said, "but maybe this isn't . . . my path. Maybe this isn't how *I* help people."

"Sometimes our path is not clear to us, and we have to break through our fears, through those things that terrify us the most."

"But aren't there some other energy exercises we can do?" Alaura asked weakly. "I'm sure there are some things about my past I haven't told you yet—"

"Now is the time to *act*. Now is the time to move *forward*."

Alaura realized she was back in her cubicle, sitting in her chair, almost as if she'd been teleported here. She looked around her; Thom and his musky odor had evaporated.

But who could she call?

Oh God, she was on the verge of tears. She had to have friends who wouldn't think she was entirely psychotic for calling them about the Reality Center.

She thought again of Jeff. She had his e-mail address memorized. But God, what the hell had she been thinking? She'd been minutes, inches from seducing Jeff. It had been wrong, so wrong. Disgusting. She was over ten years older than him. And now he probably hated her, which she certainly deserved.

Finally a name popped into her head. Helen Silber, customer account number W443521. Helen always rented two *Bob the Builders* and the latest British comedy. She seemed sad, always that tired slump to her shoulders, always that same strained smile, so Alaura tried to be extra nice to her, tried to keep her away from Waring. Maybe Helen would benefit from Reality.

Another name: Bill Scranton, W423222. His son had Down syndrome. A nice man. Always asked how business was going. Never got frustrated when his son misbehaved, but still he always seemed exhausted by his life.

And another: Ed Clyde. She couldn't remember his customer number, but he always hung around, wanting to talk movies for hours. Jesus, he seemed so lonely, no one better to talk to than the tattooed girl at the video store.

She knew the names and stories and rental histories of a hundred Star Video customers. Sometimes, out in public, at bars or in grocery stores or on the sidewalk, customers would approach her and ask how she was doing, and more often than not, she could not remember their names—outside the confines of the shop, she was helpless. But now her memory seemed to crack open, a treasure trove uncovered in desperation, names rushing before her like the late-return list emerging from the Star Video printer.

This is a mistake, she thought. *I won't call them.*

But she Googled anyway, found their phone numbers easily.

They all like me, she reassured herself. *And some of them seem like they could really use this.*

All she had to do was call.

The moments inside the Reality Center transpired for Jeff in painful confusion. But he had promised Waring that he would not leave his side, would not try to escape before they found Alaura.

Waring pulled the Dodge to a skidding halt, sprawling slant-wise across two parking spaces. Waring hopped out of the car at once, and Jeff followed, hands thrust in his pockets, trying to look nonchalant. The structure in front of them that corresponded with the address in the phonebook was a dull, two-story building composed of an unidentifiable brown material and flat black windows and was surrounded by perfect maple trees that might have been clipped out of a magazine from the 1950s. The place looked like it had been designed to house an assortment of offices—optometrists, therapists, tax preparers—and not a weird life-training cult.

A sign above the building's main entrance, written in a font worthy of an evil corporation from a 1980s sci-fi movie, read:

WELCOME TO REALITY

"Let's do this," Waring said.

"Okay," Jeff said.

Waring led the charge. He pushed through a revolving door, and they found themselves in an expansive, immaculately clean lobby with black marble floors. It was warm in the building. Lined on the walls around them were several flat-screen televisions, all of them showing slideshows of people smiling, holding hands, walking around lakes, and doing trust falls.

"Ew," Waring said.

They kept moving. A moment later, they'd passed through a brightly lit hallway and entered a wide-open, empty conference room. The ceiling here was thirty feet high. Upon a small stage to their right stood a lonely microphone stand, like both a musician and her entire audience had just fled the scene.

"What the hell is *that?*" Waring said, pointing upward.

Above them, running along the wall below the ceiling, was a series of weird quotes printed on large white boards.

"The Future Is Now," Jeff read. "Isn't that, like, a contradiction in terms?"

"Yes, Jeff," Waring said, smiling and nodding at his employee. "That's absolutely fucking right."

Then a woman appeared in front of them. She was a well-put-to-gether business type with an impossibly tight ponytail. She asked politely, but with a note of concern in her voice, if they needed help. Jeff was too embarrassed look at her, but he heard Waring say steadily:

"I'm Alaura's brother. We have a family emergency."

"Alaura is unavailable, sir. I'll give her a message as soon as she's free."

"No," Waring said, his tone quickly rising, angry. "This is a *real* emergency."

"Sir, I—"

Waring walked past her.

Jeff muttered an embarrassed apology and followed.

They moved down a hallway. Waring tested several doors.

"Sir!" the woman called after them.

Around them spanned more posters:

REALITY IS NOW

TECHNOLOGY IS A TOOL

PROGRESS IS FREEDOM

"Ugh," Waring muttered, holding his stomach as if nauseated. "You'd think they'd avoid all this *1984*-type shit."

Finally they entered a large room divided into cubicles.

"Alaura!" Waring called out.

All at once, twenty heads popped into view, and Jeff found Alaura's face near the center of the room. Her eyes were wide open and bloodshot, and Jeff noticed that all of the people, even Alaura, wore suit coats. The women's hair was all neatly in place. The men were all cleanly shaven. Jeff became immediately aware of the scruff on his own chin, tinged a rebellious red. And he had not visited a barber in over a month—the unattended hairs on the back of his neck seemed to gain weight, pull at his skin. He knew he looked terrible, grungy, unkempt. More like Waring than anyone else here. Had he even showered that morning?

Waring stepped forward and began to navigate the cubicles. Jeff followed, and soon they reached Alaura. She was standing there, facing them, clutching her purse—as if ready to leave. And for the second time since meeting her, Jeff saw that her heavy eyeliner was dripping down her face. She had been crying.

Then, even more confusing for Jeff, Alaura said to Waring, "Why are you here, you fucking assholes?"

"I'm Thom Trachtenberg," announced a deep voice. "What are you people doing?"

The voice had emerged from a solid-looking man who had materialized a few feet away from them, in the center of the main walkway between the cubicles. To Jeff, the man looked both ridiculous and frightening; he had a feathered mullet and chiseled jaw, and his arms were spread wide as if he were attempting to perform a miracle.

"We're taking Alaura home," Waring snarled at the man.

"It is *her* choice to be here," Thom said.

"It's *my* choice to take her home, you sack of shit."

Thom crossed his arms, raised his strong chin. "We are helping guide Alaura into the future."

A moment later, Jeff saw that several young men and women—Alaura's classmates, including a gorgeous redhead with mesmerizingly full lips—were standing behind Thom. And like Thom, they all crossed their arms.

Jeff heard Waring snort.

The snort quickly turned into a chuckle.

The chuckle into cackling laugher.

"Did you hear him, Jeff?" Waring finally managed to say. "He said they're . . . they're—"

"Is this a time for laughter?" Thom's voice boomed.

Waring leaned forward, held his stomach, and whaled—Jeff didn't know exactly why his boss was laughing, yet at the same time, it made total sense.

"Yes, I think it *is* a time for laughter!" Waring said. "I think you guys are fucking hilarious!"

Jeff realized Alaura was standing next to him. Her head was pressed against his shoulder. Like that night last week, on the couch in her apartment. He looked down at her, but her head hung so low that he could not see her face. He placed his hand on her waist, felt her weight give way into him.

"We've heard all about you, sir," Thom was saying to Waring. "You are most certainly Alaura's drunken, abusive employer. I can smell the alcohol and cigarettes on your person. Why would you try to impede Alaura's progress in improving her life?"

Waring, still laughing, turned again to Jeff. "They're standing there like they're the fucking Boondock Saints!"

Jeff looked at the group of suits standing in front of him—Waring was right, they did look like a nerdy little military—and Jeff found himself beginning to laugh as well.

"Sir," Thom continued, "isn't it obvious that the modern world will be one of interconnectedness? That those who shut themselves off from the world, those who push away their problems and drown them with means of escape, will be left behind? Look at everyone here. We're all trying to *connect* with others. You *must* know that with your unhealthy influence and your dead-end business, you are holding Alaura back from achieving her full potential."

Waring's laughter stopped instantly.

He stepped toward Thom.

"Her full potential?" Waring said in a low voice. "Look at her."

Alaura was now completely curled under Jeff's arm, bent forward, near collapse.

And with a voice harsher, meaner, and sincerer than Jeff had ever heard him use, Waring said slowly:

"Alaura wants her money back. And if you ever mess with her again, if you ever call her, mail her, anything, I promise that I . . . will . . . kill . . . you."

For a moment, Thom held Waring's intense stare.

"I'm sorry, Thom," Alaura said softly. Jeff looked down at her; she was still huddled weakly against him.

"Alaura?" Thom said.

"I need to go home."

"But you've come so far, Alaura. You've been so strong. You're one of us. All we've asked of you, Alaura, is to be yourself. And to make some phone calls."

Alaura glanced at him. "Thom?"

"Yes?"

"Thanks for everything, but if I hear you repeat my name one more time, I think I might kill you myself."

The man with the feathered hair scowled, his lips curling inward like a spoiled little boy who'd just overheard his parents insulting his mediocrity.

A moment later, he seemed to recover; donning an obviously fake smile, he turned to the other classmates and raised his hands, cleansing himself of this fiasco.

And without another word, Waring turned to Jeff, nodded, and they walked out of the room with Alaura between them.

Five minutes later, Waring piloted his Dodge back onto I-40 and headed west toward Ehle County. Jeff sat on the passenger side. Alaura lay in the backseat like a sick child. Waring had no idea what to say to her. He wanted to fix everything. But he knew that if he spoke, anything he said would be wrong. The interstate traffic had picked up—Raleigh rush hour. People driving home in their little air-conditioned bubbles, singing along to their radio or yammering into their cell phones. Waring's car was by far the oldest and rustiest on the road, and it rattled and squealed every time traffic forced him to decelerate. At this rate, it would take them over an hour to get home.

"Alaura?" Waring said finally, unable to stand the silence.

"What?" she murmured.

"I want it to be known—I could have massacred that asshole."

Alaura: no response.

"I could have," Waring went on. "I wanted to. He looked like Khan, by the way. I can't believe you paid them."

"Not now, Waring. Please."

"Of all your religious excursions, this is by far the stupidest. I can't believe Karla fell for it, too. You'd think that with a body and face like hers she'd be smarter—"

"Please," Alaura said, sniffling. "Just don't."

"Leave her alone, Waring," Jeff said.

Waring glanced at Jeff. "Okay, freshman, just calm down."

"I am calm."

"And did you actually do a trust fall?" Waring said to Alaura, as if he hadn't been interrupted at all, looking at her in the canted rearview mirror. "I thought you were over that religious crap."

"It's not a religion."

"What's wrong with religion?" Jeff asked.

"It's . . ." but Waring's voice trailed off.

"What?" Jeff persisted.

"It's just wrong, okay, Jeff? It's the twenty-first fucking century. Religion is part of the whole human thing."

Jeff laughed, and he turned to look calmly out the window at the lumbering traffic. "Man, what are you talking about?"

"The Reality Center isn't a religion," Alaura muttered.

"Alaura understands," Waring said. "Or she *should*, after today's fucked-up experience."

Now Alaura's breathing had gone wet and heavy; she was crying. "Stop it," she said.

Waring looked at her in the rearview. "Alaura, are you really—"

"Just stop it! Please don't be an asshole, Waring. Please!"

"Fine," he said.

"I know it was fucked up, okay?" she said. "I put a lot of money on my credit card. I bought this stupid outfit. I bought a damn iPhone. Why? What am I going to do with an iPhone? How am I going pay off my credit card? I'm such a fucking idiot."

"No, you're not, Alaura," Waring said quickly. He felt his face stinging, like he might start crying himself. "Stop it, sweetie. Everything's going to be fine."

"And I almost called . . . a few . . . of our customers." Alaura heaved for breath. "I looked up their numbers. I was going to call them. But then . . . then . . . then you guys showed up. But I was going to call. I really was." She blew her nose into a napkin she'd found on the floorboard. "I'm pathetic. So pathetic. I don't have any friends. I don't have *any* friends."

Long silence.

"Alaura?" Waring said.

"What?"

"You have friends."

Jeff turned in the passenger seat and smiled at Alaura.

Over the next few moments, her crying gradually stopped.

She sighed. "Thanks for coming to get me." She swiped at some makeup running down her cheek. "Waring?"

"Eh?"

"What's going on at the shop? Jeff told me that things were sort of, well, falling apart."

"You just rest for a bit. I'll catch you up when we get back to my house."

"Your house?"

"Yeah. I need some help with things there. There've been a few developments. I've made some big decisions since your desertion of everything that really matters in this topsy-turvy world."

Alaura flipped Waring the bird.

Beat.

All three of them: pressure-relieving chuckles.

THE
BURIED
MIRROR

A NEW HOPE?

Alaura awoke with a snort. Her face was pressed against cracked, tobacco-stained pleather—the backseat of Waring's Dodge. A cool breeze streamed through open windows and played on her forehead. Sunlight angled close to level. Late afternoon.

As the day reorganized itself, she realized that the car was parked on the rutted gravel driveway of Waring's house. She climbed out, stretched her fingertips skyward, and with arms aloft she saw that she still wore the dark blue suit coat that, along with matching pants and old-lady business flats, had cost her over three hundred and fifty dollars. Three hundred and fifty dollars she did not really have.

Then she remembered what had happened at the Reality Center, and a dull pain rippled through her abdomen.

She leaned forward, half-crouching, pressed her palms together between her knees. She groaned.

A minute later, still hunkered in this standing fetal position, she turned her head and saw, by the street in front of the house, a green and yellow sign hanging from an inverted wooden L. The sign read, "House For Sale," and below that, diagonally, "Sold!"

She approached the sign, touched it to confirm its solidity.

Voices. Murmurs from Waring's house. His small sloping ranch, with its pinkish bricks and perpetually clogged gutters. Over the years, she had spent many drunken nights here, binge-watching obscure films or Hollywood crap or entire television series, talking with Waring, fending off Waring's harmless romantic advances, passing out on his couch. The slim concrete porch—she would sit with him for hours, stoned or hammered, listen to him complain about this awful customer or that awful movie, laugh at him without restraint whenever his wacky diatribes culminated in successful punchlines. (As the only genuine authority figure at Star Video, she resisted laughing at his jokes in the presence of other employees, but here, at his house, she let herself go.) And sometimes she even made *him* laugh, said something wily and provocative that caught him off guard, and his cranky exterior would break, and he would squeal like a child, a high-pitched giggle stunning in its sincerity, entirely gleeful, beer sluicing from the can in his fist.

But he had not been laughing lately. Nor had she. How long had it been? Months? Years? His drinking had increased, so had hers, and they had bickered more and more about stupid nonproblems. Their laughter had all but vanished.

She approached Waring's open front door. The murmurs rose, separated—it was not the television playing some movie, as she had assumed, but Waring and Jeff talking.

"These posters," Jeff said excitedly. "*Billy Jack*? I don't even know that movie, but the poster's awesome. And the whole cast autographed *Apocalypse Now*. Martin Sheen, Robert Duvall, Dennis Hopper. And he actually wrote *Larry* Fishburne! These should be in frames, Waring. The corners are all crunched."

Alaura edged closer to the house, and she visualized Waring's collection of warped dry-mounted posters leaning against the wall near his couch, posters he had never bothered to frame, hang, or sell—*The French Connection*, *The Night of the Hunter*, *Sunset*

Boulevard, many more. Then she heard Waring grumble as if distracted, or disinterested, or both:

"Never got around to frames."

"But you should."

"Oh, I should, should I?" Waring said, now seeming to find interest, or annoyance, in the topic. "You should focus on packing, which I'm paying you good money for."

"I wouldn't say *good* money," Jeff retorted with a laugh.

Jesus, Alaura thought. *Are they getting along?*

"I see," Waring said, a playful lilt in his voice. "No one's holding a gun to your hairless testicles."

"Gross," Jeff said.

"Alaura likes hairy men."

"Huh?"

"Hairy chests, hairy bottoms, hairy balls. Bearded faces and genitals, that's her."

Jeff laughed again, this time in disbelief—a mocking-but-friendly guffaw. "Do you listen to yourself?"

"My voice is the only entertaining part of this exchange."

"I guess."

"And anyway, if you had a chance with Alaura, you've missed it."

Jeff seemed to mull this over for a moment, then he said, "Actually, Alaura and I hung out in her apartment, like, a week and a half ago."

"Doing what?"

"We watched a movie."

And Waring's voice rose to a mock-Shakespearean timbre: "A *movie*!?"

Then they both laughed.

Yes, Alaura thought, this is what I've gotten myself back into.

She tiptoed off the porch, returned to the Dodge. Inside the car, she found her new, expensive iPhone. She called Star Video's voicemail line, and she cringed as she listened to the strange resignation she had left that morning, only a few hours ago.

What the *hell* had she been thinking? Leaving Waring in the lurch. And quitting before even beginning to search for another job. After she'd just run up her credit cards again.

But the message had still been listed as "Unheard." So quickly she pressed "5" to delete it. Waring would never know.

And all at once she thought, I want my mind back. I want to erase Reality. Waring had been right: once again she had gone wacko for some stupid ideology. Which meant it was time, she supposed, for a new tattoo, which had always been an integral step in deciding which facets of any kooky religion to retain or discard . . .

But why did getting another tattoo feel so . . . foolish?

Because she was too old for this shit. Because she was twenty-nine years old and had naively, idiotically believed that the Reality Center would present the final answers. That all the cogs of her life would fall into place.

And worse than that, she'd revealed her core weaknesses, once again, to Waring. She'd shown Waring that she was still that same stupid girl she'd always been.

Later later later, she thought. Think about it later. I'll figure it out. Maybe selling the house means that Waring is, against all odds, making some reasonable effort to save the shop. Focus on Star Video. She slammed the car door hard, so that the guys would hear. A moment later, they appeared on the porch.

Pointing to the "For Sale" sign, and switching at once into Star Video manager mode, Alaura said:

"Explain!"

Jeff continued boxing up Waring's belongings while Waring caught Alaura up on Star Video's status—the grand conspiracy designed to purge West Appleton of its noble independent video store, the identity of Blockbuster's franchise operator, the Board of Aldermen meeting, the eminent domain hearing scheduled for October 29 (three weeks away), how Waring's house had sold in less than four days but for nowhere near the asking price, so he was still short a significant amount of cash—for lawyer fees, for mounting operating expenses, and especially for the recently revealed back taxes—even if he slept on the couch in *The African Queen* at Star Video, which Alaura quickly realized was the extent of his big freaking plan.

Waring concluded by morosely quoting the amount of cash he would need to keep Star Video open for the short term.

"Ten thousand dollars."

Long pause.

"Ten thousand?" she said.

"And that's only for the next few months, roughly. With the higher rate we'll probably have to pay a new distributor, if we can even *find* a new distributor, the truth is, the store is losing money. I'm totally out of options."

"Out of options?"

"I'm out of money."

Her mouth parted slightly, and her eyes widened. "You don't have anything else hidden away?"

"No."

"Nothing at all."

"No."

"Wow."

"Brilliant," Waring said, and he gazed with a deranged Joker grin at the bowed plywood roof of his porch. "She says 'wow.'"

"I'm taking this in, Waring. You know, you've always been pretty secretive when it comes to—"

"I need ideas, Alaura. Costumes and two-for-one deals won't cut it. Jeff was suggesting we could put a café or a screening room or a popcorn machine in the shop. But obviously that's, I don't know, stupid."

"It's not stupid," she said.

"No," he said. "You're right. It's not stupid. Blad's actually been pretty helpful. But still, we can't put in a café without, you know, money."

"So you're saying?"

"I'm saying the only answer is a cash infusion."

"A cash infusion?" she asked.

"I need a shit-ton of cash that I'm under no obligation to pay back. Or I'll have to close Star Video."

Alaura emitted a breathless curse.

"I concur," Waring said.

They didn't speak for a few minutes. A chill passed over Alaura. As much as she had wanted to avoid the obvious, she'd known this day was coming. Only an idiot could look at Waring's tiny house, crumbling apart and unfit even for a squatter, and believe that he had the financial resources, let alone the wherewithal, to keep a struggling business afloat. To evolve in the ways he would have needed. Or even to accept Star Video's decline and fall with something resembling grace. She knew she shouldn't be surprised. But it was heartbreaking nonetheless. They'd both be set adrift in a world where everything they'd ever cared about, everything they knew, had gone out of style. The world was moving on. The future was now.

She glanced at Waring's pale face. He chewed on his cigarette, its strings of blue smoke trailing into the yard like the smoking caterpillar's hookah in *Alice in Wonderland*. He frowned. To the casual observer, Waring might look simply angry. But Alaura knew he was frightened, hurt, devastated.

Who is Waring Wax without Star Video? Where can the monster live if not in his own enchanted cave?

She reached out and placed her palm on the back of his hand. Without looking at her, he turned his hand over and clasped hers.

They sat like that for several minutes, holding hands, silent.

Later, after a phlegm-obstructed cough, Waring cracked open a new pack of cigarettes. He offered her one. Alaura accepted.

She had avoided all toxins for the past three weeks, and a cigarette sounded great.

"Oh, did I tell you?" he said after giving her a light. "I have a
fool-proof plan for saving the shop."

He was speaking, she knew, in his gearing-up-for-a-joking-bull-
shit-rant tone. "That plan would be?" she said, humoring him.

A devilish grin flitted on his lips, though he still looked as tired
as they both felt. "Well, filming in Appleton for that movie starts
soon, right? And surely with just a smidge of their budget, probably what they're going to pay a two-line supporting actor, or one
day of catering, we could save the shop. So after a lot of personal
debate, and deep inner struggle, I've decided to bite the bullet and
finally become an actor."

Alaura was already a little dizzy from her cigarette, but still she
found herself playing along, nodding, eyes wide like she'd never
heard anything so brilliant.

"Am I right or am I right?" he continued. "I'd make a fantastic fucking actor. The comic relief. Tabitha Gray's snarky uncle
or something, who gets murdered at the close of the second act. I
can see my name on the poster. Alex Walden, Tabitha Gray, Celia
Watson, and Waring Wax star in *The Buried Mirror*, a tale of something or other, intrigue and sex and other things—"

"Wait!" Alaura yelled, and her body jolted forward in the
unsteady rocking chair.

Had Waring really just said . . . ?

"*The Buried Mirror?*" she blurted.

Waring's tone dropped. "For fuck's sake, Alaura, can't a guy
finish a stupid joke?"

"Did you say *The Buried Mirror?*" she repeated sternly. "I'm
serious. Is that the name of the movie filming in Appleton?"

"Jesus, yes," Waring said. "That's what they said at the Board of
Aldermen meeting."

"Did they say the name of the director?"

Waring: palms flipped upward in incomprehension.

"Of *The Buried Mirror*? Did they say the name of the director at the Board of Aldermen meeting?"

"No, they didn't say the name of the damn director."

But Alaura knew. She had not paid attention to his career for the last few months, hoping to save herself from the embarrassment/pathos/physical pain she had felt after seeing his last film, *Changeless*, a misconceived and overly long Buddhist-sci-fi thing that had been a critical and commercial flop. She hadn't wanted to witness the collapse of his Hollywood dreams, because even though they'd fallen out of touch, she'd of course been rooting for him all along. Both Hollywood and time had been hard on him. He had once been trim and handsome, but in the most recent photos of him she had seen, on the Internet, at the New York opening of *Changeless*, he had looked exhausted, worn down, jowly, and in fact, rather ugly. Of course she owned all three of his movies on DVD, and she'd watched them all again and again, even *Changeless*, which was quite terrible but not nearly as terrible as everyone said, and she still recommended his movies, even *Changeless*, to any and every customer at Star Video, trying to do her own little part to bolster his flagging career.

But she hadn't checked his IMDB page in months. She'd had no idea what he was up to.

That he was making *their* movie.

"I don't believe it," she said breathlessly. "Waring, I might know someone who can help us."

She scrambled for her iPhone—the details of Star Video's new hope were possibly a frantic Google search away.

"What are you talking about?" Waring asked.

The director of *The Buried Mirror* could only be one person— Match Anderson, the local boy from her hometown who'd gone on to Hollywood acclaim. Her high school sweetheart.

•   •   •

After using her iPhone to confirm on IMDB that Match Anderson was indeed the auteur behind *Not Tonight, Joséphine!*, which was categorized on the website as "filming" and which was too ridiculous a title *not* to be fake, and after a round of calls confirming her suspicion that the cast and crew of the movie would be staying in Appleton's nicest hotel, the Siena, and after calling the Siena and extracting from the front desk drone that the production had recently arrived, Alaura grabbed Waring's keys, jumped in his Dodge, and sped (as fast as the Dodge would allow) across town.

But Match couldn't be in Appleton. This just wasn't possible.

The only thing that explained it, that made this all not completely absurd, was *The Buried Mirror*. Match had written the first draft of the screenplay when he and Alaura were in high school together, in Sprinks, over a decade ago. She had helped inspire *The Buried Mirror*. They had worked on it together. Developed it together. And the story was set, she knew, in Appleton, the town to which they'd made more than a few teenage expeditions over the years, after meeting as high school freshmen. The movie's lead characters, a wife and husband, were both Appleton University professors, and the Historic District was intended as the picturesque, *Stepford Wives*-y backdrop to the intense, hypersexual storyline.

Now Match was here, filming the movie! Alaura had to remind herself that she didn't believe in Fate. There was no Reality Center magic about any of this. She had done nothing to bring about this result.

Because if she really got down to the truth of the matter—and *I better get shit straight quick*, she thought—if she was totally completely honest, Match had not been her "high school sweetheart," as she often thought of him. She'd only conferred that passé label on their relationship in retrospect, years later, *after* he'd become famous. In fact, they had only "been together" during the summer following their high school graduation. Before that, they had been best friends . . . she had been a tomboy, and he had been the sort of geeky, artsy rich kid who would hang out with a tomboy. They had watched movies together, constantly, for years—in fact, watching movies was all they did. Movies were Match's entire life. And she hadn't minded at all. As freshmen, they'd become quickly inseparable. But it was not until their final summer together that they began kissing, holding hands, sleeping together, calling themselves boyfriend and girlfriend—actually, though she didn't think about it often, the intimate side of their relationship had only lasted a few weeks. He was handsome, but for some reason, she'd never been that attracted to him, he smelled a bit funny, and he was maybe a bit *too* fascinated with movies . . . so she'd always thought of him as more of a brother, and their ultimate summer coupling had been less romantic and more like a submission to what seemed proper teenage protocol. They were about to go their separate ways—she thirty minutes to Ape U and he light-years to Los Angeles for film school. So they got together, and in a flash, the summer had ended.

Then, for some reason, she never contacted him. She never e-mailed or called or wrote, waiting for him to make the first move. But he made no attempt to contact her either. His parents moved away from Sprinks, so he'd never returned to the town for holidays. Within a few months, she was deep into partying at Ape U, drinking and smoking weed and getting piercings and tattoos and sleeping with guys like it was going out of style, and soon it was too late to be the one to break the silence.

She had always known he was special. His name was special—"Match," a cool Anglicization of the Scandinavian "Mats." His grandparents lived in Europe, which was the coolest thing she had ever heard. He'd been born in Massachusetts, had lived for years in Boston, and he was the only kid in Sprinks—where his mother had moved to work at nearby Research Triangle Park—who didn't speak Redneck. He was ideologically opposed to hunting and manual labor. He wore black band tee shirts and baggy jeans, and he loved to read fat books and to watch movies, always movies.

These traits, as well as his waifish frame (he'd weighed no more than 125 pounds at the time) so differentiated him from her other classmates that he was the logical choice as her companion, because by that point, she was already "too smart" and "too weird" for Sprinks. And Match hadn't minded that she was poor, that she lived in a rusty trailer. He introduced her to a new world: a world beyond Sprinks, a world of culture and insight. They developed their own shared history, their own inside jokes, their own lexicon derived from film that only slightly resembled Piedmont English. They rented movies from the nearby grocery store and watched them on his family's VHS player and huge television. They cackled at their own obscure movie references, while other kids thought their antics were offensively nerdy. As far back as freshman year, Alaura had felt that their souls were platonically linked.

The Buried Mirror, she remembered, had started as a joke between the two of them during that final summer. On a Saturday road trip to Appleton to see an old film (*The 400 Blows*, she recalled), they had wandered downtown (which to them was Greenwich Village compared to the ratty stoplight of Sprinks) and into an independent bookstore. There they had chanced across a used Spanish history book called *The Buried Mirror*, and into her head popped the idea that it would be a good title for a movie. She told him this. He agreed and said that it sounded like a Hitchcock thriller. The idea stuck. On the drive home that day, they worked out some of the story details. She proposed Appleton as the film's setting and suggested that the main character be a stifled housewife with dangerous sexual longings. He suggested that her husband could be carrying on an affair with an underage girl living on their immaculate Historic District street, and that when the stifled housewife discovers the affair, she engages in her own self-destructive escapades, including some backwoods rednecky drug-den scenes, ending in disaster. Alaura insisted that the actors must be real-looking people, not Hollywood types, and he agreed enthusiastically, registering all of it, a creative blaze roaring behind his thousand-yard stare.

Over the next few days, he outlined a story, and a week later, he acted it out for her on his back porch. They critiqued the outline together, then made love for one of the very last times, and then he sat down to write the entire thing.

If he was making the film now, in 2007, that meant that *The Buried Mirror*—a Lynchian/Cronenbergian thriller she had helped inspire—had been growing inside Match Anderson for over eleven years. And now he was home, in North Carolina, in Appleton, to film it.

She didn't believe in Fate. But at the moment, it was hard not to.

With just a little more luck, Star Video had a chance.

It was seven p.m., just after sunset, when Alaura arrived at the Siena Hotel, which was a four-story Italian-style building that rested in a verdant corridor of oaks and maples at the bottom of the eastward slope of Appleton, two miles from campus.

A large crowd had gathered at the hotel's ornate front gate.

Alaura parked the Dodge, walked across College Street, and found herself amidst a throng, a bizarre collection of middle-age and teenage females—autograph hounds, she realized. She pushed through the heavily perfumed crowd, her head down, gaze locked on the sidewalk, and she realized again that she was still wearing this stupid blue business suit.

Keep going, she told herself.

She reached the head of the buzzing mass, where activity seemed loudest, most violent, and to her surprise, she was admitted without comment past the literal velvet rope, ushered in by an armed security guard wearing a lemon-yellow polo, his massive hand gently touching her back.

Why had she been admitted? Did Match know she was coming?

It was probably the tattoos on her neck and her pomaded hair combined with the business suit—that she looked so unlike the bubble-gum swarm of Southern women—that the security guard had assumed she was part of the crew.

She walked quickly toward the hotel.

The front doors of the Siena opened and closed with a pleasing sci-fi whoosh, and once inside, she found herself amidst another maelstrom. She had been in this lobby once or twice, for a wedding maybe, or on a night out drinking (there was a restaurant/bar in the back), but she did not recognize the space now. Piles of crumpled cardboard boxes and various bits of alien film equipment filled the room, and packs of people churned in seemingly random directions, chattering, laughing, cursing. Several loud debates went on at once, fingers pointing at computer printouts, men and women rubbing forefingers and thumbs against temples. A man with wild white hair sat in a suede easy chair, his legs crossed, and berated several young crewmembers. Another man stood next to a potted holly tree and looked over the room with a scowl that seemed to betray sinister intentions.

Then Tabitha Gray, Academy Award winner and international tabloid star, entered the lobby—she was flanked by three body-guards, firearms holstered.

Alaura had never been so near a celebrity. Fifteen feet. Ten feet. Five. Tabitha Gray, known affectionately as "Tabby" (though she was reputedly a sadistic anorexic) was even more striking in person than on screen. Her brunette hair seemed to sparkle. Her face was flawless and Photoshopped. Her neck was as long as the neck of that alien from *Close Encounters of the Third Kind*, and her figure was the work of some sadistic deity bent on torturing all of malekind.

As she passed, Tabby smiled at Alaura, and a blue firework exploded inside Alaura's chest.

But the blissful moment evaporated as Tabby floated by and as Alaura discerned that the room had quieted in deference to her raw power, to her beauty and fame and familiarity to audiences. Tabby knew her own power, and the crew knew it, and she hated them for it, and they hated her. Alaura felt the vehemence at once—there was nothing but sexually charged hatred in the air, until Tabby finally exited in the direction, Alaura now remembered, of the hotel's indoor swimming pool.

"May I help you, miss?" a voice asked.

A huge guy in a yellow security shirt stood to Alaura's right. His hair was up in a high, clean, perfect Kid 'n' Play box cut.

"No," she said, confidently looking toward the center of the room.

"Are you a part of the crew, miss?"

"Absolutely."

"The hotel is off-limits to non-crewmembers, miss. We've rented the entire building."

She knew it was unwise, but hoping to scare off this square-headed titan, she decided to channel Waring:

"Quit waving your beef burrito in my face, dude, and don't call me *miss*."

"Miss, I know everyone on the crew, miss."

"I'm a friend of the director," she said.

"Do you have a security pass, miss?"

"I just arrived, didn't I?"

"Miss, I'm going to have to ask you to leave."

"Call me miss again," she said, preparing herself to be arrested and placed into handcuffs. "I triple-dog dare you."

One hour later, Alaura was sitting in a small, sterile conference room in the depths of the Siena Hotel, a room that she imagined was used primarily for the hiring and firing of employees. Another uniformed security guard—this one slickly handsome and donning the Eurotrash fauxhawk that was all the rage that year—stood in the corner of the room, hands cupped in front of him as if protecting his genitalia. The guard had not spoken to Alaura, nor moved a muscle, since the other guard with the box cut had left to check her insane story. She had removed her suit coat and was leaning forward, her elbows propped on the ovular conference room table.

Endowed with a confidence born wholly from the absurdity of this situation, Alaura said to the guard, "You know, I work at a video store. If you bring Match Anderson to me, I'll give you free rentals for life."

No response.

"I bet you get one or two crazies like me a week."

Nothing.

"This time it's actually true, though. I really *do* know Match Anderson."

"Get me a screen test?" Fauxhawk said in a bored voice.

The door opened, and a potbellied man with a scraggly salt-and-pepper beard entered.

"Match?" she said.

He wore a rumpled brown blazer, and his eyes seemed twice the size that she remembered. Altogether, Match looked like a different person. His face sagged under his beard, even more than in the most recent photos of him she had seen, like he'd attempted to pull back his skin for a facelift only to terminate the operation unfinished, leaving the stretched-out material to flop downward. His formerly waifish frame had remained spindly at the chest and shoulders, but it had bloated dangerously in his midsection. And his hands twitched nervously, like he was tickling an invisible monkey wrapped around his waist.

She noticed that his forehead was sweating, little beads dripping from hairline to brow.

"It's me," she said gently. "Alaura."

He stared at her, unresponsive. Neither like he recognized her, nor like he didn't—almost like he was frightened. Then he looked off to the corner of the room, as if someone there was about to speak to him.

Alaura shot Fauxhawk a nervous smirk.

But a moment later, a shy smile emerged behind the thick tendrils of Match's short, uneven beard. It was an expression Alaura immediately recognized from the halls of Sprinks High.

"It's me," she said again, standing up.

"Alaura?" Match's voice—creaky and childlike.

"I've missed you, Match."

"Oh, wow."

He reached out and touched her: the squid tattoo on her right arm.

She brought her opposite hand up to meet his, and in the same movement, she caught a breath of his familiar scent: a woody sweetness that she'd always associated with bookshelves.

"I just found out that you were filming in Appleton," she explained. "I asked around and found out this is where the crew is staying. I came right away."

"Man," he said, and he looked down at the floor. "*The Buried Mirror* script was originally set in Ehle County. Do you remember?" He glanced at her, smiled, then swiped at the sweat on his forehead with the back of a hand. "Of course you remember, Alaura. You were there in the beginning. Since that first draft I wrote in high school. You *know* that the setting was always Appleton."

"Sure, I remember."

"But the studio thought Charleston was more exotic and recognizable. *Midnight in the Garden of Good and Evil*, et cetera, though of course that was filmed in Savannah. And so but anyway *The Buried Mirror* is set in Charleston."

"Okay?" Alaura said, struggling to follow the relevance of this story.

"But then, when we were location scouting, Ehle County made us an amazing offer. Maybe because I grew up around here, I don't know. But so, boom, we're filming here, in Appleton, but hanging fake Spanish moss everywhere, trying to make the streets look all flat and Charlestony. And now here *you* are. Alaura Eden. Standing right in front of me."

She didn't quite understand what he was talking about, but nonetheless, she hazarded: "Yes, here I am."

"Alaura Eden," he repeated. Then, in a peculiarly secretive murmur, he said, "Alaura, I'm so glad you're here. I have to tell you something. Something I've only told one other person."

"What is it?"

"I can trust you, can't I?"

She squeezed his shaking hand, which she now noticed was clammy under hers. And she realized that even though he was looking at her, his eyes were almost completely unfocused.

"You can't repeat this to anyone," he whispered.

Alaura glanced suspiciously over Match's shoulder at the security guard, who was now inspecting the reflection of his fauxhawk in the conference room's tiny window, completely unimpressed that Alaura had not turned out to be a lunatic.

"I won't tell anyone," she said.

"I need your help."

"*My* help?" she asked, thinking at once of Star Video, and that she had come here to ask for *his* help. "What do you need?"

"It's like . . . it's like Fate that you're here," he muttered.

She smiled nervously.

"Can you help me?" he asked.

"Why do you keep asking me that, Match?" she said, edging away from him a little bit. "Is this about the movie?"

"No," Match said. "It's about me."

"What is it, Match?"

He sighed. His voice lowered even further. "Alaura," he whispered, "I don't know how to say this . . . but I've been seeing the ghost of Alfred Hitchcock. He's sitting in that chair right now."

Alaura looked at the chair, clenched her jaw, and tried with all her might to see what simply wasn't there.

EVERYTHING YOU ALWAYS WANTED
TO KNOW ABOUT MATCH ANDERSON*
(*BUT WERE AFRAID TO ASK)

Waring and Jeff, alone again at Star Video. Next-to-no business. Jeff had just taken a short break and strolled out to College Street, trying to absorb the full extent of today's events: the Reality Center, holding Alaura while she wept, helping Waring pack up his house, and the insane revelation about Match Anderson. It was all too much to process.

Then Jeff smelled something. Butter. He looked down the street in the direction of the intoxicating odor, and he noticed that Blockbuster's parking lot was nearly full. Two posters swayed in the breeze beneath the huge Blockbuster sign. One of them read, "Rent TWO Get ONE Free," the other, "And FREE Popcorn!"

Jeff walked back into Star Video, having resolved not to mention this brilliant marketing offensive on the part of their enemy, nor that he had suggested the exact same maneuvers to Waring not two days earlier.

"I can't believe it," Jeff said, sitting on a stool close to Waring, who, as always, was seated in his director's chair.

"What?"

"That Alaura knows Match Anderson. And he's here in Ehle County."

"Yes," Waring said. "She never told me that either. Never mentioned she knew a Hollywood director. It's all a rather improbable turn of events."

"Crazy."

"Some might say far-fetched."

"Uh-huh."

"Contrived even."

Jeff nodded.

"If it happened in a movie," Waring said, "I probably wouldn't believe it."

Silence.

Minutes later . . .

"Have you ever seen *Annie Hall*?" Jeff asked.

"Have I ever seen *Annie Hall*? Let me think, Jeff." Waring clenched his eyes shut, searching his memory banks. "Yes," he said finally. "I recall watching *Annie Hall* once or twice."

Jeff chuckled. "I've never seen it. Can we watch it now?"

"'Sfine."

They watched *Annie Hall*.

Ninety-four minutes later, as the final white-on-black credits faded, Jeff turned to Waring and asked, "You believe what Woody Allen says?"

"Mm?"

"How life is full of loneliness, misery, and suffering, but it all ends too soon."

"So?"

"So do you believe him?"

"What's not to believe?" Waring asked.

"But it's so cynical. Seems like a miserable way to think about life."

Waring turned to Jeff. "Think about it," he said. "Cynical

implies that because life is meaningless and painful, we should be miserable. Woody is kind of suggesting the opposite. That *because* life is shit, we should try to enjoy ourselves while we're here."

Jeff considered this, and he was preparing to ask if Waring believed this notion himself—because it seemed very out of character—when Waring added:

"Of course, Woody married his stepdaughter, which is gross."

"He did?"

"You don't know this?"

"No."

"Christ! We could fill up the Grand Canyon with what you don't know."

Jeff flipped Waring the bird, the first time he had attempted this gesture after witnessing Alaura do it to Waring fifty times.

Waring smiled, as if in appreciation.

"By the way," Waring said. "Rose has a crush on you."

Jeff frowned, having been completely caught off guard.

"Seems pretty obvious," Waring went on. "The way she's always, you know, talking to you."

"Rose barely talks to me at all."

"She never says a word to anyone else."

"But I thought maybe her and Farley were—"

"Rose is a much better fit for you than Alaura. I'm just saying. Completely objective viewpoint here."

Jeff flipped Waring the bird again.

Waring rolled his eyes, disappointed by the repetition.

"I can't believe Alaura really knows Match Anderson," Jeff repeated.

"Yes, so amazing," Waring said with a sudden grimace.

"*Losers* was a great movie."

"Yes, it was. But it's been a while since *Losers*."

"I didn't see *A House on the Edge of Reason* or *Changeless*," Jeff said.

"Don't."

"I hear they're . . ."

"They are."

"They don't rent much."

"That's a good sign of a bad movie," Waring said knowingly.

"But I mean, maybe he can help, you know, with the store?"

Waring sighed loudly, his patience with the subject of Match Anderson apparently exhausted. "By the way, Sasquatch, call him Woody. Not Woody Allen. Just Woody."

"Why?"

"Video store etiquette. Woody."

Jeff nodded. "By the way, Waring, you're repeating yourself."

"What?"

"That's like the tenth time you've called me Sasquatch, which doesn't even make sense, by the way, if I'm quote-unquote hairless."

"I'll remember that, teenage Ed Begley Jr."

BEING MATCH ANDERSON

Match Anderson's immaculate room at the Siena Hotel looked like it had been ransacked by goons searching for top-secret government documents. The mattress of his four-poster king bed sat askew on its box springs. Several dinner trays and takeout cartons were strewn over the floor, along with a carpeting of yellow and white papers, hundreds of them, many with Match's messy handwriting scrawled over them. It was a wonderful room—mahogany furniture and brass fixtures and a sixty-inch flat-screen television—but the place was a complete disaster, as if Match had been holed up here for months.

Alaura sat quietly and watched as Match traipsed around, quickly, crazily, in completely random routes amidst the clutter—the Tasmanian Devil who had clearly caused the room's devastation. Now that she'd spent an hour with him, during which they'd shared a quick meal in the hotel's restaurant, and during which he'd been constantly accosted by fifty crewmembers asking him a hundred questions, all of which he seemed to answer correctly, but with intense anxiety and annoyance . . . she couldn't believe the general character of his behavior, nor how he looked, nor how he sounded.

His voice was scratchy, like a smoker's, and he lapsed occasionally into strange phrasing, odd elocution . . . a million parsecs from his sharp boyishness back in high school. And he looked . . . well, he looked awful. Skeletal in the shoulders, haggard and sallow in the face, and more of an unhealthy distribution of flesh around his waist than she had originally noticed. He was sweating profusely, and mostly, it seemed, from his forehead. And his huge, glassy eyes— freaky and detached like Gollum in *Lord of the Rings*.

The problem was: how to bring up Star Video. She hadn't figured out how to do it yet. There hadn't been a calm moment.

"So the thing was, I couldn't get money for the movie," Match said, after he'd been silent, but walking violently, for quite some time. "For *The Buried Mirror*. The studio was balking at the eleventh hour, there just wasn't funding, so I had to say sayonara to my lead actress, who is a great fucking actress, by the way, and she would have played the role perfectly, this obscure Irish chick I bet you'd know. But [name of film studio omitted] said that I had to go for someone with a bigger name, just ten days before initial exteriors in LA, and what the hell am I supposed to do? I don't have a lead actress. So I float my interest to agents and shit, and then it comes about after a *lot* of rigmarole that Tabitha Gray is interested. I mean, Tabitha Gray! And though honestly she isn't right for the part, I agree to meet with her at this restaurant overlooking Central Park, this private club, and she's read the script, and she's super interested, which really doesn't mean anything, because they're always super interested, but I'm hoping, because I've been wanting to make this movie since fucking high school, you know? I mean, I know I'm only thirty years old, but still, that's a long time."

Alaura nodded, smiled. But Match was frightening her. He was tramping around and not looking at her and smoking cigarettes and sweating and holding a clinking glass of bourbon and monologuing.

"I can't express how wrong Tabitha was for the part," he went on. "*Is* for the part. But I walk in to meet her, at this fancy club, and what do I see standing at the bar? *Who* do I see? Here it is, Alaura, are you ready? Here it is: I see this amazing fucking Alfred Hitchcock impersonator. I mean, he's absolutely stupendously perfect. You know how into Hitchcock I was. Am. I've watched every second of every movie and all the interview footage and every episode of *Hitchcock Presents*. I know what the man looks like. He's one of my heroes. And there's this impersonator standing there, at the bar, all chubby and shiny like a white seal in a black suit, his teeth jutting forward and craggy, ugly as all sin. Around sixty years old, placing him at the height of his powers, you know, *The Trouble with Harry. The Wrong Man. Vertigo. North by Northwest. Psycho. The Birds.* Six great films in eight years." Match sipped his bourbon.

"So what happened?" Alaura asked timidly.

"What happened?" Match said. "What happened is I waved to him. And he waved right back. Then he starts mouthing words at me. He's standing fifteen feet away, from here to that wall right there, but he's not saying anything, like he can't make the words come out. Creepy. So I think, must be a drunk impersonator, right? Must be some dude who stands down at Times Square to get pictures taken with tourists. Never mind that this theory doesn't make a damn bit of sense. Here is this impersonator in an ultra-private uptown club, a club so private that they virtually probed me to let me in to meet Tabitha Gray, because the dude at the front, the maître d', he didn't recognize me, and I don't dress very fancy to boot." Match took another tiny sip of bourbon, just touching his tongue to the golden liquid. A line of sweat trickled down his left cheek. "Anyway, Tabitha shows up. She sort of explodes silently into the room the way movie stars do, and I click into action. I play the conflicted artist with her. I play the snooty intellectual. I tell her how amazing she is, but then I tell her, to catch her off guard, that I think she's *wrong* for the part, that she's too attractive, too famous, too damned striking. Which is all true, of course, because the part calls for a sort of frumpy housewife type, someone so dull that you'd never expect her to do the things she ends up doing, as I know you remember, Alaura, all the sexual stuff. I say all this to Tabitha, honestly not knowing whether I'm trying to scare her off because she's so wrong for the part or if I'm playing that frankly honest card hoping to bait her into it."

Alaura was struggling to keep up with Match's frenetic pace, to hold everything in her mind. Not to mention that his room smelled distractingly like an intensified version of him, those musty old bookshelves, but with an unfortunate dash of mildew thrown in.

Focus on Star Video, Alaura thought to herself. Star Video needs money. Not even a ton of money. Just a little boost. Waring's finally trying. We can survive. We have to. There's no way bookstores and record stores and the fucking Postal Service can outlive Star Video . . .

"And as I'm babbling away at Tabitha," Match continued, "I keep looking at the fat bastard at the bar, and I notice that the bartender hasn't said a word to him. And then I know, I just *know*, pow! I know that I'm looking at Alfred Hitchcock's ghost. And I know for a fact that he's here to see me. It's a shock, obviously. But I keep my focus on Tabitha. And I even notice that she's flirting with me a little, which is hilarious, given how I look and how she looks and that her last boyfriend was that French soccer player. Anyway, I leave Tabitha *in medias res*, I walk away, which is as good an approach with a car salesman as it is with an overhyped actress . . . and I plan to poke Hitchcock in the chest just to see how real this ghost fucker is. I reach the bar. But he's not there. I look back at Tabitha Gray, who's looking at me with the sad puppy-dog thing, and there's Hitch sitting across from her. But she doesn't see him!"

"Match?" Alaura said softly when he had been silent for a few seconds.

He turned to her and smiled pleasantly, like he had momentarily forgotten his old friend was in the room.

"Do you realize that this sounds . . . well . . ."

"Crazy?" he said. "I know."

She nodded, relieved that he had provided the word.

The question now became, crazy how? Had he sustained a blow to the head? Was he legitimately schizophrenic? Was he strung out on pills and booze? Was he dangerous? Alaura didn't believe she was in any danger herself, though, unfortunately, the fact that the thought had crossed her mind was more than a little worrisome.

"Clearly, I've gone nuts," Match said, as if directly addressing her thoughts. "I've been working too hard. Nonstop for, like, five years. More like ten years. More like always. I've never stopped. So it's mental exhaustion, or something, and now I'm seeing the ghost of a dead director. And of course it has to be insanity, because *The Buried Mirror* is my Hitchcock thing, that's how I think of it now, not like Lynch or Cronenberg, but like Hitch. This is my attempt to be both artistic and entertaining, just a straight out-and-out thriller, but done artfully, and with the sex stuff, too. You know, Alaura? You remember, don't you? You were the first person who ever read *The Buried Mirror* five thousand drafts ago."

"Of course I remember," she said in a daze.

"So the first thing I do is call my brother. You remember Finn?"

"Yes," she said. "He used to masturbate all the time."

"That's right."

"I walked in on him once."

"I've walked in on him jerking off so many times I could pick his dick out of a lineup."

And Alaura knew he was referencing *Porky's*, the scene where the angry gym teacher proposes a penis lineup to determine the identity of a flasher.

Was this a good sign? That he was capable of a joking reference?

"So I call Finn," Match said, "and he's really concerned. He coproduces things with me. Did you know that?"

"Yes, of course. I've kept up with your career."

"Finn is concerned," Match said, not acknowledging her comment. "Concerned for Match's well-being. But we have to keep it quiet because we're supposed to start shooting in ten days. So Finn discretely arranges for me to see this neurologist, this Indian or Pakistani guy with a pencil-thin mustache, who does these brain scans, in Brooklyn, and he interviews me, and he can't really find anything wrong, but he gives me some pills. My brain doesn't look like a schizophrenic's brain, he says, and typically visual hallucinations are not as defined and consistent as what I'm experiencing."

"And?"

"And the pills work. I don't see Hitchcock. But only for a little while. When we start filming, all of a sudden, like a week in, I start seeing him again. Hitch at the food services table. Hitch sitting on the couch in my trailer. Hitch on set, standing behind me, watching me direct. Hitch everywhere, like fifty times a day!"

"Oh, Match!"—she wanted to reach out to him, embrace him, calm him down. But he was still whirling around the room, bumping into the nightstand, kneeing the antique chestnut coffee table but still moving, not reacting in pain.

"And I can't tell *anyone*," Match said, his voice grumbling over the final word. He took a sip of his whiskey, a big sip this time, and he sighed in pleasure-pain after swallowing. "That's the rub. I shouldn't even have gone to a doctor because if [name of film studio omitted] finds out that I'm seeing a ghost, that I'm *crazy*, then they could rip me right off the movie. I mean, I don't own the rights to the script, I sold it to them, I have very limited creative control. And to be honest, the bigwigs don't care for me. After *Changeless*, they weren't too thrilled to bankroll another Match Anderson project."

This was the fourth or fifth time Match had referred to himself in the third person, and Alaura was concerned that this sort of linguistic disassociation might be symptomatic of . . . of whatever was going on with him. She rubbed her hands together. She watched him and noticed again that he was scratching himself repeatedly, sort of a Toshiro Mifune nervous habit, though Match's scratching carried none of Toshiro's oddly masculine charm. She felt an incredible sadness welling up inside of her, a cold balloon rising through her belly, both for Match, who was clearly suffering, and for Star Video, which she sensed getting lost in the cloud of this madness.

"*Changeless* really screwed things up for me in Hollywood," Match said. "Eighteen months principal photography, twenty million over budget, and it was a damned flop. Like two weeks in the theaters. I'm embarrassed to even think about it. A sci-fi time-travel reincarnation romance? I mean, I think it's beautiful, but I thought it would be a classic, you know, that sort of movie that no one sees but critics call a classic and in twenty years normal people will call a classic, too. Terrence Malick, that sort of thing. But the critics hated it more than the public. I mean, they fucking *hated* it. Twenty-six percent on Rotten Tomatoes." He looked at Alaura and said, "I can tell that you hated it, too."

Alaura cringed behind a tight smile.

Yes, if she was being honest, she'd hated it.

"I didn't hate it," she managed.

"So I've got no wiggle room," Match went on, his voice cracking again, pained, and he began another circuit around the room, moving off in the direction of the cockeyed poster bed. "Because Doris Day signs on, right there in the restaurant . . . wait, did I say Doris Day? I meant Tabitha Gray. Sorry. Tabitha Gray signs on, she says yes, so we get the money we need. But damn it all, it's like the project is beyond my grasp now. Thank God there's only twelve days left of principal photography. Thank fucking God. Because now I'm like a hired hand on my own movie. It's horrible. If Tabitha doesn't like something, it gets changed. She's not playing the part frumpy, she's playing it sexy from beginning to fucking end. Which makes no sense. She wouldn't cut her hair. The bitch wouldn't even consider bangs. And Alex, he's amazing, he's a force of nature, but he makes no fucking sense with Tabitha, he's too old and fat, maybe thirty-five-year-old-Tom-Clancy-movie Alex, but not sitcom Alex, fuck. He arrived on set on day one like fat Brando in *Apocalypse Now*, when of course I'd asked him to slim down. And I wanted the crew to live out in the woods somewhere, in some shit-hole redneck motel, or even in Sprinks, I actually hoped, because I thought Sprinks might get everyone into the feel of the movie, you know, the *feel* of the South, even if we're filming in Appleton. But Tabitha or someone waves their magic wand, and we're shooting in HD, not in Super 16, and there's all new hair and makeup people, and she's not comfortable saying this or that, and Alex is not comfortable saying this or that, so the script gets altered. And we're staying at the Siena, the ritziest place in Appleton. And I wanted to keep the details of the production secret to create some buzz, but that pissed off the Ehle County authorities, so they're giving the studio a hard time, which pisses off the studio, so they're giving me a hard time. And even though our budget has virtually doubled, I'm not allowed to do half the set-ups I had planned, the long tracking shots, the in-camera stuff, et cetera, because *time* is so fucking important now, and they'd rather clean things up with CGI. I don't know what's going on. I'm seeing Hitchcock, and I'm making a shitty summer blockbuster."

"Match," she said softly. "You need to calm—"

"But there's only twelve days left of shooting," he said, then he exhaled loudly. "Twelve days. Then it's postproduction, thank God, back in LA. Things will slow down. I just have to make it to postproduction. Twelve days."

He had completed his latest trip around the room, and he suddenly collapsed next to her on the baroque burgundy quite uncomfortable couch where Alaura sat. Their hips touched. She smelled his musty books. She looked at his disheveled curly hair. She wanted to remove his dirty brown blazer, massage his neck, straighten the mattress, put him to bed.

"I'm rambling," he said. "Sorry."

She took a breath. "Does he talk to you? Hitchcock?"

"No. He tries, I think, but I can't hear him."

"Do you see him now?"

"Not now. Down in the conference room, when you first arrived, I saw him. And he's always there when Tabitha is near."

Alaura nodded, unsure of the implications of this comment.

"Jesus, Alaura!" Match jerked up on the couch as if his own words had startled him. "I've only been talking about myself! If I'd known you were still here in Appleton . . . Alaura, I've missed you. I think about you. All the time. I think: Alaura would love LA. You'd love it there. You should come visit me sometime. You know, high school might have been the last time I was completely happy, watching movies with you. It's hard to believe that you're here, that you're real. Alaura, what've you been doing for the last ten years?"

And despite everything—despite the cyclone of Match Anderson and her resultant bewilderment—Alaura found herself smiling. That Match thought of her, perhaps often, shot her through with an odd surge of pleasure.

So she gathered herself and confessed, though she was unable to conquer her embarrassment about it, that she hadn't been doing anything worth discussion with her life. He prodded further, politely but insistently, and she finally admitted that after graduating from Ape U, she had kept working at Star Video, and she had been there ever since. Which all sounded pathetic, she knew, following the exciting, rambling—if technically insane—tale of the past few months of his life. But it felt good to tell him, because . . .

As she spoke, she noticed the crazy glaze temporarily vanishing from Match's face. His eyes seemed to focus on her. His forehead stopped sweating. He leaned back in the lumpy couch, relaxed, like the boy she had known so many years ago.

"And the tattoos?" he asked calmly.

"Just things I've picked up. They've each got a story."

"They're beautiful. You're beautiful."

"Um," she said, and she couldn't help cringing a little. Thankfully he was now staring off into space and not at her. "You remember we used to talk about getting tattoos?"

"Beautiful," he repeated. "That one on your arm is from *20,000 Leagues Under the Sea*, right?"

"That's right."

"Any guys in your life?"

"Um . . . occasionally? Nothing that stuck."

Match looked toward the ceiling. "I think it sounds like a great life. Working in a video store. Ordering movies, watching movies, talking about movies. You get the best part of the movie business: the movies themselves."

She didn't know what to say, and wishing she could direct the conversation in some other direction, she needled him with a playful elbow. "Shut the fuck up. It is *not* a great life."

"I'm honestly envious."

"All we do is sit around and bitch that *Parker Louis Can't Lose* isn't on DVD."

He sighed. "Sounds like heaven."

All she could think to say was: "But Match, you're famous."

He chuckled amiably. "I don't want to be famous. I really don't."

Again he stared off into space, and she wondered if he was seeing Hitchcock—she looked toward the center of the room, half-expecting to find the fat director sitting on the bed.

"Match?"

"Uh-huh."

"You asked for my help."

"Yes."

"What kind of help do you need?"

"Oh. I don't know."

"You're seeing things," she said.

"That's true," he said. "I am seeing things."

"I'm your friend," she said. "I want to be here for you, for whatever you need. It's . . . sort of what I do for my friends."

Match looked at her, nodded. "That would be nice."

"Is there any way you can, I don't know, take a break? A short vacation?"

"No way," he said. "With only twelve days left, I can't leave now. Just a bit more shooting. Then we'll be done."

She nodded. Twelve days. Could they make it twelve days?

"Alaura?"

"Yes?"

"I've thought about you a lot over the years. You're very pretty."

"I . . ." she stammered. "Match, I just got out of a relationship. I'm not really looking for anything, you know, new?"

Match flinched. His eyes seemed to cloud over.

"Nothing romantic," she said quickly. "I'm sorry. I hope that's okay."

"Oh," he said. "No, that's fine. But could you, I don't know, stay here with me?"

"Here? In your hotel room?"

"There's a roll-out bed in the closet. I could sleep on that."

She looked toward the closet door, which was huge, nine feet tall, like she was visiting in a giant's lair.

"I really do need your help," he said.

She smiled. He was looking at her now. But his forehead was sweating again. He scratched at his beard with his fingernails.

"Of course I can stay," she said. "Whatever you need."

Then she remembered. If she didn't say something now . . . this was as good a time as any to bring it up . . .

"Match, there's something else. I wish I didn't have to."

"What?"

"I hate to ask. I really hate to bring this up."

"You can ask me anything, Alaura. You're helping me, after all."

"Okay," she said, and she took a centering breath. "The thing is—my store needs money. Star Video, where I work. The video store industry is really struggling, as I'm sure you know. We really need to raise some money, or we might go out of business."

Match frowned, confused, like she'd just spoken in Chinese.

"No," she said quickly, realizing it hadn't come out the right way. "I don't want money *from you*. I'm not asking *you* for money. I just thought, I don't know, with you in town. With Tabitha Gray and Alex Walden and Celia Watson, I don't know, maybe we could organize some sort of . . . fundraiser? A benefit? For Appleton's struggling independent video store."

She buried her head in her hands. She couldn't believe what she was saying—that she'd found herself in this insane situation, that her old friend was on the brink of madness, perhaps *over* the brink, that a fundraiser was her big plan to save Star Video, and that she had handled it all wrong.

Then she felt his shoulder press against hers.

"I have an idea," he whispered.

Y TU TABITHA TAMBIÉN

Four days later, Waring authorized the purchase of a small but theater-worthy popcorn machine for Star Video. It was a dingy old monster, and it made a ton of racket—essentially, it was the concession stand equivalent of Waring's Dodge. Jeff had found the thing on Craigslist being sold by an old movie theater, three towns over, that was going out of business. Jeff had driven in the Dodge to pick it up that morning, and he'd paid for it with funds raised from selling some of Waring's least-damaged posters on eBay, including the autographed *Apocalypse Now* poster for four hundred dollars.

Now the red, yellow, and faded-chrome device was sitting on Star Video's counter next to the Cashier du Cinéma. It hissed and burbled, and white starbursts of popcorn tumbled out of the metal pot suspended at its center. To Waring, the popcorn smelled incredible. Like his youth—like every movie theater he'd ever gone to with his mother, who had always, without exception, bought them a large popcorn to share.

Waring looked at Jeff and Alaura, who were both watching the machine and smiling like it was the Narnia wardrobe.

Highlander played on the store's central television.

"This movie reminds me," Waring said in their general direction.

"Huh?" Jeff said.

"I'll go ahead and say it: I don't believe in global warming."

Alaura rolled her eyes immediately, but Jeff frowned in confusion. Waring suspected that the pimpled peon had been raised by his conservative mountain family to be skeptical of global warming, but that now, as the recipient of two months of a liberal Ape U education, he had converted to a staunch believer.

"No way!" Jeff said, confirming Waring's suspicion.

"Don't take the bait, Jeff," Alaura said after a brief chuckle. "He's just yanking your chain."

"Nope," Waring said. "Doesn't seem much hotter."

"But levels of carbon in the atmosphere?" Jeff said. "And heat waves? And ice caps melting?"

"Just a hoax, I think," Waring persisted. "Last winter was maybe the coldest for a hundred years. How do you explain that?"

Jeff could not explain, as Waring had anticipated, but the kid eventually stammered that major weather fluctuations might be triggered by global warming.

"So now *cold* temperatures are caused by global *warm*ing?" Waring countered. "That's loco, homeslice."

"You're obviously in a better mood," Alaura said to Waring, her lips now protruding in that sexy, annoyed pout of hers, but with a hint of a smile. "What got you onto this?"

"You mean besides my general distaste for ideological Hollywood fads spurred by flavor-of-the-month liberal documentaries? *Highlander II. Highlander II* got me thinking about it."

"*Highlander II?*" Jeff said, bewildered.

"It's an awful movie, obviously. Truly awful. I caught it on Spike the other day. There's a scene where the Highlander, and I've never understood why they cast Christopher Lambert, who sounds about as Scottish as Kevin Costner sounds British in *Prince of Thieves*, anyway, there's a scene where the Highlander uses the great power thing he won in the first *Highlander* movie," and Waring pointed to the television, "*this* movie, to save the world from the destruction of the ozone layer. The sky is red, and people are all but bursting into flames in the street. Just got me thinking."

Alaura was ignoring him, and she started unwrapping the classic red and white popcorn tubs that they'd be using to hand out free samples to customers.

"But the ozone layer was a real thing," Jeff said to Waring. "Wasn't it?"

"Yes," Waring said, smiling at his flustered employee. "Remember, I was cognizant while all that ozone business was going on. You were a wee baby, Alaura. And you, random extra from the town in *Footloose*, you weren't even sperm."

"But what does that prove about global warming?" Jeff said, his voice cracking slightly   the kid seemed totally at a loss, which of course had been Waring's intention.

The front door of Star Video opened, and Match Anderson entered.

The man gazed wide-eyed at the store and stroked his beard, Waring thought, like a dazed wizard.

"Match!" Alaura said, rising from her stool.

Match's eyes widened, Waring saw, as if he was surprised to see her. "Oh, hello there!" the young director said.

Waring watched Alaura sprint around the counter. She was smiling like an idiot. She hugged Match, kissed his cheek. Waring sneered. He didn't like the cut of this guy's jib, not one bit. Match's clothes looked like he'd spent last night in a bus station. His beard grew unevenly on his drooping face. He was not, in general, nearly attractive enough for Alaura, and on top of that, an offensive arrogance oozed off of him. If his nose were raised any higher, he'd fall backward.

Alaura had supposedly been sleeping in Match's hotel room for the past few days, though she'd been pretty tightlipped about the whole thing. Like usual when it came to men.

"I came here to see you," Match said after a long pause, looking around at Star Video's high ceilings and tall shelves and nodding authoritatively. "This place is really great."

"Thanks!" Alaura said.

"Smells good, too. It's cool you have a popcorn machine."

Alaura grinned at Waring, who forced a smile back at her like a haunted mirror.

"Are you done filming for today?" Alaura asked.

"No. Waiting for magic hour. A few more shots on campus. Tabitha running across the quad. Jimmy Stewart running after her."

Alaura looked at him quizzically. "Jimmy Stewart?"

"No," Match said, shaking his head and laughing at himself. "I mean Alex Walden. Alex Walden running after her."

Waring's director's chair groaned as he stood to escape to *The African Queen*.

"Oh!" Alaura said. "Let me introduce you to the guys. Waring!"

So Waring submitted to introductions and hand shaking, as he knew he should. He knew he had to play nice, just like he was reluctantly polite at the Open Eye Café in order to secure his daily red eye.

"I'm supposed to thank you," Waring said, remembering that Alaura had instructed him to thank Match profusely at his first opportunity. "What you're doing for Star Video. I appreciate it."

"Doing?"

"The celebrity auction?"

Match swiped his index finger through the air between them, scrunching his face and laughing. "Dumb Match! Of course, the celebrity auction!"

Waring studied the bizarre bearded man, who had directed one excellent independent film and two awful Hollywood abortions. Match seemed, to Waring, brimming with that numb-brained smugness he'd always expected of filmmakers. Or was it worse than that? Match's mouth hung open as he gazed again around the store, now totally disengaged from the conversation his entrance had initiated. Glossy bloodshot eyes. And from the expression on his face, it almost appeared that Match hadn't at all remembered that only four days earlier, *he* had suggested the celebrity auction to Alaura as a fundraiser for Star Video—auctioning off dinner with his lead actors, as well as discarded props from the set of *The Buried Mirror*.

"Anyway," Waring said, straining behind his mandatory smile, "like I was saying, please thank the actors for us. We've set up a display, right over there, to feature all of their films. And your films, of course. We'll also be auctioning a bunch of these old posters I have. And of course, mmm, it's great that, you know, the studio is willing to rent out the Siena for the event and to match the bids—"

"Oh, don't worry about that," Match interrupted. "Good PR for everyone. We've had issues with the local government, which has ticked off the studio. Anyway, I'm hoping that a few hours of the actors' time will buy us some community support."

"Mm," Waring said, nodding and still smiling furiously.

"Actually, I just remembered," Match said, now looking at Alaura. "I came here for two reasons. First, do you have aliens?"

"Aliens?" Waring said.

"The sequel to *Alien*," Match explained. "I've always loved the *Alien* movies. And the studio has approached me about directing another sequel."

This surprised Waring, who had believed that the *Alien* franchise was dead and that Match was not really a director in demand.

"*Aliens* is my favorite movie," Jeff announced.

Waring turned and stared at his moronic young employee, who was standing behind the counter.

"Your favorite movie?" Waring asked. "Of all time?"

"It's one of my employee picks."

"Wow, Jeff. That's ridiculous."

Jeff shook his head. "At least I believe in global warming."

"Who doesn't believe in global warming?" Match said.

"*Der Führer*," Alaura said.

"I'd get fired if I said that in Hollywood."

"See!" Waring said, delighted that his earlier point had now been scientifically verified.

"I didn't say *Aliens* is the best movie ever," Jeff explained. "I said it's my favorite. There's a difference. It was one of the first R-rated movies I ever saw, and I thought it was the definition of cool. Great effects. Kick-ass protagonist. I've watched it hundreds of times."

Waring turned up his hands, then let them drop—totally exasperated by Jeff's defective reasoning. "Next you'll tell us that you enjoyed the *Star Wars* prequels more than the originals."

"No," Jeff said, his mouth twisting like he'd sipped turned milk. "I'd never say that."

"And now I'm thinking about Jar Jar Binks," Waring said. "Thanks for ruining my entire day, Jeff."

Jeff shrugged, unwounded by this exchange.

"Hell," Waring went on, "I think Match's first movie was a better action flick than fucking *Aliens*."

Waring slowly realized that this comment was not the rousing endorsement of Match's first film he might have hoped for, and that, in addition, Waring had also implied a subtler judgment against Match's later films. Waring hadn't meant it that way, because he'd actually liked *Losers*. A lot. It was a solid, solid movie. Waring bit his upper lip, trying to think of a way to erase what he'd just said. Match frowned down at his standard-issue black Converses—Alaura shot Waring a vehement look—and Jeff seemed to take this as his cue to walk to the back of the store and shelve movies.

"So can I check out *Aliens*?" Match said, smiling painfully.

"Sure," Alaura replied, and after glaring again at Waring, she darted away to retrieve the show box.

"Well?" Waring said, now alone with Match (and much less nervous than he'd expected to be in this situation). "What was the second thing?"

"I'm sorry?"

"You said you came here for two reasons."

"Oh, yes. The second thing." Match pointed a finger at Waring—and his embarrassment seemed to vanish instantly. "It was to ask you a huge, huge favor."

"Me? Favor?"

"Yes. I was wondering if you could recommend a bar."

"A bar?"

"A place where people drink," Match clarified. "For the cast and crew. Things have been a little tense on set. For various reasons. I was hoping to have a gathering. A party. I mean, our wrap party's in, like, eight days, but still, I thought a night out drinking would be good. For morale. You know, at a local place. Nothing fancy. I was wondering if you could take everyone."

"Me?" Waring repeated. "*Take* them to a bar?"

"Yes. I just figured, you know, since we're doing you a favor with the celebrity auction thing. Everyone wants to go. Including all the actors. I'm giving them tomorrow night off."

"Tomorrow night?"

Alaura reappeared with *Aliens*. "Match," she said, "I'm not sure that's a good idea."

"Well, I've already told everyone that it's happening, so . . ." He looked again at Waring. "What do you think, man? Can you help us out?"

And as if mentioning the actors had ripped open a hole in the space-time continuum, Tabitha Gray and Celia Watson, flanked by a security detail of six muscle-bound men, entered Star Video. Waring's legs went gelatinous. He gripped the counter for support. Celia Watson, who was perhaps the smallest person Waring had ever seen, and who made him feel immediately disgusting for finding her deliciously attractive, because until just last year she'd played a bubbly teenage detective on that stupid Disney Channel show, though he was fairly certain she'd recently turned legal-years-old . . . Celia Watson disappeared at once into the labyrinth of Star Video.

Tabitha Gray—the most beautiful woman in the world— approached Match Anderson. She did not look at Alaura or Waring, curled her fingers around Match's hand, and kissed his cheek. Then she smiled at Waring in perfect imitation of herself.

"Guys," Match said, looking in awe at the celestial being holding his hand, "meet Tabitha Gray, star of *The Buried Mirror*."

Meanwhile, Jeff stood in the Mystery/Suspense section, organizing movies that didn't really need organizing because he'd already organized them twice that week. But after Waring's disastrous comment about *Losers*, Jeff had felt a blinding spasm of embarrassment, similar to moments at church talent shows when a well-intentioned old lady would sing painfully off-key. So Jeff had retreated, and he was lost in his work, making space for *Mystic River* and reflecting on why he should feel such embarrassment if he wasn't the one who'd misspoken, and then contemplating, for some reason, if he'd ever make it back to Tanglewood Baptist, because he hadn't been to church in weeks, when he heard the *click-click* of high heels somewhere nearby.

"Hi," said a clear, flutey voice to his left, near the Drama section.

"Hello?" Jeff said, turning to look.

It was Celia Watson, the young supporting actress from *The Buried Mirror*.

Jeff stared at her. His voice was paralyzed in his throat.

Celia Watson began to giggle. But it was not a cruel giggle. At least, Jeff didn't think so. Her unexpected appearance—it was surreal, as if the image of her in front of him was too flat, a poor copy of Celia Watson. She was only a little over five feet tall in heels, and frightfully skinny, and strangely she wore a neon green dress over blue jeans. Was that in style these days? Her hair was longer than he'd ever seen it, and it was platinum blonde instead of the brunette he'd been expecting. And as his vision adjusted to the uneven store lighting that seemed to cast Celia into silhouette, he realized that her head seemed several sizes too large for her body.

But her luminous smile made his intestines quiver.

He had never been a fan of Celia Watson. Was anyone? he wondered nervously. When he was in elementary school, all the girls had watched her Disney show religiously, and their parents had driven them in caravans to her corny concerts. Since then, Watson had starred in musicals and teen movies. Terrible, laughable movies. Yes, she was famous, but most intelligent adults thought she was a joke.

"How's it going?" Celia Watson said.

"Uhhhhh," Jeff said charismatically.

"What are you doing back here? Working?"

Taking a breath, Jeff finally found the wherewithal to answer in English: "Shelving movies. I mean, I work here."

"This must be a cool place to work." Celia stepped forward, picked up a random DVD show box—*Memento*. She considered it without judgment, as if she didn't recognize the movie, or perhaps knew everything about it, then set it back in place. "Hey, are you the one who put together that nice display of my films at the front of the store?"

Jeff nodded. He was doing everything he could to keep his eyes on Celia and not to scale the Mystery/Suspense section in terror.

"Yes," Jeff said. "I made the display."

"Oh, thanks!" she said genuinely. "I know they're just kids' movies, but thanks."

"So you're in this Match Anderson movie or whatever?" Jeff managed.

"*The Buried Mirror*?"

"And you're filming around here?"

"Yeah," she answered. "Later today on campus. Very pretty, campus. Not much to do at night though, huh?"

He nodded, doubting that there was much to do.

"So you're in college?" she said. "What year?"

"Freshman."

"That makes you eighteen? Me too."

"Cool," he said.

"Anyway," she said. "I hear your boss is taking us out tomorrow night. To a local bar or something. You coming?"

None of which made any sense to Jeff. "Me?" he said.

"Sure. Why not?"

Why not? Dear Lord, was Jeff successfully managing a conversation with Celia Watson? He didn't want to blow it, so he tried to figure out *why not*, to figure out some way that Celia Watson's question was not enthralling. In fact, there were a thousand reasons why not. He was not of legal drinking age. He had never been in a bar. And he knew, if he really dug deep into himself, that he would never be able to maintain this charade and converse at any length with Celia, who was a Hollywood star, whose parents had been Hollywood stars and had thus bestowed upon her a charmed life, and who must not yet have noticed Jeff's acne, or his stupidity, but who was staring at him now, swaying at him, glowing at him, her lips glistening as if covered in magic jelly.

Then he heard Alaura's voice whispering from the front of the store, beautiful Alaura, and he imagined her standing with Match Anderson. Though Alaura was working regular shifts again and organizing the celebrity auction—which would save Star Video— Jeff could not help feeling painfully jealous of Match Anderson, who was ugly and dirty and hardly able to hold a conversation, but who was obviously brilliant or else he would not be a Hollywood director, would never be able to land a girl like Alaura—

Jeff realized that he'd been silent for too long, and he found himself blurting at Celia: "Sure, let's go out!"

Celia's body shook in surprise. Her already large eyes widened even more. "You're cute," she said enthusiastically, as if flirting with an interviewer at a press junket. "Cool. I like tall guys. We'll have fun."

"How's, uhh . . ." Jeff scrambled through the recesses of his consciousness for anything to say. "How's the movie going?"

"The movie?" she said. "Oh, it's fine. I'm thrilled to be in a Tabitha Gray movie, of course. It's a great move for me." Celia looked down at her green dress, which she was worrying at with her tiny fingertips. Her voice lowered. "I think it's going to be great. I *hope* it's going to be great. Match Anderson is, you know, he's great. The screenplay's crazy, though. Really, really crazy. And it's weird, of course, because I'm playing this sexual role. My character has an affair with Alex Walden! Gross, huh? He's ancient. Like forty-five years old. I mean, ew. And overall, honestly, I'm not even sure I understand the screenplay. Do you know the story?"

Jeff shook his head no.

"No?" Celia said, her perfect eyebrows raised. "Apparently your coworker, Alaura whatever-her-name-is, she helped Match write it. She's the one with the tattoos, right?"

"Sure," Jeff said. "She's my friend."

"She's been hanging about with Match, I hear. Staying in his hotel room?"

"I don't know."

"It's just, this celebrity auction thing's a little weird," Celia said. Her voice was now deep and worried, and she was sticking out her lower lip, like a little girl denied her favorite toy. "They're saying the celebrity auction was Alaura's idea, too."

Jeff nodded. He tried to think of a way that the celebrity auction *wasn't* weird, though until just now he'd considered it a brilliant plan.

"It's just, my agent and parents, you know?" Celia went on. "So far, I've only starred in kids' shows and movies. Sure, *The Buried Mirror* is supposed to be my first adulty thing. A big breakout thing, a change of image, et cetera. But still, who's going to bid on me at some celebrity auction? Preverts, that's who."

Jeff found himself chuckling. "Preverts? That's funny. *Dr. Strangelove.*"

Celia giggled, and she swayed toward him. "That's right!" she said brightly.

Then she reached out with her short arm and tiny hand, and she squeezed his forearm.

Jeff felt a cold shock radiate through his entire body.

"You're so cute!" she said.

Looking up at him, she nibbled her lower lip, the same one that had just been puckering out at him.

"I really hope you'll come out tomorrow night," she said softly.

"Uhhhhh," Jeff said again. "Cool."

She turned, looked at him coyly over her small shoulder, and swished toward the front of the store.

Jeff: King of the World.

After Match Anderson left with Tabitha Gray and Celia Watson, all three conveyed in individual SUVs, Waring called a conference with Alaura in *The African Queen*. Alaura surrendered and trudged up the steps carrying a carton of fresh popcorn, though she didn't feel like talking to Waring—she needed to process what had just happened with Match.

For four days, she'd been taking care of her old friend, reconnecting with him late at night when his perpetual director duties went on pause. For four days, they'd hung out and watched movies, like old times, joking and laughing and confessing secrets and sleeping together in his bed, but nothing more than sleeping. But just being with him—and helping him in any way she could—had been enough to bring about, for both of them, she believed, a sense of calm. Match was going to save Star Video. And helping Match had helped *her* shroud the residual shame she felt attached to the Reality Center, of getting lost in something so ridiculous.

The point was, she was really helping Match. She made sure he ate healthy food. She mixed him smoothies and juices. She told him when to take his pills. She'd convinced him to cut down on the bourbon and the cigarettes. The result: He'd told her that he hadn't been seeing Hitchcock nearly as much and that things were going well on set. He hadn't mentioned hallucinating, nor ranted manically, for the past seventy-two hours. She was fairly sure he wasn't sleeping much, but altogether, he seemed to be improving. And there were only eight days left of principal photography. Three days until the celebrity auction at the Siena Hotel. They were almost there.

But then the door to Star Video had opened, and in had walked . . .

"Tabitha Gray," Waring said, his breath especially rank and boozy this afternoon. They settled on *The African Queen*'s crusty couch. "We just met Tabitha Gray," he went on, "which needs to be discussed at length. For example, I couldn't stop staring at her *teeth*, which were, like, perfect."

Alaura devoured a handful of buttery popcorn, which was absolutely delicious.

"And I'm not sure I actually *heard* anything that she actually *said*," Waring went on. "Did you? She was here, wasn't she? I'm not imagining that, right?"

"Is there anything important you want to discuss?" Alaura garbled, her mouth full.

"Yes. So I have to ask you—what the hell was going on with Match?"

She sighed—so Waring had also noticed how suddenly Match's demeanor had changed when Tabitha Gray entered the shop. It was like all the good work Alaura had done dematerialized in an instant. Seeing Tabitha Gray, Match had immediately started sweating, and scratching, and talking too quickly. Tabitha had kissed Match's cheek, and thereafter he had followed her around as if connected by an electrified leash. He'd stared off into space. He'd laughed at all her jokes, which Alaura, like Waring, had barely heard, because Tabitha *was* completely overwhelming.

All at once, Match was wearing that strange, frightening glaze. Alaura knew he was seeing Hitchcock again. She just knew it. And Tabby, somehow, was the catalyst.

"So what's going on there?" Waring asked.

"I don't know. He hasn't really mentioned much to me about Tabitha—"

"It's like he's on drugs," Waring interrupted. "*Is* he on drugs? I'm not used to being more sober than other people."

"Oh," Alaura said. "That."

"What do you mean, *that?* Your boyfriend is one seriously weird dude."

"He's not my boyfriend. And he's not weird. He's stressed out by all his work."

"Is that how he always acts? Is this the guy we're relying on to save my store?"

Alaura picked up the remote control with her butter-smeared hand, turned on *The African Queen*'s flat-screen—but the DVD player was empty.

"Shit, Alaura. What's going on?"

She knew he wouldn't leave her alone about it, because Match had been acting, for his entire visit, and not just after Tabitha Gray's arrival, like a crazy person. And anyway, she *had* to tell someone.

So Alaura confessed to Waring about Match's Hitchcock hallucinations. She told him about Match's rambling monologues, and his speaking about himself in the third person, and his too-frequent aphasiac swaps of actors and actresses who had appeared in Hitchcock films . . . She let it all out, trying to keep her voice down so no one below *The African Queen* would hear.

As she spoke, Waring's scruffy face slackened in astonishment. His bloodshot eyes widened.

"Holy fuck!" Waring said when she finished. He leaned forward and began scrounging the empty cigarette packs on the small coffee table. "I pinky-swear I won't tell a soul, Alaura. But you can't hang out with him anymore. If he's really hallucinating—"

"Keep your voice down. It's fine, Waring. He just needs my help. There's only eight more days of shooting, and then he can get some counseling or whatever. And by helping him, I help Star Video."

A thought that suddenly made Alaura sick to her stomach—that she might be putting Star Video's survival ahead of Match's.

"But if he's hallucinating," Waring said, "if he's seeing Alfred Hitchcock, then he might be dangerous."

"I said keep your voice down! He's not dangerous, Waring. He's a good guy, a *really* good guy who's having a hard time. He's been better these last few days. Almost back to normal. We have fun together, okay? We always did. And I'm just helping him out. Just for another eight days."

Waring had abandoned his cigarette search and was now looking at Alaura with concern—then, when she fell silent, he reached out and took her hand. She did not pull it away.

"It's okay, Alaura," he said with an un-Waxian tenderness that stunned her. "You're right. The celebrity auction's in a few days. We can make it until then. I'll take the cast and crew to a bar tomorrow night. It will probably be best if you occupy Match, keep him at the hotel. Seeing as he's insane. They'll be gone in a few weeks. Match'll be gone, and we'll have the money we need. The end. Simple as pie, right?"

Simple as pie, Alaura thought.

SH** HAPPENED ONE NIGHT

The following night around nine p.m., Waring and company burst into Hell, a basement dive bar in West Appleton. They were a horde of fifty consisting mostly of nerdy crewmembers. The place was empty. For a while, they'd have it to themselves.

"Hell" was in many ways a generous appellation for the bar. For example, the true home of Satan most likely has functional plumbing and doesn't flood every time it rains upon the surface of the earth. But the drinks here were plentiful and cheap. The décor was all retro band posters and demon-themed dioramas. The regular patronage was half blue-collar local, half Ape U literati, and, thankfully, no prepsters. There were four beer-stained pool tables, an air hockey table, and a pompous jukebox for which Super Furry Animals would likely be too mainstream. It was the perfect shitty dive bar into which to bring a Hollywood film crew, if one was hoping to show off how perfect a shitty dive bar can be.

Cigarettes were lit. Drinks were ordered. Waring watched some guy with a braided beard hand Jeff a Red Bull and vodka. Then Jeff walked over to Waring and held out his drink. They cheersed.

Jeff said something that Waring didn't catch, and Waring said, "Go on, have fun, don't get killed."

As Jeff scampered away, the juke sprang to life, blasting an eighties punk song and leading quickly to a small, arrhythmic dance party. Soon the crew had divided into age groups, twentysomethings, thirtysomethings, and older. Only the actors maneuvered between the groups, materializing for a few minutes to command attention, to tell a dirty joke, to degrade a crewmember for some physical or social shortcoming, only to then apologize with jocular camaraderie, thus cementing a new friendship for life. And while the actors were the revolving torrents of light in the otherwise dank space of Hell, the mood, Waring noticed, was one of equality, of, "We're all in this movie together." The few heated squabbles that broke out (inevitable with such a high concentration of creative minds) ended as quickly as they began.

Celia Watson was there, wearing a ridiculously skimpy white dress. Alex Walden was there, too. So were a few of *The Buried Mirror*'s lesser-known actors. Even Tabitha Gray made an appearance, but only for five minutes, accompanied by five bodyguards, before retreating quickly to her SUV.

Waring watched the scene from the corner of the small room. He sat alone at a dirty black booth constructed from cheap plywood, and he started on a crossword puzzle, a pint of dark, hoppy beer in his left hand. He took in a mouthful of the beer, winced as he gulped it down.

Alaura wasn't here. She was with Match at the Siena. Waring had instructed her (and for once she had obeyed him) to stay with Match that night, thinking that Match in public could only lead to disaster, such as the cancellation of the celebrity auction, and Star Video losing its ridiculous, gimmicky chance for survival.

But what does it matter? Waring thought. Even if the celebrity auction was a rousing success, which was a big *if*, they'd probably lose the eminent domain battle in court anyway.

Everything was falling apart. What the hell was Waring going to do?

"Our noble host!" a voice cried. Waring looked up. It was Alex Walden, who had just detached from a group of dorky, giggling makeup artists playing pool on the corner table, and who was now strutting toward Waring's booth.

Alex Walden—a big actor with a big voice and a big reputation as a drinker and a yeller. Recently he'd been arrested for public intoxication in Canada, Waring remembered, and in his now-infamous mug shot, Walden had grinned like he'd wanted to kiss the camera, or eat it.

He now turned the same expression on Waring.

"You look grim, my friend," Walden smiled.

Without thinking, Waring retorted: "And you look older than ever."

"Ouch!" Alex Walden laughed loudly, a yawp that drew the attention of half the bar. "A dagger to my heart! Your name is Waring, correct?"

"Mm."

Walden took a seat across the booth, and without asking, he removed a cigarette from Waring's pack, lit it with Waring's lighter.

"Help yourself," Waring said.

"Tell me, what *is* the deal with deep-fried sandwiches in this town?"

"Mm?"

"Every where I go, every take-out menu, its deep-fried turkey sandwich this, deep-fried bacon sandwich that. Deep-fried custard sandwiches sprinkled with powdered sugar? I actually saw that on a menu. What the hell, man?"

Waring shrugged, didn't answer, wondered how many deep-fried sandwiches that Walden saw had ultimately reached his belly. Walden was not as thin as he used to be. He had recently made the transition from features to television comedy, a definite backslide in his career, and his waistline showed it.

"We don't fry like this in California," Walden explained, still smiling his million-dollar smile.

"Methinks the fat man protests too much."

Alex produced a Technicolor eye twinkle, studied Waring for a moment. In a low voice, he said, "I like you, sir. You say what you mean."

"Is that rare?"

"Of course. No one's honest in Hollywood."

"Next thing you'll say is that I'm *real*," Waring said with a sneer. "That you don't meet *real* people anymore."

"Ha! That's what I mean! I'm envious of you, my friend."

"Mm."

Waring lit a cigarette of his own. Walden looked off into the bar, still chuckling to himself, his internationally known profile—like an exquisitely designed mountain range unmarred by caloric intake—displayed perfectly for Waring's viewing.

Of course the celebrity's presence intimidated Waring. It had simply taken a few moments for this intimidation to register. And that Alex Walden seemed, at least for now, to find Waring entertaining excited him more than a little. But after spending a few stuttering minutes in Tabitha Gray's presence the day before, and seeing that she, like all human beings, was made of flesh and blood—if perhaps a more expensive vintage of those basic commodities—Waring for some reason wasn't as nervous as he knew he should be. Waring could look at Alex Walden (and it was hard *not* to look), and he could see the actor's many iconic characters: the noble CIA operative aboard the stolen Russian submarine, the evil doctor, the manipulative and sadistic real estate salesman . . .

But Alex Walden was still *just a man*.

Or was he? That Waring was thinking about him this much, and was thus unable to maintain his normal thought patterns . . . maybe there was something intrinsically *more* about Alex Walden. So Waring decided to maintain his sneering expression, and with forced boredom, he looked down at the table in front of him, where he'd forgotten that he'd been working a crossword.

People always tell you to be yourself around celebrities—so Waring would continue to be himself.

"Know any jokes?" Alex Walden said.

"No jokes," Waring grunted. "I intend to get drunk tonight. That's all."

"Cheers to that. Perhaps I'll get drunk with you."

"Suit yourself."

And even though another ripple of giddy nervousness passed through Waring, he stifled it with a sip of dark beer.

Alaura and Match were lying in bed, in Match's hotel room at the Siena. They were on top of the sheets, fully clothed. A movie played on his gigantic television: Truffaut's *Bed and Board*.

Over the past few days, Alaura had cleaned the room. She'd picked up various papers off the floor and had done her best to organize them. She'd thrown away all the take-out cartons from Lee's Chinese, Pizza My Heart, etc. And she'd even, that night, forced Match to shave. He'd been reluctant, but submissive, and the result, unfortunately, was a too-great revelation of his jowls, giving him a Peter Jackson look that would have been better left masked by a full beard.

"Match?" Alaura said.

Match's eyes were closed. He hadn't spoken in quite some time.

"You're not drinking the juice I ordered you, Match."

"I'm not thirsty."

"Did you take your pills?"

"Yes."

"You're not watching the movie."

He sighed. "I'm listening to it," he said. "It's nice just to listen, even though I don't speak French. But if I open my eyes, I see him.

Hitchcock. And I have to prepare for tomorrow. Mentally prepare. We've got a big scene to shoot."

"But . . . I thought you weren't seeing Hitchcock as much."

"Oh," he said, and he opened his right eye to glance at her.

His face was so sweaty that it looked like he'd just swam in the hotel pool. His one-thousand-thread-count pillowcase was soaked.

"I wasn't being completely honest about that," Match said, his voice strained. Then he closed his right eye. "I *have* been seeing Hitchcock. But I knew you didn't want me to. I'm sorry."

She shivered.

Had she been any help to him at all?

"Why didn't you tell me?" she asked.

"Because I have a lot on my mind, Alaura. There's just seven days left of principal photography. One week. But it's a big day on set tomorrow. A big scene for Tippi Hedren."

Alaura took a breath. "Do you mean Tabitha Gray?"

"Huh?"

"You said Tippi Hedren," she said, her voice a bit frightened. "But I think you mean Tabitha Gray."

Long pause. All at once, Alaura wanted more than anything to escape. To be back at Star Video, working the floor, talking about movies with customers, giving Waring a hard time.

"Match?" she finally said.

"Yes."

"Can I ask you a question?"

"Okay."

"I've noticed that whenever Tabitha Gray is around, you start getting, I don't know, different."

"I do?"

"Yes," she said.

Match rubbed his forehead, did not open his eye again. "Whenever I see Tabitha, whenever I even think about her, things get kind of fuzzy. I don't know why. I'm sorry. I'm tired. I want you here, Alaura. You're helping me. You know I love you. We're friends."

Alaura sat up on the bed. She shook her head. "I'm not sure you realize how confusing that all sounds, Match." She reached across her body with both hands and massaged both shoulders. "I'm really worried about you, Match."

"It's fine. Honestly, seeing Hitchcock . . . it sort of, it relaxes me. I like seeing him."

Another breath escaped her. "You *like* hallucinating?"

"Well, it's just that, you know, it feels like I'm in a movie. Which feels good."

Now she was tearing up. "Oh, Match, please don't say that." Nothing she'd done had changed anything. "Match, if you say things like that, I'll have to call your brother. I'll have to call Finn."

"Just seven more days," Match muttered. Now he was scratching his chest, as if harboring fleas. "But wouldn't that be wonderful, Alaura? To *live* in a movie. Before they all go away. To jump inside a movie and live in it forever."

Alaura covered her face with her hands. She thought she might explode. Finn was apparently flying to North Carolina soon. Maybe Finn could help.

"Please, Match," she said. "Just rest."

"I'm sorry," Match said—though he didn't sound sorry. "I'll stop."

"Just rest now, Match. You need to sleep. Keep your eyes closed. If you sleep, you'll feel better."

She reached out and stroked his sweaty forehead.

For some reason, Alex Walden was talking about his parents; Waring did not know how the subject had come up—he certainly wouldn't have brought it up himself.

"My old man was a champ," Walden rambled in a Mickey-to-Rocky grumble. "A class-A champ. He worked the Hollywood system, you know. Didn't have the looks to be a star, but he mastered his craft and clawed his way into bit parts, eked out a living on the stage. You've never heard of him—"

"I own a video store, sir," Waring interrupted, somehow employing playful condescension. "I've heard of your father."

"Bullshit."

So Waring quickly listed the all the films he could remember that featured George Walden, a supporting actor for his entire career. The list reached ten movies, twelve, and as Waring spoke, Alex Walden leaned back in his seat, raised a clenched fist to his wounded heart.

"He was good," Waring concluded. "Even in commercials, he was good."

"That's right, my friend. Even in commercials. He was an asshole son of a bitch, but he could act his way out of a paper bag—"

"Unlike most people in the business."

"That's fucking-A right."

Alex Walden and Waring shared a long, significant stare.

"What about your pops?" Walden asked.

Waring belched, looked stage left.

"Come on, Mr. Wax. I get it, you aren't the type to get all weepy."

"Am I still *real* if I'm not weepy?"

"Fuck you, Waring, you magnificent bastard!" Alex Walden pounded the table. "This is what men do! We sit and drink and say meaningful things about our fathers!"

Waring shook his head. "Fine," he said. "My father was a prick. A distant but demanding prick. He pushed me into finance, when all I really wanted to do was be a fuck-up and study film. He wanted me to get married, have kids, have a good job. The complete Manhattan storyline. So I tried that for a while, for quite a few years, but, well, you see where that got me."

Waring held out his hands to his sides: *This* is where it got me.

"And your mother?" Alex Walden said—his gaze was fixed and intent, engrossed in everything he was hearing.

Waring took a deep drag of his cigarette. He thought of his mother, the failed actress. How she'd gotten pregnant too young, and how his father had thereafter talked her out of pursuing her acting ambitions. How she had never forgiven his father, and how she'd never been happy again, not for a second, except at the movies, with Waring.

"No," Waring said. "I'm leaving."

In utter astonishment, Alex Walden laughed. He called out: "And I'm coming with you!"

Waring and Alex Walden and Walden's three bodyguards walked up the slope of Henderson Street, past the thirty-foot-long mural of a yellow number 2 pencil, toward the main drag of College. The bodyguards made Waring feel like he was visiting a politician in a war zone—but the man was not a politician, he was Alex Walden, and the two of them were joking, laughing, talking about movies. Walden clearly loved Hollywood. He referenced movies like a veteran video store employee, and he provided unbelievable insider tidbits about actors and filmmakers, people whom he had worked with over the years. But he also listened to Waring, egged Waring to tell him more about Appleton, about Ape U, about the history of this small town and about Waring's individual history, as if this place and this precious moment on College Street were worthy of study. And though Waring suspected, knew, that Alex was simply gathering material, either for *The Buried Mirror* or for some other movie, he didn't care—Alex Walden was laughing with him, and laughing genuinely.

They turned onto College Street, and in the distance, Waring saw a crowd of stick-figure college students waiting outside of bars. As they approached the first line, in front of a shoddy West Appleton dance club called Olive or Twist known to serve underage drinkers, Walden continued talking to Waring and asking questions and listening with rapt interest and smiling, but Waring could see how faces from the passing mass began to turn in their direction.

The first of them to approach was a group of three sorority girls, eighteen if they were a day, and gorgeous. Excitedly they asked, all in unison,

"Oh my God, are you— are you—"

"Yes," Alex Walden replied, smiling congenially.

And soon a swarm was upon them. The bodyguards were pressing people away, and though Walden and Waring continued to make progress up College Street, Waring sensed a sort of choreography about all this, how hands holding pens and bar napkins were allowed to straggle over for Alex Walden to sign, a torture to which he submitted with much humility, and how boys and girls ran in front of them and while backpedaling took pictures of the throng with cell phones, pictures of which Alex was the primary subject, centered in the frame as he often was on celluloid or digital video. There was even a hint of falsity in how Alex repeatedly apologized to Waring for this inconvenience (with a chagrinned smile). But Waring didn't care. The bodyguards repeatedly muscled the two of them together, protecting them from being ripped to shreds, and Waring was speechless, completely unable to step out of the moment, to look at it from above, to see the ways in which any of this was ugly, because he could not find a single ugly thing about it.

Meanwhile, Jeff had been adopted by the crew of *The Buried Mirror*. All of them, every single one, were film nerds. Their referencing abilities were off the charts. The guy with the braided beard, whose name was Delaine and who was *The Buried Mirror*'s Best Boy, had apparently taken on the role of looking after the young video store clerk. So Jeff sat at the bar with Delaine and several other guys from the lighting team, and they talked, and they laughed, and they drank.

They bought Jeff drink after drink. They regaled him with stories from shoots around the world, with star gossip, with elaborate self-hyping descriptions of their upcoming projects. Several of the lighting guys would be on B crew for a new Spielberg movie ("A comedy," one of them said, "A guaranteed bomb!"), but most would be working on independent productions for little or no money. They spoke of Los Angeles with off-handed reverence, as if it were a golden city. They didn't ask Jeff very many questions, but he didn't mind, because he was happy just to be in their presence, to absorb their passion. What most impressed Jeff, as he studied them, was that they seemed completely at peace with who they were. None of them were attractive, all of them were chubby and poorly dressed, but they carried themselves like visiting dignitaries. Every move they made, every word they spoke, implied that *The Buried Mirror* was paying them well and that they were emotionally invested in completing it and that they had no regrets about the course their lives had taken.

If only Jeff could find something to be so passionate about.

After three drinks, Jeff was feeling tipsy. He'd been drunk before, a few times in Murphy with his redneck cousins, as well as that one night, not long ago, at Alaura's apartment. It was nice to be feeling that again: like a warm blanket wrapped around his neck. He hadn't worked up the courage to insert himself into Delaine's conversation, but he was more than happy to laugh along with their stories. And he found himself laughing louder than he'd have ever thought was socially acceptable.

A bit later, Jeff felt a small weight on his right shoulder. A hand. It was Celia Watson. He realized that he had stopped looking around for her, stopped following her with his gaze as she moved from group to group around the room . . . his attention had half-drunkenly lapsed into conversing with these cool guys. Now he smiled at her. Celia was wearing a white tube dress that ended high on her thighs and low on her chest, that held her body like a latex glove, and that was way too expensive for a bar in Ehle County called Hell. But her smile was as cool and casual as everyone's in the lighting crew.

Celia was speaking to him. But Jeff could barely hear her voice over the roar of the bar:

". . . come . . . you . . . outside."

"Whuh?" Jeff slurred.

Celia turned and walked away.

Jeff was a lot of things, but he wasn't a total idiot. He stood up, zeroed in on Celia Watson's amazing figure, and advanced through a neon stream of bar lights and faces and laughter.

He heard Delaine call out behind him, "Go get her, champ!"

Which was followed by a room-wide whip of laughter.

Jeff followed Celia's path out of Hell's exit, then up the stairs to street level. A moment later, he deposited himself against a brick wall in the dark alleyway above the bar.

Celia's tiny, hourglass form consumed his entire field of vision.

"Hi there," he said.

"I thought we could have some privacy up here," she said.

"Privacy. Sweet."

Jeff looked around. They were standing in what was little more than a brick cave. A ratty juniper tree sprouted from a small patch of earth to his left. A Dumpster to his right reeked of shrimp.

"So what's *The Buried Mirror* about exactly?" he managed to pronounce.

Celia rolled her eyes. "I really have no idea," she said. He pulled her into sharper focus. She was standing less than three feet away from him. "I was actually hoping you could tell me."

"Huh?"

She ran a small hand through her long, perfectly styled blonde-white hair.

"Things have been kind of bizarre on set," she said. "Has your friend Alaura said anything about Match?"

"About Match?"

"I mean, if it was just a weird screenplay, but the director was acting like a sane person, then I don't think I'd be worried. But it's like he's on acid, all the time."

Jeff found himself laughing, which he knew was inappropriate, given the situation.

She placed the tip of her forefinger on his lips. "Hush," she whispered. "You don't have to say anything if you don't want to."

"What?"

"But will you do me a favor?"

Anything! he thought.

"If I take a picture of the two of us making out," she said, "will you post it on your Facebook page?"

Now laughter would have been appropriate, but Jeff couldn't laugh. He looked down at Celia Watson. He noticed that she was holding an iPhone. And she was nibbling again on her lower lip.

"Make out?" he said.

"Yes," she said.

"Take pictures?"

"Yes."

"I think it would be physically impossible for me to say *no*," Jeff said.

A second later, Celia Watson had pulled Jeff down by his shirt, and she was sticking her small tongue into his mouth. At first Jeff staggered, but then he gained control of his senses, and he took Celia into his arms. Her mouth was cool and minty. He worried, for some reason, about smearing her makeup. He heard a clicking sound, which he determined to be her phone, held out at arm's length and capturing photos of their tryst. He heard blood rushing through his ears. He reached down and, like he'd seen in movies, placed a hand on the small of her back. He pulled her against him.

He wanted to pick her up. He wanted to take her to bed. He felt her teeth on his lower lip, just like she had been nibbling on her own.

Then she pulled away.

"This is perfect!" she said. "You're a good kisser, by the way."

Jeff's eyes opened. Celia was looking down at her iPhone. She was scrolling through the photos she had just taken.

"These are *awe*some," she said. "Thanks, Jeff."

He was giddy that she remembered his name, though his body felt ripped apart because he was no longer touching her.

"You wanna kiss some more?" he said, not caring how stupid he sounded.

"Oh," she said, and she looked up from her phone. "Well, the thing is, I have a boyfriend."

"What?"

"Zac Efron, the actor? I'm sure you've heard of him."

"Oh," Jeff said, nodding as he took this in.

Celia was now performing for Jeff a pitying look, but she spoke politely, sincerely: "I'm sorry, Jeff. The thing is, my agent and I thought it would be a good idea to, you know, put some pictures of me partying out on the Internet, you know? Because I'm about to do this adult movie, with sex in it and everything. I need to alter my image. But I don't want anything more."

"No," Jeff said, looking down at the scuzzy alleyway under his feet. "No, that makes total sense."

"So if I e-mail you these pictures, will you post them for me? I mean, I doubt it'll even make *Entertainment Tonight*, but we should still try, right?"

Jeff nodded. He felt his soul being shredded. He gave her his Ape U e-mail address, and he looked down at her as she sent off an e-mail with the pictures attached.

Then she turned to walk back into Hell.

He called out to her, "Celia!"—three syllables forced into a desperate, descending plea.

She turned back.

But Jeff realized, as he had feared all along, that he had absolutely nothing worthwhile to say to Celia Watson.

They stared at each other for a long time.

Finally he blurted: "So I hear Match Anderson is hallucinating. Weird, huh?"

Celia Watson eyed him with her huge, famous eyes. "What?" she said. "What are you talking about?"

"Match Anderson is seeing things. Like a crazy person."

"What do you mean?"

Jeff thought about it—yes, this was all true. He was not making it up. "I overheard Alaura talking with my boss," he explained. "After you guys left Star Video yesterday."

Celia nodded. "And?"

"And Alaura said that Match is, I don't know, seeing the ghost of Alfred Hitchcock."

Celia's eyes widened. "Is that fucking true?"

Jeff managed a nod.

She stepped toward him. He froze. She reached up with both hands, placed her palms gently on his checks, and guided him down. She kissed him, this time with her mouth closed, this time soft and sweet.

Then, before he knew what was happening, she had turned her back to him again—he wanted her to stay, he wanted to put his arms around her. But his mouth had gone limp and useless.

A moment later, she was gone.

Jeff closed his eyes, phased into another dimension—all he wanted was to hold her. Maybe lose his virginity, sure, but just holding Celia would have been enough.

He stood in the alleyway, wobbling like a flagpole in the wind.

. . .

Two a.m., Star Video. The bodyguards mumbled downstairs while Waring and Alex Walden sat in *The African Queen*, drinking. Walden smoked a fat cigar, and they watched *Charade*, starring Audrey Hepburn and Cary Grant, because three times that evening Walden had pronounced the phrase "Cary Grant was a god." So Waring had listed as many Grant movies from Star Video's catalogue as he could, and when Walden had confessed that he hadn't seen *Charade*, Waring had guffawed and said, "You're fucking kidding me, you've never seen *Charade*?"

So they watched and marveled and laughed together at the immaculate banter between Hepburn and Grant.

Later, Waring caught something on the screen.

"Hey," he said, and like an old pal he elbowed Alex Walden, who had just nodded off to sleep.

Walden snorted awake.

"Looksie who it is," Waring said. Using the remote, he rewound the movie a few seconds. Hepburn and Grant, over coffee on a Parisian riverboat, were engaged in yet another witty exchange. Their young waiter, whose head slid into view only for a moment—a moment barely long enough for Waring to capture with the "Pause" button—was George Walden, Alex's father.

"Shit," Alex Walden said, sitting up straighter. "I didn't know he was in this."

Waring watched Walden. The actor's face was oddly blank, but there was a crumpling of the skin below his mouth—Waring had seen this expression before, in countless movies: this was one of the subtle ways Alex Walden conveyed sadness.

"I didn't know he was in this," Walden repeated.

Then his head rolled back onto the couch cushion, and his eyelids fell shut.

Waring lit a cigarette, his last of the night. He removed Alex's smoldering cigar from his fingers and set it in the ashtray. Then a boozy tide rocked him forward until his elbows rested on his knees.

How, Waring wondered, had Alex Walden not known that his own father had an uncredited role in *Charade*? It was exhilarating, he thought, to have been the one to deliver this information.

But there are always truths rippling beneath the surface, clamoring to break into our awareness, yet we do not see them. Not all movie revelations are bullshit plot devices. And again Waring thought of that plane ride, twelve years ago, how he had bitched and moaned to the guy sitting next to him about how *unreal* it was for his wife to have left him—and he thought about the hotel room—why rehash this now?—Waring did not know. It was probably because Star Video might be saved and Alex Walden, celebrity, was Waring's new drinking buddy—it was probably because for once, if Waring let himself, he could feel good—but what fucking right did he have to feel good?

In the hotel room, drunk, after the disastrous interview in Charlotte, the phone rings. The caller is Waring's wife. He tries to hide that he is overjoyed to hear from her, but she has called with single-minded purpose—and with false excitement he begs her to go right ahead, to explain everything, especially the "Dear John" note currently residing on his hotel bed stand, transported with him from New York, read hundreds of times. She explains. She tells him that she has wanted a divorce for years. She tells him that he has failed her in every way. She hates his drinking and his constant television watching. She tells him he is horrible in bed and that she has seen a doctor and *he* must be the one who is infertile. She tells him his money isn't enough. And finally she confirms what Waring already suspects, that she has been sleeping with his former boss, Ethan, and that is why Ethan had him fired, and that she is moving in with Ethan, and they are starting a family right away.

The emotion of the moment was painfully vivid—he'd rarely recalled it through the years, he'd successfully avoided reliving it, but it had remained unaltered, sharp, noxious. His wife. Helena. They hadn't spoken since the divorce.

But what if Helena could see him *now*? Sitting in his wonderful, crappy video store?

She would laugh at him. She would take one look at Star Video and roll her eyes and laugh and thank her lucky stars that she had gotten out while the getting was good. The only person who thought this crappy video store was wonderful was Alaura, whom Helena would also, he knew, dismiss with searing displeasure.

No one cared about Star Video. There had been no community movement to save his store. Like his marriage, the video store's time had passed.

He nursed the hurt of it.

He sucked hard on his cigarette.

What was he supposed to do with his life?

Everything in the universe—technology, finances, local government, everything—was pointing him away from Star Video. But he had no idea *where* they were pointing. He looked off into the black space of his shop—the dusty warehouse ceiling, the rectangular gridded lights, all of it dark.

Then his attention turned again to *Charade*. Beautiful Audrey Hepburn, the most enchanting creature ever to live.

A dream blazing in the darkness.

MATCH POINT

At six a.m. that morning, there was a knock on Match Anderson's hotel room door. Match was showering in preparation for that day's big shoot, and when Alaura answered the knock, a young male intern asked her to come downstairs on an urgent matter. Alaura dressed quickly, followed the intern, and was led into the small conference room where she had been reunited with Match a week before. And like a week before, she was instructed to sit and wait.

Five minutes. Ten minutes. Twenty.

Finally a woman wearing a slate-colored business suit entered, and she introduced herself as a [name of film studio omitted] executive—Alaura did not catch the woman's name or her specific title at first. But the woman meant business. She was short and boney, had the sunken cheeks of a corpse or a vegan—a female Harry Dean Stanton. Alaura was too confused to be scared.

"You've been spending a lot of time with Mr. Anderson?" asked the executive, who stood stiffly in the middle of the small room, arms crossed, looking down at Alaura.

"Yes," Alaura said.

"Sleeping here every night?"

Alaura gulped. "I don't think that's your business."

"I'm the executive producer of *The Buried Mirror*, so everything is my business."

Trying to counter the woman's rude aggressiveness, Alaura said quickly, "I want to go back to Match's room."

Harry Dean Stanton squinted, and her voice lowered. "Is there something you want to tell me, Ms. Eden?"

How did Harry Dean Stanton know her name? Looking around the room, Alaura wondered if she was being Punk'd. Doubtful, she decided. "What are you talking about, ma'am?"

"I think you know what I'm talking about."

"Aren't you listening to me?" Alaura said—a tremor had entered her voice. "I don't know what you're talking about."

"Ms. Eden, are you aware of any mental problems that Mr. Anderson is currently experiencing?"

At this, Alaura shrunk in her chair. Her face warmed over, her stomach curled. "No," she finally managed. "I'm not aware of any . . . problems."

Harry Dean Stanton nodded, and she left the conference room without another word. A moment later, Alaura was escorted back to Match's room, where she found Match sitting dumbfounded on his bed. He was wearing a blue bathrobe, like Bill Murray, she thought, in *Lost in Translation*. His hair was still wet from showering, and on his feet were wedged two cheap hotel sandals. The bathrobe hung from his shoulders like a towel on hooks, and it pooled in a mass of fabric atop his potbelly. He did not seem to have noticed her entry into the room.

"It's all over," he said, gazing at the floor with an oddly beseeching look, as if he expected the carpet to answer.

"What do you mean?"

"I think I need a lawyer. Have you spoken to a lawyer?"

Alaura did not understand—why would *anyone* need a lawyer? "No," she said. Then, almost as a joke: "Have *you* spoken to a lawyer?"

"No." His gaze moved from floor to ceiling, slowly. "I took some phone calls. But except for Hitch, I haven't *seen* anybody since they took you away."

Alaura closed her eyes, but only for a moment—she threw back her shoulders and nodded resolutely. "Match, I talked to this woman who said she was your executive producer—"

"Oh, man, *she's* here?"

"Yes. She's a bit intimidating. She mentioned something about . . . about mental problems. But I didn't say anything. She didn't mention Hitchcock, so I think if we just say that you're mentally exhausted or something, then maybe we could avoid—"

"Thank you," he said breathily, as if relieved—but he added, "Don't worry about it."

"What?"

"We'll work it out. We'll place a call, get things rolling."

"We?" Alaura said. Did he mean his brother? Tabitha Gray? Hitchcock?

"I don't need your help, Alaura."

She stood up, but she sat back down immediately. "No," she said weakly. "I want to help you."

"Don't get involved in this." Match looked at her directly for the first time since she had reentered the room. "You're too good for all this, Alaura. For me. I'm going to quit the movie."

Around Alaura, the walls of the room seemed to shudder.

"But why? The celebrity auction, Match. We need the celebrity auction to save Star Video. You promised."

Match interlaced his slender fingers, pushed his fingertips back and forth over the tendrils on the backs of his hands. "I'm a terrible director," he said, as if that made any sense.

She tensed her legs, tensed her arms—willing herself to stay calm. "No you're not, Match. You're a great director. You're just having a rough time right now. It's just exhaustion. That's what we'll tell her. We can get through this."

"No, we can't."

"Tell me the truth, Match. What's going on?"

Match rolled his spindly shoulders, and he reached up with his bony hands and massaged his puffy, recently shaved face. His eyes were large, bloodshot. His chest seemed concave, and he breathed quickly, deeply, almost panting, as if possessed by the demon in *The Exorcist*.

"What's going on," he said, "is that I got a call this morning, before you woke up. It was my agent. He told me that he could no longer represent me because of some rumors. I don't know what rumors exactly. Though I can guess. I don't know how the secret got out. I thought only Finn knew about Hitchcock, and I doubt he would tell the studio. But he must have. Or the doctor in New York. Or you, Alaura." He shook his head. "But I know *you* didn't tell anyone. I just don't understand."

Alaura covered her mouth with a tense hand; had Waring mentioned Hitchcock to someone? No, she thought. Impossible. Not even Waring was that stupid.

"We just have to make it another few days," she said. "The celebrity auction, Match. Star Video."

Silence. Tears swelled in her eyes for a moment. But Match did not notice.

She heard Match mumble something.

"What?" she said, looking back.

"I said perhaps it's for the best."

"The best? How is quitting the movie for the best? How the hell is giving up for the best?"

"Because I'm exhausted, Alaura. I'm so tired. Even if I don't quit, they'll fire me. No matter what. They're going to take *The Buried Mirror* away from me."

"They?"

"The studio. Everyone will know about Hitchcock. It'll be on Twitter and the blogs by this afternoon. And then it'll follow me forever. Everyone will know I went crazy—"

"Match!" she said, trying to curtail his wandering mind.

"And it's a relief, really. That I'm quitting."

"No."

"Because it's shit, isn't it? This movie is just shit. It's my fault, Alaura. It's a terrible screenplay. I'm sorry to admit it, but it is. I've just been working on it too long. They'll finish it. They'll film in California somewhere, on a shoestring, and release it. They never wanted to come to North Carolina in the first place. But the movie will bomb. I know bombs. I've already directed a few. *The Buried Mirror* is a bomb."

Alaura stood, almost leaping from the bed, and she walked to the far side of the room to the big bay window. Outside the window sprawled several beautiful homes: Appleton's Historic District mansions, where family fortunes as old as the hills churned and turned and tumbled, always making more money, always growing, while those damn beautiful houses stayed exactly the same.

"Take it," he said, and she turned back to him, saw him pointing to his cluttered desk where a tattered copy of *The Buried Mirror* screenplay lay. "Read it," he went on. "It's a terrible, barely functional screenplay. And it's the best I could do. And anyway, Alaura, what's the point? I'm asking myself, not you. What's the point? Of any movie? Simple characters. Ridiculous circumstances. Pseudorealities where everyone is beautiful and everyone speaks perfectly and says perfectly interesting things, and no loose ends allowed, unless they're interesting loose ends, when who are we but the summation of our loose ends? And even when movies are at their best, when they're artful or challenging or original, they're still just a way for the audience to forget how shitty the world is, to experience something that resembles real emotion, only to be returned safely. Movies are a drug, a sedative. We trade in a controlled substance. You watch a movie and laugh and cry and jump in fear, and your brain thinks it has experienced something real. But it's bullshit, it's all a mirage—"

"No!" she yelled. "Stop it, Match. Movies are—"

"Movies are dying, Alaura. That's the truth. Every year, box office numbers go down. It's a dying industry. Everyone in Hollywood knows it. No one says it, but we all know. It's not just video stores, it's the movies, too."

"Match," she said softly. She recrossed the room and dropped to her knees in front of him—she couldn't give up—not yet—not on Match. "You *are* a good director," she pleaded, setting her hands on his legs, squeezing the fabric of his bathrobe. "You just have to stick with it. Your movies help people. They've helped me. They really have. Movies are important, Match. They are! You're a good director."

"That isn't true," he said.

"Yes, it is."

The door to Match's hotel room opened—the female executive with dead eyes, Harry Dean Stanton, entered.

Alaura returned to the bed beside Match.

"Mr. Anderson," Harry Dean Stanton began, taking position in the center of the room. Her feet were shoulder-width apart, hands clasped behind her back. "Thank you for your patience. Let me begin, Match, by saying how sorry we are for this inconvenience. But we've received some information that we must take seriously. In the simplest terms, Match, we have been informed that you're hallucinating, seeing the dead film director Alfred Hitchcock."

"Oh, I see," Match said—his voice now weirdly calm, composed.

"Yes, very strange," the executive said. "Please understand that I'm not asking you whether this rumor is true, though if you choose to tell me that it's true, I'd be required to report that information to the studio. Insurance, obviously, is a major issue. Fortunately we have an indemnity for cases such as this, which we're now being forced to exercise. But if you are deemed mentally unfit and were to continue directing, we'd lose our insurance. Not to mention that someone hallucinating is not terribly likely to direct a profitable movie. Also not to mention that the buzz from your dailies has been, frankly, unbuzzworthy. Legally, I think we'll have no problem removing you from the picture, though of course an arbitration procedure is more than within your rights—"

But Alaura couldn't follow Harry Dean Stanton's words—this was all too dreamlike. How had they learned about Hitchcock? Why wasn't Match trying to defend himself?

And was there any way to keep the celebrity auction going?

"—and we expect your decision within the hour," Harry Dean Stanton concluded some time later. "I'm sorry, Match. Thank you for your cooperation."

Harry Dean Stanton left the room.

Alaura turned to Match. "Okay," she said, regaining her composure. "Everything's fine. We'll call a lawyer. We'll find out how this rumor started, and we'll refute it. We'll go to arbitration or something. I'll tell them whatever I need to tell them—"

"No," he said. "I've made my decision. It's best if I resign."

Alaura's breath left her; her chest twisted into a painful void.

"They'll cancel the shoot in Appleton," he said. "I'm sure of it. The production will leave North Carolina, probably by tomorrow. It's all over."

"Over? But what about Star Video?" she said, her voice cracking.

Match did not respond. He simply stared off at nothing in that singularly vacant way of his, lost in his own crazy thoughts, seeing Hitchcock, totally unmoved by her pleading mention of Star Video. He didn't give a shit. He had never given a shit. He had just wanted to keep her around, to use her for her company, just hoping to finish the movie.

She stood up, spotted the small suitcase she'd brought with her to the hotel, on the floor by the bed. But she decided to leave it. Then she saw the mangled manuscript of *The Buried Mirror* on Match's desk.

"I'm leaving, Match," she said.

"Do you . . . do you really like my movies?" Match asked pitifully, his huge, bloodshot eyes wavering up to face her.

She felt her heart sink into her stomach. She was close to tears. She wanted to tell him to go to hell, that he had ruined everything, that giving up on the movie, and on Star Video, meant giving up on her.

But then she caught her own reflection in a gilded mirror on the wall. She was surprised to see the angry expression there. The rage that twisted her face. She couldn't believe how ugly she looked.

She took a deep breath.

Then she walked to the desk, picked up the copy of *The Buried Mirror*, and walked toward the door, where she stopped and turned back to him.

"Yes, Match," she said, knowing that she could completely decimate him now, but also knowing she didn't want to. "You're a very good director. Never forget that. I hope things work out for you. I'm sure they will. Don't . . . don't give up. But now I need to go, okay?"

"But Alaura, I'd really like it if you—"

"I'm sorry, Match."

And instead of slamming the door, as she had intended to do seconds earlier, she closed the door slowly. It clicked shut quietly behind her.

INTO GREAT SILENTS

That morning, Jeff walked across Appleton University's campus toward the central library. The air was cool, and Jeff noticed that a few branches of the university's mighty oaks were tipped with russet. Summer was a distant memory. Autumn was here. It was a Wednesday, and those students who had foolishly signed up for early morning courses were now stumbling, like confused ants, into buildings.

Jeff had class, too. But his thoughts were too scattered to even consider it.

He entered the five-story yellow-brick library, which was one of the newer buildings on campus, and he quickly made his way up the elevator to the glitzy computer lab. He wished that he'd been able to upload the pictures from Celia Watson with the ancient laptop he'd inherited from his cousin, but the machine had a terribly slow Internet port, so he knew he could only get the important work done at the library's computer lab.

He walked around a corner, saw the long bank of IBMs, several of them attended by tired-looking students who had probably been working all night. He found an empty station, sat down.

The photos of him kissing Celia Watson were undeniably real. He had not dreamt it. You could see her face, clear as day. His hands clawed at her white dress. Her tongue was in his mouth. Her perfect little breasts were pressed into him. Her tanned arm, stretching out to hold her phone, constituted a quarter of each frame.

Now, sitting in the computer lab, he couldn't help laughing. He doubted that anything so amazing would ever happen to him again, and fortunately, he had photographic evidence to back it up.

He quickly uploaded the photos to his Facebook page, along with the tag: "Yep, this is me and the beautiful Celia Watson, living the dream."

Then he opened another window, and he signed up for a Twitter account. He had no idea what Twitter was, or how it worked, because it had only been around for a few months. But he'd heard all the kids on campus talking about it. So he created a profile, uploaded the photos, and waited for the world to take notice.

A few minutes later, Jeff logged off the computer, walked out of the library into the cool autumn air, and headed toward Star Video. He was scheduled to work later that morning.

Jeff crossed Star Video's parking lot—lost in thought, lost in another replay of Celia Watson's body against his—and he stepped up to the shop's front door. The white sun hung like an amulet, low in the sky, and it reflected brightly against the shop's front windows. But when Jeff pulled at the door, it rattled stiffly, immobile.

The shop lights were dark, and a sign in the window written in Waring's scrawl read: "Closed, Staff Development."

Using his key to enter the dark shop, Jeff saw bluish light emerging from *The African Queen*'s flat-screen TV. He ascended the spiral staircase, and on the couch he found Alaura and Waring watching an old black-and-white movie.

Waring's arm was draped over Alaura's shoulder.

Jeff realized he had never seen them touching.

"Jeff!" Waring said with a baffling, toothy smile. "Now *this* is a movie you should watch while you have the chance." He pointed at the screen. "*Sunrise* by Murnau. I know it's a silent movie, and that it's black-and-white, and that it doesn't star Tom Cruise or Meg Ryan or whomever you kids watch these days—"

Alaura burst into laughter. "Meg Ryan?" she said.

Waring grinned. "Are my references no longer culturally relevant?"

"I like Meg Ryan," Jeff said, feeling a little defensive about it.

"And here, Jeff," Alaura said. "If you want a real giggle, give the old *Buried Mirror* a read." She handed him the screenplay. "It's a yuck-fest."

"I thought it was a romantic thriller."

"In the sense that *The Room* was a romantic thriller," Waring said, "yes, *The Buried Mirror* is a romantic thriller."

"It's awful," Alaura clarified.

"Awful awful," Waring seconded.

Jeff set the awful screenplay on the loft's cluttered table and said, "Are you guys drunk?"

"Actually, no," Waring said.

"I wish," Alaura said, "but I haven't been drinking for almost a month."

"Is that true?" Waring said, and he seemed truly surprised. "Shit, I hadn't noticed."

"I'm actually thinking of laying off booze for a while longer."

"Did you fall and hit your head or something?"

Alaura shook her head, smiling, and she patted Waring good-naturedly on the thigh.

To Jeff, they both certainly seemed drunk.

Finally Alaura, wearing a sarcastic smile the whole time, explained the reason for their bizarre behavior—how all was lost because of everything that had happened with Match Anderson, the Hitchcock hallucinations, that the executive had found out, that Match had quit the movie, and that the film crew was leaving Appleton, thus ensuring the cancellation of the celebrity auction.

"Oh my God," Jeff said. "Oh my God."

"What?" Alaura said, who immediately seemed to notice that his reaction to the news was more intense than it should have been.

Jeff sat down on the top step, where he had been standing. He couldn't breathe. He glanced again at Waring—for whom he had kept the stupid secret about the bicycle gang. And Alaura—to whom Jeff had never worked up the courage to confess his feelings.

His body felt tight, pressured. He didn't need to say anything—they would probably never find out—

"It's my fault," Jeff blurted.

"What?" Waring said.

"I . . . I overheard you guys talking about the Hitchcock thing. Up here in the loft, day before last. And I told Celia Watson about it. Last night." Jeff looked guiltily at Alaura. He winced in intense pain. "She kissed me, I'm sorry, and I was drunk, and it sort of . . . flew out."

Silence.

Waring stood up in *The African Queen*. His face flushed red. His scraggly black hair shivered atop his head.

Sitting behind him, Alaura leaned forward and gave Jeff the nastiest look in the history of the world.

"I didn't mean to," Jeff said, almost crying now, and he stood as well, terrified, took a few steps down the stairs. "I'm sorry, Waring. I'm *so* sorry—"

"You're sorry?" Waring said. "You're sorry?"

"Waring . . ." Jeff whimpered.

Then, with frightening calmness, Waring said: "Jeff, you've ruined Star Video. Which means you've ruined my life, and Alaura's life, and—"

"Waring, I'm sorry!"

"—and if you don't leave right now—"

"Waring! I really didn't mean to! I'm so sorry!"

Alaura knew how ugly she appeared. She knew her expression was twisted with anger and disdain, and that her face looked even worse now than it had in Match's hotel room mirror earlier that morning. She knew she looked like a monster. But she didn't give a shit. She didn't give a shit that Jeff worshipped her, that he looked up to her, that he was probably in love with her. Jeff had ruined everything. How had she ever, even for a moment, considered kissing him? Match had only needed to make it a few more days, and Jeff had blabbed like the stupid little teenager he was. So she scowled at him. She felt her lips ache and her jaw clench painfully. Jeff cowered pathetically in front of her. The moron. The tears on his face only solidified her fury.

She glanced at Waring, whose countenance was bent into Waxian attack mode. Alaura wanted him to attack. Everything had been leading to this point. If they'd just made it to the celebrity auction, then everything that had happened might have been worth it. She looked at Jeff and thought of Pierce, her shitty ex-boyfriend, who had used her for an entire summer and then dismissed her like a servant. She thought of Thom and Karla, those culty weirdoes, who'd implied that everything Alaura had ever done with her life was a waste. And she thought of Match—that Match was insane didn't relieve him of his responsibility to be a good person, to be compassionate, to help her.

She hated all of them. And she hated Jeff.

"Fuck you, Jeff!" she spat out.

The kid was crying, and she was glad.

"Tell him, Waring," she said. "Tell him he's fucking fired."

. . .

But what was going through Waring's mind now? Yes, he was infuriated. Jeff deserved every awful thing that would ever happen to him for the rest of his life. And this was a perfect opportunity to scream, because how often do we actually have a chance to act in *truly* righteous anger? To let our rage explode? The kid needed to suffer. He needed to understand the extent of his inanity. When people do awful things, they *must* be punished, or the world will devolve into chaos.

But Waring realized he couldn't do it.

He looked down at Alaura, whose normally beautiful face was cinched into disgust—it was a magnification of the look she had given Waring many times. Though he'd always acted like he didn't give a shit whenever she was angry at him, he did give a shit. And Jeff, the dumb young kid (emphasis on *young*, Waring thought), was in love with Alaura, or whatever passed for love with dumb *young* kids, so Waring knew what that look must feel like to Jeff, how it must be burrowing like a steak knife into the middle of Jeff's stomach.

So instead of yelling, Waring sat down next to Alaura.

"What is it?" she said angrily, twisting on the sofa, craning her tattooed neck toward him. "Aren't you going say something? Aren't you going to fire him?"

Waring reached for the remote and pressed pause, silencing the silent movie's score.

"For fuck's sake, Waring," Alaura snarled. "Jeff fucked everything up. We should be getting ready for the celebrity auction. I should be with Match *right now*—"

At the mention of Match's name, however, Alaura's voice seemed to leave her. She fell back into the couch, looked off into space.

"We're going to need Jeff," Waring said flatly, to both of them, to neither of them. "I can't fire him because the store is closing, so he won't have a job anyway. But we're going to have to sell off all the movies and—"

"No," Alaura said weakly, and her body folded. She collapsed downward onto her own knees, as if preparing for her plane to crash.

But Waring nodded—his mind was made up. "You knew this was going to happen," he said softly to her. "I knew it, too. And if we didn't know, we were idiots. Jeff might have done the stupidest thing in twelve years of stupid Star Video moves, which is saying something. But it doesn't make any sense to fire him."

Waring looked at Jeff.

The young man's hands had dropped from his face. He now donned a wet, hopeful expression.

"You didn't do it on purpose," Waring said. "Did you, Jeff?"

"I'm really sorry," Jeff said, his voice shaking.

Waring nodded. "Apology accepted."

And Waring watched his two employees gasp, as they considered the many implications of this unprecedented act, and as they both comprehended that, in the end, what his apology really came to was . . . a final admission of defeat.

Star Video was finished.

Alaura said in a weak voice, "But Ehle County needs an independent—"

"No, Alaura," Waring said gently. "Thank you, but it's time. We weren't going to make it anyway. Maybe a few more years, but that would have been it. People want different things now. And yes, Jeff made a stupid mistake. But look at him. He can't help himself. He's stupid."

Long silence.

"I still think we should fire him," Alaura murmured, and she shot Jeff another piercing glare.

"Well, I think it's still *my* store," Waring said—lacing the comment with more of his old-fashioned cockiness, hoping to calm her down.

"But Waring," Alaura said. "What are *you* going to do? What the hell does Waring Wax do without Star Video?"

He looked at her, and he thought about making another snarky joke. Ten possible comments filtered in front of his eyes, each snarkier than the last. But he didn't say anything. He just sat there, his big idea now bobbing through his mind, forming and reforming and bifurcating and taking on nuance. He visualized his future. But instead of saying anything, he just looked at Alaura, beautiful Alaura, the girl he loved.

She shook her head.

A mischievous smile flitted on his lips.

A dream blazing in the darkness.

THE
LAST DAY
OF
STAR VIDEO

The shelves were nearly bare, and Star Video, or what remained of it, now seemed twice as large as it ever had. Over half the shelves had already been dismantled, their remaining DVD and VHS show boxes shifted toward the front of the store. The remnants of the shelving now lay in a gigantic metal heap, over eight feet high, near the entrance to the Porn Room. *The African Queen* had also made its final voyage. Its wooden hull was now a splintered shipwreck covered with a large blue tarp. The result of all this was a new, strange, wide-open space that made Star Video look more like a business at its earliest stages than at its end. The room now echoed. Fully half the floor space was bare, a gaping hole where one could now do cartwheels, run sprints, lie down and take a nap on the cool linoleum. In this rear section of the store, at least, the battle against the dust bunnies had been won.

Today was Star Video's last day of business.

But where the hell is everyone? Alaura thought. Where are all the regulars?

Alaura had informed them (those twenty or so most faithful cinephiles) that Star Video would be closing early tonight, and for good. That they could all bid adieu by having the last grab at the remaining DVDs and VHS tapes. One dollar per title. Fifty cents. Free. Who cared.

But none of them had come.

Only the dregs of cinematic history remained, of course. DVD collections of *The Real World* and *Road Rules* and *Big Brother* and *The Bachelor*—because no one cared about watching reality shows several years after that reality had transpired. And there was *Garfield: The Movie*, *Crash* (not the 2004 movie by that title, which had inexplicably won Best Picture, but the 1996 *Crash*, by Cronenberg, which alone should have gotten it sold), Spielberg's *1941*, *Mac and Me*, *Junebug*. And *Gigli*—they'd tried for years, literally, to sell their last DVD copy of *Gigli*, but it had all been for naught. Every disc remained of *Wire in the Blood*, a British mystery series that Alaura had actually quite liked but that no one else seemed to know about, even the nice old ladies from Covenant Woods. Hundreds of old comedies remained, and hundreds of old dramas, and a somewhat higher percentage of indie films, like *The Trouble with Perpetual Déjà-Vu*, *The Mystery of Trinidad*, and *Death and the Compass*, movies with promising titles that had turned out to be mind-numbingly awful—even though Alaura had always touted the merits of independent cinema, there was no denying that quite a lot of those titles had been simply unwatchable.

And it had not escaped Alaura's notice, and it made her throat clench to see: *Changeless*, Match Anderson's failed sci-fi epic, was her lone remaining title on the Employee Picks shelf.

For five weeks—since the production of *The Buried Mirror* had closed up and left town—every movie at Star Video had been on sale. Liquidation. Classics and new releases (everything from *King Kong* to *Casino Royale*) had been gobbled up first, and as she and Waring had aggressively reduced prices, more and more of the store's impressive back stock had evaporated. Porn, of course, had gone like cocaine pancakes (Waring's term). Then those television series popular with the Ape U intelligentsia: *The Sopranos*, *The Wire*, *Homicide: Life on the Street*, *Deadwood*, *Black Adder*, *Black Books*, *Fawlty Towers*, *Firefly*, *Arrested Development*, all the others. Then the Criterion collection. Then everything else. Several customers had spent over a thousand dollars each, toting away laundry baskets filled with DVDs. And the fanatical collectors: anime hounds, horror snobs, Peter Sellers junkies. One customer, a fat African-American man with a C. Everett Koop beard, had purchased every film in the Korean Horror section, as well as every Takashi Miike movie still in stock, insanely claiming that Miike would one day go down as Japan's greatest director since Ozu. Another customer, a hale and hearty Swedish guy with sand-blond hair who spoke less English than a tree stump, had expressed and then acted on his rather awkward penchant for black-on-white gay porn.

So many cracked personalities. At times, there had been a line of twenty or thirty at the Cashier du Cinéma. Like the old days, Alaura had thought. Financially, these had been the best five weeks in Star Video's history.

But at this final moment, this last day of business, where were all the regulars? The friends of Star Video? The former employees? The annoying barflies? The regulars who came in and hung out and talked about movies? Where was the swell of local remorse?

Were they all at home? Watching cable? Streaming movies on Netflix? Did they all have better things to do than wave farewell to their beloved shithole video store?

(And at the very least the local progressive Appleton newsrag might have assigned a reporter, seeing as Alaura had sent them repeated e-mails about this important community development. She'd even suggested running an obituary for Star Video, a clever conceit that, in her opinion, had been discourteously ignored.)

"Bring your final selections to the front!" Waring barked from behind the counter, standing where his director's chair had once stood. "Lights out in five!"

Alaura surveyed the ravaged floor. She could see through the remaining grated shelves all the way to the rear wall. Dead, she thought. Over. For years, this industry had flourished. It had begun in the early 1980s, when she was a little girl, when VCRs had first become affordable to everyday citizens, because everyone wanted to watch movies at home. At first the VCR had been about time-shifting, about recording the shows you couldn't be home to watch. But then, shortly thereafter, video stores had come along, and quickly VCRs were only used to play rented movies, bringing the movie theater to the home. It had been that simple: that was the entire story of their industry. She had started working at Star Video in 1997, when there were still those long lines on Friday nights, that sense of frantic scramble for the newest releases, and that giddy tingle to discover a movie one remembered from one's youth ("They have *The Dark Crystal*? No way!"). Watching movies had never been like this. Before the 1980s, people only watched films in theaters, or they were hostage to whatever aired on television. If you wanted to see *Rashomon*, you had to wait for a Kurosawa retrospective at your local university, like that ever happened, like people even cared. If you wanted to watch every episode of *Hill Street Blues*, you had to be home to catch it, every week, on time, for years.

Video stores had changed everything. And now they were dying.

Alaura sold an obese man with a handlebar mustache thirty dollars' worth of third-rate VHS nature documentaries. She thanked him, bagged his movies, and realized that he might be the last paying customer Star Video ever had.

Only four customers remained. She vaguely recognized their faces. But they weren't regulars. They just wandered the remaining aisles. Bored.

Didn't they understand today's significance?

Farley understood, and he'd been driving customers nuts all day. He'd interviewed nearly every person who had entered the shop. It was sweet watching him navigate the store (with Rose, who was apparently his new girlfriend, as well as his sound crew, devotedly at his side holding the boom mic) and accost customers with questions about what Star Video had meant to them, what Star Video's closing might mean for West Appleton, etc. Dorian had submitted happily to being interviewed—he had arrived with his new boyfriend (a flannelled musician wearing tighter jeans than Alaura's), hugged everyone (even a reluctant Waring), and after his interview departed the shop while donning, as always, his contented-Buddha smile.

"That's it," Waring called to her. "Time to lock up."

She nodded.

Six p.m.—the earliest, she was certain, that Star Video had ever closed.

Alaura moved to the front door. Her legs felt weak. She reached up and carefully yanked the cord on the neon OPEN sign. The light went out.

Jeff, simultaneously, hit the circuit breakers in the Porn Room, killing over half of the store's fluorescent bulbs.

The final customers began shuffling toward the exit.

Alaura was close to tears. Her stomach ached. She didn't want anyone to see her, but she couldn't help it. For fuck's sake. When had she become a girly crier? Maybe it was just because she was exhausted. That morning she had awoken early and worked her first shift at Weaver Street Market, the West Appleton grocery co-op Waring always made fun of. She had always half-mocked the place, too, though the food was tasty. People seemed too happy there. So enlightened, so fucking evolved. Aging hippies shopping with purple fabric bags. Taut middle-aged joggers meeting at sunrise for group runs, and cyclists, and speed walkers, and Nordic walkers (elderly women dragging weird graphite poles behind them). Bluegrass and jazz and puppet shows on its shady front lawn. Hula-hoopers. The interpretive dancer who might or might not be a lunatic.

The co-op was a community center, but Alaura had always considered it too mainstream-West-Appleton-progressive for her outsider spirit. Then, on a recent sortie for a quick lunch, only a week ago, Alaura had actually taken a moment to reconsider the place for the first time in years. The light from the large windows rushed into her eyes with the painful shock of cold water, and she had realized that she recognized many of the customers shopping around her. Of course she did. She knew everyone in West Appleton. And she knew the reason she normally walked through Weaver Street Market (and everywhere else, for that matter) like a robot, with blinders, was because she *would* recognize people but would *not* remember their names. It was bad enough in bars, or on the street, when Star Video customers would approach her and ask how she was doing, and she could never remember their names. Outside the confines of Star Video, she was helpless.

But that day, when she made eye contact with them, she remembered most of their names instantly, and they nodded and smiled, and a few even stopped to ask how she was doing, stammered for some sympathetic offering about the closing of Star Video. It dawned on her that she made them nervous. They thought she was cool. The hip girl with tattoos. Not as pretty as she used to be, no longer one of the sexiest girls in West Appleton, but cool nonetheless. That day she walked out of the co-op feeling light and popular, and after eating her lunch of tempeh and couscous and mushroom salad at a picnic table out front, she marched back into the place and applied for a job. Her interview the next day was for customer service manager. Living wage, benefits, 401(k). And they didn't care about her tattoos. Those hippy entrepreneurs have a few things right, she'd thought.

And even before finding out that she'd been hired, she'd had visions of herself—the happy, tattooed grocery-store lady, who greets customers and organizes important community events. Wearing a red bandana, like Willy Nelson, as well as a sleeveless, low-cut shirt—Rosie the Riveter with tattoos and cleavage. Assisting elderly women with their dried goods. Helping an autistic employee learn to bag fruit. The glass doors of Weaver Street Market sliding open for her husband pushing a baby carriage. Eating a vegetarian lunch with her small family in the shade of the oak trees out front. An *old* old woman with tattoos and kinky gray hair, a vegetable patch in her backyard, walking streets covered in yellow leaves from grocery store to home, a small funky house in West Appleton, a fireplace purring at her arrival.

Alaura noticed that Farley, half-hidden in the New Releases section, was filming her, and she found herself performing a teary-eyed, smiling shrug for his camera. Then she saw Jeff, who had emerged from the back room and now stood near the decimated Employee Picks section—she didn't know what else to do, so she gave the poor kid a little wave.

Oh, Jeff. I wish I'd handled you differently.

Waring appeared beside her.

"We'll need to get going soon," he said. "Don't want to be late."

She nodded.

Their final four customers, none of whom had purchased anything, left the store—they weren't regulars, they didn't understand the importance of this moment, and they exited with oblivious, cordial nods to Alaura, who held open the door for them.

She wished them all good night.

Waring, Jeff, and Alaura—bundled in various coats and scarves against the November chill—stood together, silent, on the weedy sidewalk in front of Star Video. Jeff was speechless. Waring and Alaura looked morose, bereft, bloodless. Jeff understood, of course. He felt it, too. But he'd only worked at Star Video for a few months, and he knew he didn't have any right to their level of sadness. Not after all the mistakes he'd made.

Still, in an oddly noble gesture, Waring had ordered Jeff to close money that night (which the young man had done under the watchful eye of Farley's camera), and for years he would be somberly proud that the paperwork for Star Video's final day of business would forever be adorned by his handwriting and calculations and signature.

Farley and Rose had just walked away—Farley was pleased with the footage he'd gathered, pleased at least that Waring had submitted, without much rancor, to his filming it. And Rose had seemed happy, too. Jeff might enjoy running into them sometime—former coworkers shaking hands on the street and reminiscing.

"Sure you won't come tonight?" Alaura said to Jeff, breaking the silence.

"No, sorry. I've got some catching up to do. Studying."

Alaura nodded, not looking at him, not insisting that he change his mind. But her coldness didn't really hurt him anymore. For weeks after the Match Anderson debacle, she'd either completely ignored him or snapped at him rudely for any mistakes he made in the store, and Jeff had come to understand the difference between real anger and the type of perpetual crankiness Waring exhibited, and how much more the former hurt than the latter, especially when it came from a woman you adored. Jeff longed for the Alaura of two months ago, in her apartment, wearing her long tee shirt and little shorts. But that was over, forever, and he'd grown used to it, moved on.

Then, a week ago, there had been yet another mysterious shift in her behavior—though she never actually announced forgiveness for his stupid mistake, she seemed to have made a conscious decision to be more polite. Or at least not to snap at him. She didn't hate him. She might even be his friend again, eventually.

"Waring?" Jeff said. "Good luck with everything."

Waring nodded, flicked a cigarette stub onto the sidewalk, and gazed at his shoes. "Well," Waring said, "you know, Jeff . . . for these last few weeks, working so hard during the final sale, you've been . . . I appreciate it."

"You were paying me."

"I'm saying thank you," Waring said, a bit annoyed.

"I know you are."

They shook hands.

Waring continued looking at his dusty shoes, and Jeff was tempted to hug the strange little man—but he suspected Waring might throw something at him.

Jeff turned to Alaura.

"Well . . ." he said.

"Oh, shut up," she said, her tone breezy and familiar. "We'll see you soon." Then she reached out and hugged him.

And though he tried to resist, he could not help holding her tight. Squeezing her even after she had started to pull away. He knew she would understand. She wouldn't mind the long hug. She knew he'd had a crush on her, maybe even loved her. But he didn't want to push it. Who knows, years down the line. Still, he held on. He did not let go. He smelled her hair, felt the wool of her lime-green toboggan fizzing against his face.

"Bye," he whispered, and he turned and walked away.

Moments later he glanced back, trying to imbue tragedy in the motion, but Waring and Alaura were already walking in the other direction, not looking his way.

So that was it.

Five minutes later, Jeff passed Tanglewood Baptist church— where he'd not gone in over a month, and he hadn't told Momma, and he didn't care—and after giving the tall steepled building a sidelong glance, he turned and entered a pub, a place he'd had the good fortune to be served beer several times recently. It was a dingy place named Pravda, the centerpiece of which was a huge red-on-black painting of Lenin on an exposed cinderblock wall. At 6:35 p.m., when Jeff arrived, there were only three other patrons, men in their twenties or thirties, drinking quietly and watching college football. Indie rock with an off-key singer buzzed over the jukebox.

Jeff ordered a twenty-four-ounce Pabst. He took the beer to a corner table and began studying a textbook on film criticism. Earlier that week, he had observed a film class, and he had all but decided to switch majors, from business to film, at his next opportunity. The class had been exciting—though much of the discussion was over his head. But they were talking about movies, his favorite thing in the world, and he'd learned that he might even be able to focus his studies on sci-fi and anime, genres that he now guiltlessly admitted were his true loves. Some people actually made a living studying exactly those genres! The only thing he had not understood during the class was that no one ever said that a particular movie was good or bad; they only talked about shots and sequences, used cryptic French terms he had scribbled in his notebook to investigate later.

So he had checked out this book, a large brick of paper, the contents of which, he now realized, were also over his head. Every few sentences he had to consult his mini dictionary, and some of the terms weren't even in there.

Then a group of three girls and two boys, preppy college kids, walked into Pravda, blaring voices, laughing stupidly at the kitschy decor of the place. They ordered fruity red drinks and took a table next to Jeff's, though there were ten other tables they could have chosen. He heard the girls babbling about *Gossip Girl*—of all the shows on television, that new piece-of-crap *Gossip Girl*. And the gaggle of them looked so much like what Jeff assumed fans of *Gossip Girl* would look like that he couldn't stop listening to them with anthropological fascination. Jeff caught a glare from the bartender—the bearded man shrugged. Jeff nodded in disgusted agreement. Then, after another explosion of shrill laughter, Jeff leaned over to them, cleared his throat, and said, "If you're going to be obnoxious, could you move over there?" One of the boys, the bigger of the two, started to say something. But Jeff beat him to it: "Don't talk to me, Chester. You're in my bar." (Why Chester? Jeff didn't know. And why had he said "my bar"? Because he had shared a glance with the bartender, he decided.) The guy stepped down, and the group moved to the far table, finished their drinks quickly, humorlessly, and left. The bartender then waved Jeff over, shook his hand, and gave him a free beer. Jeff returned to his book. Over the next hour, he got a bit drunk, and for the first time since—well, maybe since first getting hired at Star Video—he felt hopeful about his future.

At seven thirty p.m., cigarette and beer in hand, Waring Wax stepped from the shadows wearing a rumpled black suit that, to all those watching him, seemed a natural extension of his body. The large room opened up in front of him. Christmas lights were strung along the eighteen-foot-high ceiling, a firmament of near-linear constellations. Waring was standing upon a small stage and looking down at his audience. Forty Applets stared back at him. They were sitting on mismatched couches, or in Burger King booths, or at Formica-topped diner tables, or on the short bank of twelve theater seats that Waring had procured cheap from Memorial Hall on Ape U's campus (recently remodeled). He saw a young couple sitting in the front half of a Volkswagen Beetle that he had purchased for forty dollars in scrap, and that Jeff had painted with two cans of Rust-Oleum spray paint (Harbor Blue). He saw several of the old biddies from Covenant Woods, his morning regulars, who were holding hands cutely, looking up at him with dazed smiles. A few other people milled near the walls of the wide-open space, and in the dim creamy light, Waring saw them studying the dense collection of classic movie posters—there was the Tom Laughlin autographed *Billy Jack* poster that Jeff had marveled at, and several of Alaura's indie posters from her apartment, and all of the random wrinkly posters that had adorned Star Video for so many years. And looking to the back of the room, Waring saw Alaura behind the new glimmering concession stand. She was handing two bottles of beer and a leafy sandwich to a chubby lesbian he recognized from the store. Alaura smiled radiantly, leaned forward onto the counter, her head bobbing in some theatrical jest, locked in pleasant conversation. Waring smiled, took a drag of his cigarette.

"Welcome to Star Theater," he called out to the audience.

He announced the title of that night's film, the newest from an up-and-coming independent director, and he called out loudly, "I'll be honest with you, I watched the movie today, and it isn't fantastic. I've seen better. But when you go to a movie theater, you don't necessarily expect the greatest thing you've ever seen, right? You just want to be entertained. And I was entertained when I watched this earlier today. And the director, I think we'd all agree, he's earned the right to make a movie that isn't exactly amazing. He's made other, better films, and he dated that woman, you know, from that British pop group, the one everyone really liked, or so they tell me. And well, I guess . . ." and Waring took a sip of beer, only his third sip of the evening.

The air smelled, immaculately, of popcorn.

"This place, Star Theater," he went on, "will be a home for *good* movies. Or if not *good* movies, then at least interesting ones. And if not interesting, then at least weird. What I'm saying is, we'll show old films and new films, we'll host film festivals and other gimmicky things like that, and in general, we'll try to deal in *honest* films that contribute to the scope of film history. I know that sounds pretentious. But that's what we're going to do. That's our humble mission, et cetera."

Then he saw Farley, whom he'd known would be there that night, just as he'd been at Star Video earlier—Farley was filming Waring, as always, while Rose dutifully pointed a long-tubed microphone in Waring's direction, a finger set to one ear of her huge headphones.

Waring, unable to resist, began to flip Farley the bird—

"And the documentary!" Farley yelled, as if to forestall Waring's rising middle finger.

"Oh, right," Waring said, turning his attention again to the audience. "As my former employee has so politely interjected, two weeks from tonight, at eight p.m., Star Theater will screen a new documentary by Farley . . ." and Waring glanced at the camera and its vigilant operator. "Farley . . . Farley . . . who I'm sure has a last name, though I'm not recalling it just now. But anyway, Star Theater will screen *his* new documentary, which he promises will be ready and screenable by then, because apparently he's been working on it for months and is rushing to get it ready for festivals or something, though I'm a bit skeptical of his timeline, as it appears he's still engaged in principal photography *right now*. But whatever. The documentary is about my old . . . I'm sorry, *our* old video store, Star Video—"

A sudden round of applause, mingled with a healthy dose of doleful "awwwws" from the audience.

"Yes, yes," Waring said. He clenched his jaw, trying to drive away the surge of absurd sadness now expanding in his chest: "It's tragic. It's heartbreaking. We're all devastated. And Farley has captured all that tragedy on camera, which is just absolutely great. The documentary is titled . . . what's it titled again?"

"*The Last Days of Video*!" Alaura's voice rang happily through the theater.

"Right," Waring said, nodding. "*The Last Days of Video*. Come check it out. There'll be a reception or whatever, with drinks and chips and things like that." Waring belched behind a fist. "Oh, and some time early in January, date to be announced, we're hoping to have Alex Walden, yes, *the* Alex Walden, who is an old friend of mine, we go way back, he'll be visiting Star Theater for a discussion and a screening of some of his father's films. Alex, the old lug, has agreed to come, and we're just hammering out the details. Impressive, huh?" The audience agreed resoundingly with a round of clapping, during which Waring sucked down another gulp of beer. "Anyway, I wanted to thank you for coming, and for watching tonight's movie and drinking and eating with us. And for forgiving us for the state of the place, which will improve with time. As a treat for our first night of business, we'll stop the movie halfway through and bring fresh chocolate chip cookies to whoever wants one." A few giggly murmurs from the audience. "Really, I just wanted to thank you," he said again. "So . . . well, thank you."

Waring stepped away from the screen.

Sixty seconds later, up in the projection room, Waring turned down the houselights and the Christmas lights, and he hit play on the digital projector—he had paid for the projector, as well as for all the seating and the concession implements and the first and last month's rent for this ancient building on Watts Street, just around the corner from his old shop, with money garnered from selling his house, and from selling the property that housed Star Video and Pizza My Heart to Ehle County. He had paid off all his debts, and, depending on how business went (People still go to movie theaters, right?), he suspected he would have enough money to keep the place running for at least a few years.

The movie began, and he watched the first minute of it through the projector room window. But he had already watched the damned thing earlier that day—and you couldn't watch the same movie twenty times in a row, could you? He knew he would have to lug a television and DVD player up here, so he could watch other movies while Star Theater's films played on the big screen. The small projection room was big enough for the flat panel. It was big enough for his bed and his books and for the twenty boxes of junk he had deemed un-throw-awayable from his house. And it was just barely big enough for the crusty couch from *The African Queen*.

Downstairs he heard Alaura clunking around in the small kitchen, a remnant from this building's ancient history as a general store. Maybe he should go down and help her. But no. He was exhausted, and Alaura had said she could handle the cookies herself. At intermission, he would help her carry them out. Shit, he thought, how can I replace her? He couldn't afford to pay her what she deserved, of course, and he had been honest about that. Finally he'd been honest. Now she had a new job at that damn grocery store. He had visited her there that morning, had watched her from behind a display of organic corn chips and all-natural jellies, and to his surprise, she had seemed happy. Smiling, charming customers, fixing problems. She'd be running that store in a year. And that was a good job for her, wasn't it? They probably contributed to a 401(k), which Waring had never gotten around to setting up. That store would be around forever. People would always need food.

Cookies, he thought. Maybe intermission cookies can be our calling card. Every showing, bring them warm chocolate chip cookies.

He approached the projection room's lone exterior window, which opened vertically, swinging out and up. He sat in his director's chair, positioned by the window. He lit a cigarette, exhaled into the cold night. Smoking in the projection booth while a movie played was impossible; it interfered with the projector and cast ghostly waves onto the screen. But this was fine; he could smoke out the window. The fresh air was good for him, though he might catch his death up here when winter really hit. Whatever. He cranked up the plug-in radiator to "High" and looked northward out the window, in the direction of College Street.

West Appleton. He had loved it here since the moment he arrived, years ago, on the day after the nightmare in the Charlotte hotel room, when his wife had called to tell him she was starting a family with another man. The next morning, still drunk from the night before, Waring had driven a rental car through North Carolina. Four hours later, he had pulled into Ehle County and up to Star Video. As he would later tell Jeff, Waring had simply found the place via an advertisement in the back of *Video Store Magazine*, and he'd finally worked up the courage, just a few days before, to call the owner, who had given away all his bargaining leverage by confessing to Waring that no one else had inquired about buying his shop. Stepping out of his rental car that day, Waring looked around West Appleton, and his first thought was that he had no idea who *wouldn't* jump at the opportunity to own a store *here*. West Appleton was a young town, a college town, an imperfect town. There were restaurants, and pretty girls, and bars. And people were smiling. This was light-years away from New York, and he remembered thinking, *There are a lot of places worse than this.* So he walked into Star Video, which was tiny, and which had a laughably bland selection, and an hour later, over beer, he made the crumpled old geezer in the blue cardigan an offer on his store, and the guy had immediately accepted.

Now, looking at West Appleton from the projection room window, Waring was already forgetting what Star Video had looked like with all the movies on the shelves, all the posters on the walls. The movies were gone. His life was gone. He'd discovered what he'd always wanted to do with his life, and he'd made it happen, and then, after little more than a decade, it had all fallen apart. Maybe he should have seen it coming. But the winds of Fortune, he thought philosophically, are usually only felt after the storm. Or some such nonsense. Still, the second he'd seen a Redbox in a grocery store, he should have known. The second he'd seen a smartphone playing some Ashton Kutcher afterbirth, he should have known. But he'd never been one for foresight. He should have seen that Helena was going to leave him, but he'd been taken completely by surprise by that as well.

Helena would hate Star Theater, he thought. She'd absolutely fucking hate it.

He smiled.

Because his mother, he knew, would have loved it.

He gripped the bottle of stout beer in his hand. It had come from a thirteen-dollar six-pack, and it tasted like heaven. Or at least what he wished heaven might taste like—round, bitter in a soft way, with enough alcohol to singe nose hairs and remind you that you are alive.

"Damn it," he whispered.

He hurled the bottle from the window. It arced across the sky like a satellite, traveling on infinitely, over the cars lined on the far side of Watts Street, streetlight glinting off the bottle's surface, brown liquid twisting out in a spiral that dispersed into mist. Away the bottle went, venturing high in the direction where in two years the new towers of the Green Plaza/ArtsCenter would stand, where Star Video once was, before finally the bottle descended into the leafy branches of an ancient oak that occupied the vacant lot across the street. The bottle skipped and knocked through the branches, then plodded harmlessly, unbroken, upon the soft soil below.

Acknowledgements

Mom and Dad—despite the many creative ways I tried to discourage you over the years, you've always been ceaselessly loving and supportive. Thank you, from the bottom of my heart, thank you. I hope it will give you some measure of relief, if not a smile on your face, to know that publishing this book—even if it flops and no one attends my readings and James Wood pans it in the *New Yorker* (James Wood is a golden god, by the way, and very handsome, and a very good drummer)—publishing this book, no matter what, *has made me happy.* I wouldn't have done it without you guys. I love you.

To my fellow employees at VisArt Video, where I worked for nine glorious years, thank you for being fun and weird and brilliant. This book is for you.

To Dan Smetanka, my amazing editor. A word of advice to all upcoming writers: Dan Smetanka is always right.

Thanks to my agent, Craig Kayser, one of the most uniquely intelligent and entertaining people I've ever met. Thank you, sir, for coming into the camping shop where I worked and buying maps, or else I'm certain I'd still be lost in the woods.

Special thanks to Clyde Edgerton, an amazing writer and teacher and chicken wrangler and friend. Thank you for believing in my book and saving it from disaster on many, many occasions. Remember that serial killer subplot? Ugh.

Thanks to everyone else at UNC Wilmington: the mighty Philip Gerard (who presided over the germs of many a novel in my favorite writing class ever), Rebecca Lee, Wendy Brenner, Robert Anthony Siegel, Todd Berliner, Karen Bender, everyone in the creative writing program, everyone in the graduate school, everyone at Randall Library. And thanks to all my fellow students, especially Ariana Nash, Peter Baker, Ben Hoffman, Mitch McInnis, Kyle Simmons, Rod Maclean, Nick Miller, Nick Roberts, Carmen Rodrigues, and, most importantly, Johannes Lichtman . . . I'm humming ABBA's "Take A Chance On Me" and thinking of how much I miss you, you Swedish bastard.

Many books on film and video-store history were essential to the production of this novel, notably *From Betamax to Blockbuster: Video Stores and the Invention of Movies on Video* by Joshua M. Greenberg, *The Big Screen: The Story of the Movies* by David Thomson, and the books of David Bordwell.

I would be remiss if I didn't acknowledge the tremendous debt this novel owes to *Black Books*, the amazing British sitcom created by the genius Irishmen Dylan Moran and Graham Linehan, two of my comedic heroes. I stole liberally, but I hope lovingly and respectfully, from *Black Books*—as I'm sure will be obvious to anyone who's watched the show, which, if you haven't watched it, you definitely should.

Thank you to Flyleaf Books in Chapel Hill, North Carolina, for fighting the good fight for independent bookstores, for providing me gainful employment, and for being unlike video stores in that most important of ways, i.e., consistently making a solid profit.

Thank you to the Weymouth Center in Southern Pines, North Carolina, for providing me a beautiful and inspirational (if apparently ghost-haunted) space to work. And thanks to That's Entertainment Video, also in Southern Pines, for answering my many annoying questions and for renting me DVDs (*Grand Budapest Hotel*, *Scanners*, and *Dawn of the Dead*) in 2014.

Special thanks to the Virginia Center for the Creative Arts.

Thanks to Amanda Bushman, for the inspiration of your art, for your support of my writing, and for watching all those movies with me.

Thank you to my many amazing friends, Corwin Eversley, Mark Harrell, Huru Price, Kim and Eric Riley, Tom Raynor, Dylan Robinson, and everyone else I don't have enough space to name here . . . you are all in my heart.

To Shaw and Kinsey, I love you guys. And just because there's underage drinking in this book doesn't mean you're allowed to do it yourself. Just kidding. I know you guys drink. But as always, don't do anything racist.

Lastly, and most importantly, thank you to Hillary, my beautiful love. You're the bomb, boo. I love you so very much. Oh, and I tried to work in a reference to *Somewhere in Time* but couldn't figure out a way. Next book, okay?

HAWKINS   Hawkins, Jeremy, 523/352
           1978-

           The last days of
           video.

                          MAR 1 9 2015

$15.95

DATE			